.mbe

FLOODTIDE

A Selection of Recent Titles by Sally Stewart

CURLEW ISLAND *
THE BIRD OF HAPPINESS
THE LAND OF NIGHTINGALES
A ROSE FOR EVERY MONTH
SNOWS OF SPRINGTIME
THE WOMEN OF PROVIDENCE

* *available from Severn House*

FLOODTIDE

Sally Stewart

This first world edition published in Great Britain 1998 by
SEVERN HOUSE PUBLISHERS LTD of
9–15 High Street, Sutton, Surrey SM1 1DF.
This title first published in the U.S.A. 1998 by
SEVERN HOUSE PUBLISHERS INC of
595 Madison Avenue, New York, N.Y. 10022.

British Library Cataloguing in Publication Data

Stewart, Sally

    Floodtide
    I.   Title
    823.9'14 [F]

    ISBN 0 7278 5302 3

Typeset by Hewer Text Composition Services Limited,
Edinburgh, Scotland.
Printed and bound in Great Britain by
MPG Books Ltd, Bodmin, Cornwall.

Chapter One

REFLECTED in the quiet waters of the estuary, Derrycombe looked doubly beautiful – a grey little town huddled round the mouth of the River Derry where it met and mingled with Start Bay. A ring of wooded hills kept its inhabitants secluded from the world and therein, in Cressida Marlow's eyes, lay the only fault that could be found with Derrycombe. It was more than a trifle smug. Too small for a marina, too hemmed-in for caravan-parks and large hotels, it was as safe as any place could be nowadays from the ravening hordes of visitors who battened on less fortunate sister towns along the coast. But Cressy was aware that the world outside would have to be investigated one day and, with school-life nearly over, it would soon be time to make a start.

She broke the news in her own fashion, when she and her father were making for home at the end of a glorious day's ramble on the moor. With the green valley spread out below them, she suddenly stopped and held out her arms in a gesture that embraced the view.

"I don't know how I shall be able to *bear* leaving it," she muttered tragically.

After a respectful moment Roland Marlow ventured a question. "Do you absolutely insist on leaving? Your mother and I rather hoped you were going to be the prop and stay of our old age."

Gravity gave way to the transforming grin that sometimes made him think she might grow up beautiful. "Silly – I shall be back by then, when you're tired of running the bookshops. But I've got time to see the world first."

"Derrycombe's lovely but too suffocating . . . is that it?" he suggested, and saw her nod.

"I'm still Ben Davey's 'little maid', and everyone else is on the

1

job of looking out for Cressy Marlow as well. Even Admiral Blake watches from his tower in case Andrew and I get into difficulties out in the bay."

Her father knew better than to say that the Admiral, like all her friends, was only minded to be kind; too much kindness was exactly what she needed to get away from.

"What do you want to do . . . walk round India, go au-pairing in Turkey?"

This time she shook her head. "Mum's such a failure in the kitchen, I thought I'd learn how to cook properly."

It was true that Helen Marlow, with her mind on the next production of Derrycombe's Drama Society, made them culinary offerings that left something to be desired, but even so he looked surprised by his daughter's suggestion.

"Too ordinary – is that what you're thinking?" she asked. "I had to tell Andrew yesterday, and he turned up his long Pollack nose in disgust. Well, to be fair, I expect he thought Lady Evelyn would be horrified, and probably Bart as well . . . not quite the right training for the next Lady of the Manor!"

"Did *that* come into the conversation as well?" Roland Marlow asked, intrigued by this oblique way of touching on a subject so weighty. It wasn't his daughter's normal method of approach; she favoured directness as a rule.

Cressy frowned over the memory of that conversation, in fact of the whole day spent afloat with Andrew. It was their first sail together after the year he'd been away working on an estate in France. The weather had been fine, and it should have been an outing of pure delight, but she'd been aware of strain, of awkwardness for the first time in the company of someone who'd been her friend since she tipped milk over him at the age of five, during a children's party at the Manor.

"You told Andrew you'd be going away," her father prompted her patiently, ". . . because he had a different idea of the future?"

"He said that everyone in Derrycombe reckoned we'd finish up together. Bart had suggested waiting a year or two, because he'd be too busy learning the ropes to take on a wife as well, but *he* couldn't see the point of hanging about!"

2

Indignation coloured her cheeks at the memory of so humdrum a proposal, but Roland did his best not to smile. "First attempt, poor fellow . . . we all make a mess of *that*. But in any case you mustn't ask more of people than they can provide, Cressy love. Solid worth is what you'd get from Andrew, not poetry and high romance." He might have said she'd get courage, too. A less resolute young man than Andrew Pollack might have been persuaded to look for a different wife – one more biddable than Cressy was likely to be, with a father who owned land instead of a couple of small-town bookshops. Sir Nicholas was a kind, good squire, but well aware of what his son was worth, and Evelyn Pollack couldn't forget she was the daughter of an earl. She'd accepted her children's harum-scarum friend, but only because they'd refused to relinquish her.

"So what happened in the end?" Roland Marlow asked.

"We had a row," Cressy said bluntly. "Andrew can never see anyone else's point of view, but he was worse than usual yesterday. I was daft, apparently, to think of going to London – which he said I'd hate – when I could just as well fall into line behind his mother in a Pollack procession which he expects to last until the end of time. I told him he was a throw-back from some thieving feudal baron, and that not only was I going away, but he ought to encourage poor Lucy to escape as well, before it's too late. For the first time in our lives we parted bad friends."

"I'm sorry," said her father, aware that the rift still distressed her. She was staring at the view – committing it to memory, he thought – and he could look at her. It was no wonder Andrew had wanted to stake his claim; she was lovely already, long-legged and graceful and merry at heart. He was bound to see that with a little Pollack decorum added, she'd make him a perfect wife.

"He'll ask you again one day and make a better job of it," Roland Marlow suggested.

Cressy turned and smiled at him but, instead of agreeing, said quietly that it was time to go and break the news at home that she would be leaving Derrycombe at the end of the summer.

*   *   *

Three years later she was a trained, professional cook. Surface sophistication hid the scars of a battle with London that had almost got the better of her. But loneliness had somehow been survived, and whenever she went home to Lantern Cottage, Derrycombe told itself that little Cressy had become as smart as paint – definitely eyeable, in its own terminology.

She still visited the Manor, but only to see her friend Lucy. Andrew no longer seemed interested in whether she lowered her flag of independence or not, and she retaliated by giving the impression that she could take her pick of London lovers. She thought it a sad way for their friendship to have ended. Lucy Pollack grieved for a brother too stubborn for his own good, and for herself as well – she'd reckoned on Cressida as a sister-in-law, but it looked more and more unlikely now. What girl with the metropolis at her feet would settle for dishing out school prizes, delivering meals on wheels, and keeping the church flower arrangers from each other's throats?

Aware of embellishing her working life a little for Derrycombe's benefit, Cressy refused to admit even to her parents that homesickness still took her by the throat whenever she saw bunches of Devon primroses on a street-vendor's barrow. She enjoyed her job, felt proud to meet the exacting standards of Mrs Agatha Kenworthy's 'Helping Hands' agency, and waited for the moment when her heart said it was time to go home.

She arrived one morning at the Edwardian house that concealed Mrs Kenworthy's business activities to find her colleague Jane already at the desk.

"Morning, Cress. Thank God you've arrived; you looked peaky yesterday and I thought you might be sickening for something. We need a real cook tonight, not Anny throwing spaghetti into a pan and pouring a tin of instant bolognese sauce over it."

"Well, here I am, ready to cook ... where, as a matter of interest?"

"Flat in Chelsea. The client's name is Credland – Mrs Marguérite Credland. Funny mixture ... she sounding very French and her husband, if there is one, presumably English as can be, judging from the name."

"Devonian," Cressy felt obliged to insist. "Credland's a well-known name in the West Country."

Jane grinned at her. "I keep forgetting you'd know about such things; no one would think it to look at you!"

"I suppose you mean to be kind." Cressy laid her daffodils on the desk. "Being 'sore in doubt concerning spring', I thought these would cheer us up." It was her turn to smile at the look on Jane's face. "Sorry ... I can't help quoting poetry at you – it comes of being weaned on the contents of my father's bookshops!"

"Not your fault then," Jane agreed fairly. "Now, ducks, to business: here's what the lady wants. Looks bloody complicated to me, and if she's as French as she sounded she's bound to be difficult."

"Good. I like people to know whether I've cooked well or badly for them, instead of wolfing it down indiscriminately."

Cressy ran her eye over the menu asked for and agreed that whoever Mrs Credland was, she understood about good food. Cressy did the shopping which was part of the service offered by Mrs Kenworthy, and presented herself midway through the afternoon at an elegant house overlooking the Chelsea Embankment. On the way there she'd struggled to pin down the memory teasing her mind ever since Jane had mentioned the name of Credland. It wasn't just that anyone born in Devon was likely to have heard of the giant engineering concern in Plymouth which made everything from pruning knives to combine-harvesters; what she finally recalled was Andrew saying one day that his father had been irritated by a battle lost against the Credlands.

With a picture fixed in her mind of a coolly elegant Frenchwoman, Cressy found herself staring instead, when the door opened, at a small, auburn-haired woman tending to plumpness, although her face was delicately featured and appealing. She was dressed with continental flair and her English was faintly accented, but Cressy reckoned afterwards that her main attraction was the kind of warmth of manner that embraced a stranger and made her feel a friend. For a moment or two, though, Mrs Credland seemed doubtful about the girl standing in front of her.

5

"Good afternoon. I've come from Mrs Kenworthy's agency . . . you wanted someone to cook for you this evening."

Still Mrs Credland didn't invite her inside. "Are you sure it's *you*? You don't look in the least like a cook to me." If Cressy's imagining had been at fault, Marguérite Credland had even less expected that an agency cook would look like the girl in front of her, dressed in a dashing scarlet cape with a black fur hat cocked over a wind-blown fringe.

"I'm quite sure, and I've even got the lobsters to prove it!"

Her client's face broke into a smile at last. "Then you *are* the cook, though not at all what I was expecting."

She led the way into a lavishly-equipped kitchen and Cressy expected to be left there to ferret out its possibilities on her own. But Mrs Credland didn't run true to the usual form. "What we both need first is a cup of English tea, and *that* I can make myself!"

Cressy enjoyed the tea, appreciated the kindness that had prompted it, and listened to a description amusingly tinged with malice of the evening ahead.

"I'm not incapable of cooking dinner myself, you understand, but I cannot cook and entertain at the same time. Tonight I must entertain. For the sake of my dear son I am to convince the parents of a girl he knows that we are entirely respectable. I shall do my best, but the truth is that we are *not* quite respectable enough for Mr and Mrs Harcourt-Smith!"

It was old home night, Cressy thought. Surely here was another Devonian name she knew, conjuring up memories that suddenly made her feel homesick.

"They might turn out less dull than you seem to anticipate," she said encouragingly.

Mrs Credland shook her head. "I know them already. Lionel Harcourt-Smith will talk about his animals, his wife will talk about her Good Works, and Angela, though extremely pretty, won't talk at all. She's rather prim – not at all suitable for my son!" She shot an amused glance at the cook. "*You* don't look prim at all."

Cressy suspected that she was more prim than Mrs Credland might suppose, but pointed out instead that it was time she set to work.

6

"If I'm to prepare Lobster Newburg for you I ought to get started."

"I suppose I should have chosen a menu of roast beef and Yorkshire pudding, but Colin, at least, will adore every mouthful."

She was amusing and warmly friendly, but Cressy felt relieved when her client took the hint and went away. The menu was enough of a challenge to be interesting and she had none too much time in hand.

Five hours later, taking the last of the pots and pans out of the dishwasher, she was contentedly certain that the meal had been a success. Even if Mr Harcourt-Smith had found the lobster too exotic, he wouldn't have been able to resist a pudding largely spun out of sugar, cognac, and cream! But from now on, the name of Lionel would be for ever connected in her mind with lobsters. She was still smiling at the thought when Colin Credland opened the kitchen door. He was obeying his mother's instruction that the cook should be fetched, but the request had puzzled him. Now, looking at a slender girl with ruffled dark hair and laughter dying out of her brown eyes, he no longer questioned Marguérite's insistence that she was to be brought in to drink coffee and liqueurs with them.

"Good evening. My mother's compliments to the cook and will she please step into the drawing-room?"

"Something wrong?" Cressy asked anxiously.

"Everything perfect, I'd say. You are to be thanked, that's all."

He waited curiously to see what she would say or do . . . look flustered, insist that she must remove her apron, renew lipstick that had disappeared? She did none of these things, but her face lit in a smile that revealed an unsuspected dimple in her thin cheek.

"How kind of your mother. For most people it's enough that we're paid for what we're sent to do."

"Churlish pigs! Have nothing to do with them in future. Come here instead, where you'll be properly appreciated."

His voice, unlike his mother's, was English-sounding and his colouring English-fair, but he had the same embracing warmth and friendliness. Cressy reminded herself that he couldn't be unaware how potent such charm was, and no doubt used it deliberately, but she returned his smile all the same as he ushered her out of the kitchen.

The Harcourt-Smiths and the other male guest completing the party looked surprised at the sight of her in her enveloping white apron, but they rallied bravely and tried to pretend that entertaining the cook was something they normally did themselves.

They were pleasant, harmless people, and a glance was enough to see why Angela had attracted Colin Credland's attention; but there was no doubt that the hostess was bored. Cressy suspected that the introduction of the kitchen help had been a last desperate attempt to retrieve the evening by giving it a touch of novelty. It didn't stave off the guests' punctilious departure at half-past ten, and the relief on Marguérite's face suggested that this was what she'd been aiming for.

"*Dieu, merci!* I love you more than life, my dearest," she said when Colin came back into the room after seeing them into taxis, "but don't ask me to endure that again. If kind Cressida will make some more of that delicious coffee, we can *enjoy* a glass of brandy this time."

Cressy smiled at her. "I'll make the coffee for you with pleasure, but not stop to drink it. I have to catch the tube."

Colin, already pouring brandy, turned to look at her. "Haven't we made it clear? We always see our cooks safely home."

"Kind of you, but rash! It happens to be Chiswick Mall, but it might have been Romford or Barking."

His blue eyes lingered on her for a moment before he shook his head. "Not Barking . . . you don't look in the least like Barking to me."

The coffee was made before Cressy confessed that the name of Credland made her feel homesick for a place much further west than Chiswick. "It doesn't seem likely on the face of it, except that you know the Harcourt-Smiths, but do you have any connection with the Plymouth Credlands?"

"We *are* those Credlands." Marguérite's face had suddenly become tragic. "At least, my darling William was until he died six months ago. Now, I'm not sure *who* we are."

The odd statement was left hanging in the air, but Colin kindly supplied the explanation Cressy felt unable to ask for.

"My mother makes it sound more mysterious than it is. She was William's second wife after Jane Credland died. There was a son by that marriage as well, and my half-brother, Giles, is now the head of Credland's. I have a job there of sorts, at least until he can think of some way of getting rid of me."

Cressy stared at him, taken aback by the bitterness in his voice. "Is he really as unfriendly as you make him sound?"

"Nobody could make him sound more unfriendly and hateful than he actually is," Marguérite said mournfully. "We're only here now because we insist on escaping occasionally. Colin was clever enough to fracture his wrist on a skiing holiday, so we've had an excuse to stay in London longer than usual. Otherwise we should be back in Plymouth again by now."

Cressy felt obliged to protest. "Be careful . . . you're talking to someone with Devon blood in her veins! I've got used to London, but I was born by the edge of the sea. If I didn't live where I can see the Thames, I think I'd curl up and die for lack of water!"

"But you stay here all the same."

"Because I earn my living here. But one of these days I shall go back to Derrycombe."

Mrs Credland looked astonished. "Plymouth is bad enough, but that strange-sounding name you've just mentioned is probably a hundred times worse. It's ridiculous, this loyalty we're supposed to feel for the place of our birth. I hope I shall never see boring Brussels again. London or Paris, and perhaps an occasional glimpse of the Riviera; where else is bearable?"

Cressy abandoned a subject on which they obviously weren't going to agree and suggested instead that it was time she went home. The long-case clock in the hall was already chiming midnight and her task the following day was to cook a business luncheon for a dozen people. She said goodnight to her hostess and, in her own mind, wrote finis to an acquaintance that had been more interesting than most. She didn't suppose that Marguérite Credland made a habit of using the services of 'Aunt' Agatha Kenworthy, or that Colin's interest in a girl who earned her living as a cook would be anything more than fleeting. It was a prudent decision, but she came to it with regret.

Sitting beside him in the car for the brief journey to Chiswick, she was aware of him even though she knew it was what he wanted her to be. He wasn't strikingly good-looking but something distinguished him from the men she mostly met. He was elegantly dressed in an age when it was fashionable to look casual, but the difference went deeper than that. She decided in the end that the air that hung about him was of someone faintly dangerous to know. 'Solid worth' her father had once said of Andrew Pollack. She doubted if he'd say it about the man by her side, but solid worth could be – like Brussels, apparently – very boring for a girl who still felt the adventurous tug of the open sea.

He stopped the car where she directed him, then turned to smile at her.

"Am I right in thinking you're *not* going to ask me in? You have to rise with the lark, or your flatmates would take it amiss . . . that sort of thing?"

"Not that sort of thing at all," she said calmly. "Mrs Kenworthy doesn't approve of too much fraternising with clients, and nor do I. Thank you for the lift home. I hope it hasn't put too much strain on your damaged wrist."

She saw his eyes light in an answering sparkle of amusement. "Dear Cressida, you don't look like one of life's earnest toilers in the vineyard, but something tells me that you are! Do you share my half-brother's dreary view that only work is noble and everything else a shocking waste of time?"

"Wrong again! But if your brother dislikes skiving when there's a job of work to do, I'm bound to say I agree with him."

"Giles would approve of you . . . strange, because our taste in women doesn't usually coincide."

"He's the boss, I gather, and therefore a fair target for a grumble, but is he really as unpleasant as you and your mother make him sound?"

"He's a lump of Cornish granite, a puritanical kill-joy, a thorough-going sod. Does that answer your question?"

"I rather think it does!" She smiled and said goodnight, but took indoors with her the thought that Colin Credland wasn't quite what he seemed. The words he'd used to describe his half-brother hadn't particularly startled her, but the passion with which he'd brought them out had. A charming, pleasure-loving drifter wasn't supposed to feel with that kind of intensity. Families weren't obliged to like each other, but raw hatred had sounded in his voice, and Marguérite's wistful face was also a vivid memory.

A routine directors' luncheon occupied her for most of the next day, but she got back to the office to find Jane Carstairs waiting with a message for her.

"Last night's client has been trying to get hold of you. What did you do . . . walk off with the spoons, or poison somebody?"

"Neither. Don't tell Mrs K, but we finished up swigging brandy together at midnight."

"If the 'we' includes Mrs Credland, Aunt Ag doesn't seem to have anything to worry about! *Is* she French, by the way?"

"Belgian, in fact, and rather more captivating than most of our clients."

"Well, better find out what she wants. It's our task, dear one, to keep them happy."

On the telephone a moment later Marguérite Credland wanted to know if Cressida had to work that evening. If not, could she take pity on a lonely woman whose son would be out? A snack and a glass of wine would be waiting for her. Cressy accepted the invitation, and hung up, smiling at Jane's expectant expression.

"Nothing to get excited about; a friendly visit which will probably exhaust Mrs Credland's interest in me. I suspect she likes new faces, and is feeling bored."

The promised snack turned out to be sandwiches extravagantly stuffed with smoked salmon. They were delicious, and so was the chilled Chablis that went with them, but the real entertainment lay in her hostess's conversation. In the space of half an hour she'd demolished current fashions, and poured scorn on the décor of the flat she was staying in. By the time she'd mounted a swingeing attack on the staging of *Tristan und Isolde* at Covent Garden, Cressy began to see why Plymouth and Marguérite Credland didn't appreciate one another. She said so but immediately regretted it because the smiling animation in Marguérite's face was quenched by the reminder of Devon and her stepson.

11

"Don't talk about it," she implored. "I can't bear the thought. Colin's holding out for as long as he can for my sake, but Giles holds the whip hand."

"You both make him sound like a monster. Why should he treat you so unkindly?"

Marguérite shrugged. "I suppose because he can't forgive me for marrying his father. It isn't that I stole William from Jane Credland, you understand; she was already dead. But Giles was hostile at the age of six, and that's how he has remained. He'll never accept that Colin has as much right to Credland's as he has and, although we get only the bare minimum that William's will insists upon, he'd stop that if he could."

In spite of herself Cressy couldn't help glancing round. 'Bare minimums' were relative and, however elegantly dull, the flat was luxurious by any standards.

"Not mine," Marguérite said, interpreting the glance. "I only rent it while I'm allowed to stay in London. I have no home at all . . . the house in Plymouth was sold when William died."

Cressy would have liked to say that the late Mr Credland hadn't done very well by a wife much younger than himself, but it was clear that Marguérite blamed Giles, not William, and wouldn't thank an outsider for trying to change her mind. It was odd that she should talk so freely to a comparative stranger, but Cressy reminded herself that Marguérite wasn't English! In any case, below the surface of a complex and far from ordinary woman she detected a weight of loneliness that demolished normal reserve.

"Did your husband not realise the situation . . . guess that if you were left without him, his elder son would be unkind?"

Marguérite gave her characteristic little shrug. "He knew, of course, that we were not a united family, but busy men live in the present, not the future. William adored Colin, but my darling son isn't always as *sérieux* as he might be. It wasn't hard for Giles to convince his father that Credland's should be left to *him*. Colin is certainly less single-minded about it, but Giles refuses to see that more responsibility would give my son a greater interest in the firm."

Cressy wondered whether to suggest that his brother might be more convinced if Colin went back to Plymouth instead of loitering in London with a slightly damaged wrist that could scarcely be said to stop him working; but she remembered that he was loitering for his mother's benefit.

"I can see what you're thinking," Marguérite said with sudden frankness. "We're charming, but too spoiled for our own good! Perhaps it's true, a little. But Cressida, you don't understand how destructive it is to be with someone who despises you. That is what Giles does – slays us with contempt. He takes after his mother, because William was exactly the opposite: a warm and loving man who could make me feel that I was the cleverest, most beautiful woman alive. Because he thought so, I *was*; without him I'm nothing at all."

It had the poignant ring of truth and Cressy accepted it as such. Marguérite had needed William. Without him she was dependent on Colin for the assurance of being loved, but whatever comfort he could give, William's other son seemed intent on taking away. Cressy was suddenly reminded of Lucy Pollack – someone else who needed reassurance to make her bloom, and failed to get it even from people who presumably were fond of her.

"I'm sorry," she said at last. "I didn't understand . . . now I think I do."

Marguérite's tragic face brightened again. "I knew I wasn't wrong about you last night. I never am about people. If Mrs Kenworthy hadn't sent you here we should have met in some other way. It's all mapped out for us – in planetary influences and the mansions of the moon."

Vague as it seemed, Cressy found herself unable to laugh at the idea. Astrological goings-on might or might not have flung her into the path of the Credlands, but however it had happened she was there, and she felt too involved with them not to agree that the meeting had been 'meant' in some way.

Chapter Two

THE Credland factory on the outskirts of Plymouth was deserted except for a lighted room where a man still worked. He threw down his pencil with a sigh of relief that meant the design was right at last. The extra thrust of a little more power, counteracting weight carefully trimmed to keep running cost to a minimum . . . yes, there was no reason now why it shouldn't do all he required of it. It was time to call it a day and go home.

He let himself into his flat overlooking the Hoe to hear the telephone ringing. The sound of a French associate speaking what he firmly believed to be English exploded in his ear. "Giles, pardon me for this lateness, but I am back in Paris only one hour ago."

Giles looked at his watch. It had to be something important to keep Jules Froment from the sacred business of eating dinner. "What can I do for you?" he asked calmly.

"Come over here quickly if you can. My man arrived back from Tokyo this afternoon. The Japanese are very *discrét*, but Leblanc is a good . . . how do you say, spy! They are starting work on something very like our machine. We must make some speed now."

"All right; I or someone else will fly to Paris on Monday." He rang off eventually, thinking that it was just like the bloody French – months of talking to no purpose about a joint project that ought to have been nearing completion instead of being scarcely started. It took a threat of Japanese competition to prod them into the efficient action that would undoubtedly follow panic. He didn't resent the prospect of a Saturday given to mulling over specifications and costs, it was how weekends were often spent, but by mid-afternoon the following day the work was done. Now another tiresome task was involved, but he wasn't sorry to relax

15

in the different kind of concentration entailed in driving very fast to London.

The man he was looking for was in the process of dining with Cressida in a small, fashionable restaurant. The candle-lit room encouraged intimacy, but she was doing her best to keep her head.

"Why were you reluctant this morning when I telephoned?"

She evaded for once the question he was really asking. "There was a blizzard raging outside and you suggested a picnic or a visit to the zoo!"

"All right, so it wasn't quite the day for outdoor treats, but you didn't even sound enthusiastic about this evening's invitation. I get the feeling that although you're enjoying yourself, it's only so far as certain reservations will allow. Is it because you've labelled me a work-shy Don Juan, or do you have some other hang-up that has nothing to do with me?"

She hadn't expected him to be so perceptive or so direct. He deserved a truthful answer but it meant giving away a lot about herself.

"I don't know you well enough to hang any kind of label on you," she answered eventually. "The truth is that I'm a small-town girl at heart – I go rather sedately into new friendships."

"Because you've been well brought-up, or because there's an important *old* friend hanging around your small town?"

He said it with a teasing tenderness that didn't deride or find her ridiculously quaint.

As a result she found herself able to tell him the truth. "I won't bore you with the details, but there *was* an old friend who finally decided that it was time to write me off. The experience was painful and now I don't rush into things with quite my old abandon . . . high time too, my mother would say!"

She smiled as she said it, surprised by the confession; but a genuine interest in his fellow men and women made Colin easy to talk to. She suspected, too, that he'd had blunders of his own to survive, which enabled him to understand the muddles other people could create for themselves.

"My poor Cressida. All right, I accept the need for sedateness.

It's not my usual pace, but I can see that I shall have to humour you."

It was another surprise to find such sweet seriousness in a man who worked at the impression of being merely charming. She could even have confessed to the final stupidity of throwing Andrew's little model of *Seamew* in the dustbin when she returned from a visit to Derrycombe, and having to scrabble among the rubbish for it an hour later when she regretted it.

She was quiet when they left the restaurant, and he thought she was still haunted by the memories their conversation had called to mind.

"We're very near Cheyne Walk," he suggested suddenly. "Come back to the flat and share a last cup of coffee with my mother before I take you home? She was looking rather wistful when I left to pick you up."

If the suggestion had been phrased in a way that made it easier to refuse, she would have done so. The Credlands, charming though they were, were tiring companions to the extent that they insisted on one's complete attention. At the end of a long week, she would have preferred to go home to bed, but she allowed herself to be steered in the direction of his mother's flat.

Five minutes later they walked into the drawing-room and she was no longer sorry; the expression of thankfulness on Marguérite's face spoke of much more than the relief of being spared her own company.

Cressy registered this a split second before she saw that a stranger was levering himself out of the frail clutch of a Louis XV chair. He was so tall and broad that she was distracted for a moment by the farcical idea that the spindly chair must surely collapse beneath him. But there was nothing comic about the man who now stood staring at her. Unexpectedly blue eyes in a swarthy face looked her over with insolent thoroughness before they moved on to fix on Colin instead. The current of animosity flowing between the two men was immediate, and as dangerous as a high-tension wire. Though no introduction had yet been made, it gave her the name of the figure looming in front of her.

17

There was an awkward hiatus before Marguérite finally remembered that though the cook had achieved the status of old and trusted friend she hadn't yet met William's elder son. The introductions were made and Cressy got a brief nod which said that it would be superfluous to hold out her hand. The conversation seemed likely to die on its feet again until Colin roused himself from complete silence to ask his brother a question.

"Why London, Giles? You normally avoid it like the plague."

"Concern for you, among other things. You've been so elusive that I was beginning to fear your ski damage was worse than you said over the telephone." His eyes moved over Colin's elegant figure. "I can see now that I needn't have worried."

Cressy had no doubt that here was both the ugliest and the most formidable man she'd ever seen, but by some perversity of nature his voice was unexpectedly beautiful. The sound of it lulled her into missing the jab of the knife, but Colin's face was suddenly tinged with colour.

"The damage wasn't great, but damned painful – a hairline fracture of the wrist. It's mending now."

"Tedious for you; still, I dare say you've been able to keep yourself entertained."

His cold blue glance swept over Cressy again, but seemed to find nothing worth lingering on. She understood now what her friend had meant when she said he had the power to shrivel her. Marguérite was staring at him like a rabbit mesmerised by a stoat, and Cressy decided that it wasn't only his physical size that intimidated her; she was overborne by a cold detachment which denied any hope of human warmth.

When he spoke again it was only to address himself to Colin. "I hope you're feeling strong enough to start work again, because someone must fly to Paris on Monday morning. It would be best if it were you – it gives us the edge with Froment to have you speaking French to him when he's incapable of negotiating in English with us."

A smile touched Colin's mouth for a moment. "So I'm of use to Credland's after all, if only because of my mother tongue?"

His brother was uninterested in any attempt at provocation.

"Yes, Can you go, or not? If not, I must go myself. The French have finally woken up to the fact that if we don't get this project off the ground soon, the Japanese will get in before us."

"I suppose I can go if I must."

He sounded reluctant, but Cressida had the impression that it was only to drive home the fact that he was needed as Credland's spokesman abroad. He had no real objection to going to Paris; probably even preferred it to the thought of going back to Plymouth.

"In that case I'll ring Froment at home tomorrow and confirm that you'll be there by lunchtime on Monday. I've gone over all the figures again, and brought them for you. Make sure you're familiar with them before you arrive. Terms and specifications to be exactly as we agreed – no last-minute haggling on Froment's part."

"You make it sound like war, not a combined project!" This was Cressy, defiantly launching herself into the conversation. She got a measured stare for her pains which plainly asked why she thought her opinion could have the smallest bearing on the discussion.

"It's not war," he said finally, "but I don't propose to let the French ride roughshod over us."

The atmosphere in the room was too tense for laughter, but she struggled with an insane desire to giggle at the idea that a battalion of Frenchmen, much less any mere single representative, could get the better of this man. She looked across at Marguérite, hoping to share the joke with her, but Mrs Credland's face looked strained and tired. Some battle fought on her own account before they arrived, perhaps, had left her defeated.

Giles flicked through papers with Colin, and Cressy watched them standing side by side. It was almost impossible to believe that they shared a father. Colin, slightly built for a man, now looked willowy against his brother's massive frame, and much younger than the six years she knew lay between them. Genetic experts could surely have written learned tracts on the effect on them of such different mothers. Colin was entirely Marguérite's son, while Cressy supposed the first Mrs Credland must have been descended from a long line of Cornish wreckers as tough as the granite they'd sprung from.

19

The fact that Colin had brought her back to the flat for coffee seemed to have slipped his mind, but she felt reluctant to remind him of it. In fact her dearest ambition was to get away. "I must go," she said smilingly to Marguérite. "I only looked in to say goodnight."

"*Chérie*, how kind. I suppose Colin is going to take you back to Chiswick now?"

She managed, perhaps without meaning to, to give the impression that their friendship was old and close. There was also a hint of something that sounded like desperation in her voice, and Cressy realised that she dreaded being left alone again with her stepson.

"I shan't allow Colin to do anything of the kind," she said firmly. "Driving a car can't be a good idea for someone with a damaged wrist and I can easily take a taxi."

Giles Credland suddenly raised his dark head.

"Chiswick, did you say? I'm going past on my way to the M4 – I'll drop you."

She feared her mouth dropped open; knew that it had because he added with a touch of malice, "I don't want Colin to be overtired by Monday."

The inference was clear, that Colin would not have only driven her home, but stayed the night with her as well. She wanted to shout at this hateful block of a man who seemed impervious to family feeling or even the most minimal social courtesy; told herself instead that the only way to deal with him was to present a front of cool good-humour against which sword-thrust or sledge-hammer would drive in vain.

"Kind of you to save Colin the trouble," she agreed with a sweet smile.

Giles thanked his stepmother briefly for her hospitality and held the door open in a gesture that said he proposed to leave *now*. Colin followed them downstairs to the street, to a parked car that looked like its owner, uncouth but full of power.

"I'll ring you from Paris," Colin promised.

"Keep the Credland end up with the wily French."

"Trust me . . . just as my dear brother does!"

If Giles heard the jibe, he paid no attention and waited impassively while Colin took his time about kissing Cressy goodnight. She got into the car feeling embarrassed but determined not to apologise for keeping him waiting.

"You're starting late if you're going all the way back to Plymouth tonight," she pointed out instead.

"No more than three hours on a clear road, and in any case I like night driving."

That seemed to be that, and she resolved to let him find the next topic of conversation. He appeared so little inclined to bother that it seemed likely they would drive the rest of the way to Chiswick in silence. If William Credland had possessed anything that passed for social grace the virtue had been inherited by Colin, not by his elder son. There was a long wait at some traffic lights and the silence in the car was becoming oppressive.

"Dangerous things, skiing holidays, so they tell me," Giles suddenly murmured. "However, you appear to have come back unscathed."

"I didn't go," Cressida said briefly.

If she'd taken him by surprise, it didn't show.

"Mediterranean summer holidays more to your taste, I suppose?"

"I rather think I *do* prefer basking in the sun," she drawled with sweet indifference. It was hard not to smile when her only experience of the high life had been a strictly working holiday at a Riviera hotel, but it gave her pleasure to help him construct a wrong impression of a girl he thought he could despise.

Giles Credland shot a glance at his untalkative passenger, irritated by the impression that an important piece of knowledge about her was eluding him. It wasn't difficult to see what kept Colin in London, but it puzzled him that she should be so markedly different from his brother's usual choice of women. Nothing opulent about this one at all; quite the reverse in fact. There was a spare grace about her that went with the delicately carved profile and cropped dark hair. If appearances were not even more deceptive in her than they were in most women, then her own judgement in choosing lovers was deplorable. Either way she was a complication he could have done without.

"When Colin comes back from Paris I'd be grateful if you didn't encourage him to hang about in London. He's got work to do in Plymouth."

"I don't encourage him to do anything," she pointed out coolly.

"You mean you don't have to? The mere fact of your being here does the trick? Are you as confident as that?"

They hadn't exaggerated, Marguérite and Colin. Thorough-going sod didn't nearly cover him, she now realised.

"I mean that Colin hasn't been staying in London because of me. I met him and your stepmother for the first time last week."

She waited for the man beside her to remember Colin's deliberately lingering kiss and call her a liar.

"I believe you," he said unexpectedly, "in which case it looks as if my brother might have met his match at last. I should rejoice if it weren't for the fact that you're obviously a distraction, and he's got to do some work or get booted out of Credland's for good."

Cool good-humour didn't stand a chance. It was shrivelled in the consuming blaze of anger that made her shout at him. "Why not admit that you can't wait to find an excuse to wash your hands of him, and of Marguérite too? If your father made it as easy as all that for you to disown them, I hope his troubled spirit comes back from the grave to haunt you."

"I think we'll leave my father out of this discussion."

"I'm sure you'd prefer to," she agreed more quietly.

She thought it was touch and go whether he opened the car door and pushed her out. But violence had to be contained because the lights changed at last, the car behind them hooted peremptorily and he could do nothing but put the car in gear and drive on.

"This is Chiswick, I believe. Direct me, or we'll go round in circles all night."

He pulled up outside the house she indicated and switched off the engine. Cressy resisted a temptation to open the door and run; mutual disengagement was allowable, but fleeing from the field of battle was not.

"You accused me of trying to shuffle off my father's family . . . is that what you've been told?"

She was at a loss for a moment, reluctant to admit that Colin or Marguérite had talked about him. "It's the feeling I have," she said eventually, "and instinct is usually more reliable than facts, which can be twisted to present a travesty of the truth."

"I agree with you, so we'll part company on this unexpected note of harmony."

In his richly beautiful voice it sounded misleadingly urbane, but there was nothing genuinely civilised about a man so rough-hewn in feature and shape, so unmanageably large, and brutally powerful.

"I know next to nothing about your family's affairs," she said slowly, "but it's hard to believe that Colin doesn't have as much right to a share of Credland's as you do. Is it so impossible to make room for him? About your stepmother I think I *do* know, although I only met her a little while ago. For the world at large she tries to keep up an appearance of bright, brave cheerfulness, but she's lost without your father. Doesn't it occur to you that he'd have wanted his wife and son helped, not treated as enemies?"

"What occurs to me is that you're meddling in things you know nothing about. You're either credulous beyond belief or concerned to grind some axe of your own."

"I have no axe, only anxiety for people I have learned to like. Marguérite needs loving kindness as plants need water. It's no good telling her to swallow a dose of self-reliance three times a day and settle in to some village or other to become a pillar of the Women's Institute. She doesn't even want to go back to her own country to become a pillar of anything there. Can't you make any allowance at all for other people's weaknesses?"

"Only if I know they can't help themselves. You see my stepmother as the fragile survivor of a marriage that ended too soon. My own opinion happens to be that she's as tough as old boots."

For the first time in years Cressy thought longingly of physical retaliation. It would have been a relief of the sweetest kind to do him some kind of hurt that would diminish, even if it didn't destroy, his arrogance.

"I hope they *can* learn to manage without you," she said in a voice shaking with rage. "I hope your French friends run rings round you and the Japanese beat you at your own cut-throat game."

Sally Stewart

He leaned across and opened the car door. "Harmony didn't last long. If you'd like to get out we could end this fruitless conversation."

It was childish to slam the door, but she could think of nothing else to do. The car engine revved behind her and he was gone before she'd even opened the front door. There was no prospect of crossing swords with him again, but she knew that the memory of her one and only meeting with him wouldn't fade in a hurry. It had left her trembling as if with some fever, but chilled at the same time by contact with a man who seemed devoid of any vestige of human warmth.

She went to bed, but not to sleep, oppressed by a feeling of dread that refused to be reasoned away. Like some Cornish tinner of old, groping along dark tunnels in search of metal, she was alert to the smell of danger. It didn't do any good to tell herself that she need never see any of the Credlands again. Whatever quirk of fate or cosmic impulse had seen fit to draw her into their affairs, the fact was that she now felt irretrievably drawn. Marguérite needed help, and it would have been craven to turn her back on Colin because he had a half-brother who frightened her.

* * *

She saw Marguérite only once in the following week, but they went to a theatre together and she found that cheerfulness had been restored again.

"You've recovered," Cressy said when they were standing in a crowded bar in the interval. "I was worried about you the evening I called in and your stepson was there."

"For as long as Colin is in Paris I can stay in London. Giles hates leaving Credland's so there's no danger that he'll appear on the doorstep again."

Cressida wanted to ask why Marguérite didn't make a life for herself as far from her stepson's blighting influence as possible, but the question couldn't be shouted over the noise in the bar; she would have to ask Colin. When he telephoned he sounded so buoyantly cheerful that she knew he was enjoying himself.

24

"Quite right," he admitted when she said as much. "Making a deal with Jules Froment is the sort of chess-game I find exciting!"

"I take it that his queen's in deadly danger and you're just on the point of check-mating him?"

"Something like that! Paris is my favourite city, too. If you were here life would be perfect. Darling Cressida, I miss you. I can't drive two hundred miles to see you every evening when I get back . . . you'll have to consider the idea of returning to Devon."

She didn't say that the idea had always been in the back of her mind. It was tempting to pretend that, in leaving London now, she would be doing no more than she'd promised herself. It would soon be spring at home, her parents would be overjoyed if she returned, and she might be able to ease Marguérite's life in Plymouth. They were, she knew, excuses; if she went it would be because of Colin. Even if pride could have permitted it, the tactic would be fatal. If he made a mere two hundred miles an obstacle to staying in touch with her, she was mistaking physical attraction for something more lasting. His return to Plymouth would give them both time to take a little more slowly a friendship that had gone at anything but a sedate pace.

Cressida came to this sensible decision, and sighed. At twenty-one, common sense made no appeal at all against the memory of a man's laughing mouth, and the expression in his eyes which said he found her desirable and sedateness a mistake.

Chapter Three

DERRYCOMBE was hidden under a soft grey coverlet of sea mist. The bay had become invisible, and people accustomed to keeping an eye on each other across the estuary were thwarted by the cloud that had anchored itself between them. Groping her way through the blanket, Lucy cannoned into Nat Selby, who insisted on steering her safely to the bank, a old sailor's bump of direction, he assured her, being never at a loss. When she emerged again from the bank the squeal of tyres just in front of her brought her to a halt. A car materialised out of the mist, mounted the pavement, and slowly scrunched its way over her bicycle parked at the kerb.

The man who leapt out to inspect the damage was slightly familiar – met, she remembered, at one of Helen Marlow's drama society productions. She even managed to dredge his name out of her memory, Christopher Goodhew, the manager of Marlow's in Dartmouth.

"Good morning – yours?" He pointed to the bicycle lying on the ground, buckled wheels mutely apologising for the fact that it wasn't in any state to carry her home. "I'm very sorry about that, but the alternative was a head-on collision with a maniac coming down the wrong side of the road."

"Colonel Carstairs, I expect," she said calmly. "It's nothing to do with the fog. After he's made his weekly visit to Totnes, the one-way traffic system gets him confused and he forgets it doesn't apply here."

"Thought I might have missed seeing you, and hit you as well as the bicycle," the white-faced man in front of her confessed.

Lucy smiled, shaking her head, and he revised his first estimate of her downward, although still by ten years too few; she wasn't middle-aged after all. But her frumpish skirt and jacket and brown hair dragged into an unbecoming pony-tail seemed to identify her with the dedicated feminist spinsters who despised the idea of making themselves attractive to men. His guess was that she lived with an elderly mother in a cottage on the outskirts of the town; almost certainly, she did the flowers in church, and went out with a collecting box for the lifeboat fund; she was without interest, probably without sins, and rather forlorn.

"I must get your bicycle attended to, but first I'll take you home if you'll direct me."

Lucy was put in the front of the stationwagon and her mangled bicycle in the back, while Christopher followed her directions, wondering how to phrase a tactful offer to reimburse her for the cost of hiring another bicycle while he got her own repaired.

"You're obviously not familiar with Derrycombe," she remarked as they waited for the traffic lights to change; "everyone here drives in the expectation of meeting the Colonel, so he does surprisingly little harm."

"I run Roland Marlow's shop in Dartmouth, but we're of the opinion that it's high time Derrycombe had a bookshop of its own. That's why I was here this morning, inspecting some empty premises in the Warren that might do."

"Will they?" Lucy asked with interest.

"Look perfect to me, and there are even some upper rooms that I could convert into a flat. I should dearly like to escape the octopus-embrace of my landlady in Dartmouth. Her advice on how to run my life covers everything from the brand of tea I ought to buy to which local girls should be avoided at all costs!"

She looked at his profile – beaky nose, firm mouth, and decided chin; he looked entirely capable, she thought, of running his own life. "It's hard to know what to do with the advice of people who think they're being kind," she agreed with feeling.

A *dominating* elderly mother, he amended to himself, and felt sorry for her. "Where now?" They were moving again, and coming to the outskirts of the town.

"Up the hill, as far as you can go."

Living this far out, she needed her bicycle; he began to think he should just offer her a new one straightaway. He would have

28

driven past the entrance into a stableyard that came into view, but she said quickly, "In here, please; we don't bother to use the front drive more than once in a blue moon."

In bemused silence he drove under the archway, cut the engine, and stared round him. On one side of them stretched a row of brick stables surmounted by a handsome clock now chiming eleven; on the other side of the yard the domestic quarters of the Manor sprawled in muddled, unselfconscious charm. So much for the cottage he'd been imagining, and the frail but domineering old lady sitting by the fire.

"There's no need to worry about the bicycle," Lucy said gently. "My father has a very good mechanic who looks after all the farm machinery. Mick will probably be able to fix it. Come in and have some coffee before you go. I'm Lucy Pollack, by the way; I think Helen Marlow introduced us once."

She was tactful enough not to say that she remembered his name, but he felt sure that she did – it was the sort of bloody attention to social detail that the daughters of people who lived in places like Derrycombe Manor were trained from the cradle to observe. He followed her glumly through stone passages into a vast kitchen, where a woman in a flowered overall was spooning jam into a row of pastry shells in front of her.

"Cathy – are you too busy to stop and make us coffee?"

Still feeling sore because he still felt ridiculous, Christopher wondered why she bothered to ask the question. If Miss Pollack wanted coffee, coffee there would have to be. Cathy obviously thought so too, because she smiled and agreed that the jam tarts 'wouldn't harm by waiting'. They drank the coffee in a pleasant panelled room overlooking a paddock picturesquely dotted with grazing horses. Nothing was missing, he thought savagely, not a single bloody thing.

Lucy was accustomed by now to talking to people she didn't know, but she could still be quenched by an attitude she felt to be hostile. This man who had seemed outside the bank both gentle and kind was now hostile for some reason she couldn't understand. She thought Cressy would have asked him bluntly what he was miffed about.

"If you work for Roland Marlow you must know Cressida," she said to break the silence that had fallen. "We met at a children's party here when she was five years old, and we've been friends ever since. She mostly lives in London nowadays, but I still miss her."

"Her parents miss her too," he agreed. "In fact, she's very missable altogether – one of those people with the gift of painting life in brighter colours for the rest of us."

Lucy nodded, and thought his landlady needn't have worried about local girls. If the warmth in his voice when he spoke of Cressy was anything to go by, he wasn't even noticing what Dartmouth had to offer.

"She always promised to come back to Derrycombe, but I can't help feeling we've lost her for good."

Christopher Goodhew didn't seem inclined to pursue this subject either, and she made no effort to detain him when he stood up to go.

"I don't like leaving the bicycle to you. Are you sure I can't do something about it?"

She declined the offer and led him back to the stableyard. On the point of driving away, he suddenly looked at her through the wound-down window of the car. "Thank you for the coffee – I hope Cathy was right about the jam tarts." He took away with him the memory of Lucy Pollack's puzzled face and of something else besides; he'd been wildly and ludicrously wrong about most things, but not about the fact that there was something forlorn about her. A moment later he was thinking about the new shop again and the plain daughter of the Manor was forgotten.

*   *   *

When Cressida's telephone in London rang it was barely seven o'clock in the morning. She stumbled to it, half-awake, happy to think that it was almost certainly Colin ringing. Nobody else but he would suddenly decide that the day couldn't properly begin unless he talked to her first. But it wasn't his voice she heard at the other end of the line.

"I hate to wake you, darling, but I couldn't wait any longer." Helen Marlow sounded ragged with tiredness and strain. "I'm at the hospital in Totnes . . . your father had a heart attack last night. Do you think you could come?"

"Yes . . . straightaway, of course . . . the first train I can find." Her lips felt stiff, making it hard to frame words. "How – how bad is it?"

"Last night it seemed very bad," Helen admitted, "but the doctor sounds more hopeful this morning. Your father survived the attack, you see, and that's what counts most of all. He's terribly tired, though, and missing you so much . . ."

"I'll be there by lunchtime," she said hoarsely, ". . . tell him, please, and give him all my love . . ."

She put down the telephone but stood there staring at it, unable for a moment to think what she must do next. Her flatmate, Anny, came into the room, looked at her white face, and disappeared in the direction of the kitchen. A few minutes later she was back with hastily brewed tea.

"Here you are, Cress love . . . the cup that cheers. That was bad news, I take it?"

"My father's in hospital after a heart attack. Will you explain to Aunt Ag for me? Say I'm sorry to leave without seeing her, but I can't wait, I must catch the first train there is."

"Drink your tea, then go and get dressed. I'll ring Paddington – someone must answer eventually, even at this hour of the morning."

Cressy tried to smile at her. "Thanks. You're a credit to the agency!"

"Training tells," Anny agreed. "Try not to fret, Cress. If your father got through the actual attack, chances are he'll make it now." She spoke with a confidence that was comforting. Her own father was a doctor, and they were accustomed to taking it for granted that a little of his expertise had rubbed off on her.

Half an hour later Cressy was on her way, much too early for the next train. She drank station coffee she didn't want, wandered restlessly about, and finally remembered that there was time to let Marguérite Credland know that she was on the point of leaving London.

"Will you tell Colin for me if he rings?" she asked finally.

31

"*Chérie*, of course. I'm so sorry about your father, but things often have a way of not being as bad as they seem. I expect you'll be back in no time."

Sitting in the train with nothing to do but think for the next three hours, Cressy considered a future that almost certainly didn't include resuming her life in London. Even given her father's recovery, which her heart insisted upon, she had the conviction that nothing would be the same again. To people who didn't know the ins and outs of them, country-town bookshops might not seem stressful things to run, but she knew how hard her father had always worked. Above all, she knew something of the love and energy he'd poured into catching readers young. Much of his time had been spent in schools, organising book exhibitions and competitions to encourage children to write themselves. It was vital, he'd insisted, in a television-ridden age, and Cressy knew she would have to go on with it herself rather than see his work founder. That much she could do for him, but she couldn't give him back his freedom to walk the hills or tend his garden. If life was to be stripped of almost everything that made it valuable, must she accept the bleak possibility that he might prefer not to live at all? The hands on her watch had crawled through a mere five minutes since she last looked. She went back to staring out of the window, remembering the feeling of dread that had oppressed her recently. It had been justified after all, and the only thing wrong had been her sense of the direction in which the thunderbolt would fall. Her own family had been its target, not the Credlands, who'd seemed so much more likely to attract disaster.

The train was held up outside Exeter as usual and she wanted to scream at the delay, but Totnes finally came into view, and she had the door of the compartment open while they were still running into the station.

Looking for a taxi out in the yard, the first person she saw was Andrew Pollack, so obviously watching for someone that her heart stood still.

"Have you come for me . . . to say it's bad news?" she asked unsteadily, hostility forgotten.

His hands clamped themselves on her shoulders, holding her with rough, unexpected kindness.

"Sorry, Cressy, stupid of me not to realise you'd get a shock. Your father's definitely a little better – I checked again with Helen while I was waiting for the train. We thought it would help to find someone waiting for you."

"Of course it helps." She blinked away tears and tried to smile at him. "It's good of you, Andrew." Her face was luminously beautiful with relief from the fear of a moment ago, and he wondered whether the time would ever come when he could look at her without being riven by longing.

"Car's over there," he said brusquely. "I'll drop you at the hospital."

"How did you know about my father?" she asked when they were waiting to turn out of the station yard.

"How does Derrycombe know anything? Ben Davy, of course! He saw the ambulance arrive last night. If it was black-dark and a stranger in a boat with muffled oars rowed upstream past his door, I swear he'd know who it was and why the man was there. He rang Bart, and my mother spoke to Helen at the hospital early this morning."

It was Derrycombe running true to form, but in times of trouble what often seemed like irritating curiosity became a comforting insistence on the sharing of misfortune.

"All well at the Manor?" she asked next.

"Rubbing along, thanks. Spare time to drop in and see Lucy if you can; she misses you."

Cressy accepted what she already knew; she would be welcome at the Manor for his sister's sake; on his own account he was indifferent whether she went or stayed away. He was concentrating on the traffic and she could safely glance at him . . . still only twenty-five, and a year or two younger than Colin, but seeming older, a man already set in his ways. He didn't have the menacing power that had been so unmistakable in Giles Credland, but they shared the same kind of West Country obstinacy. She knew better than to expect that he and she could be friends again; only an emergency had prompted him to offer the kindness required of neighbours.

He steered the car through the hospital gates, aware out of the corner of his eye that her hands were gripped together in her lap. Memory suddenly vaulted him back in time, and she was ten years

33

old again, stoically enduring the stitching-up of a gashed head. She hadn't been frightened by the fence he'd tried to make her and the pony jump, nor by the fall that followed, but she'd been terrified of the trip to the hospital. He could remember shouting at his mother, insisting that he must be allowed to go to the hospital too, because his friend Cressy would *need* him there. When he glanced at her now her face was composed but deathly pale. He'd have liked to think she needed him still, but now he didn't know.

She turned her head, and the affection of years ago suddenly warmed her smile. "Stupid, isn't it . . . I haven't got over hating hospitals yet!"

His hand covered hers for a moment, hurting her with its grip. "Throw your heart over, Cressy."

The childhood phrase almost destroyed her. She nodded and fumbled for the latch of the car door before she could burst into tears and embarrass him.

*   *   *

A week later Roland Marlow was out of danger and daily getting stronger. Derrycombe congratulated itself on this good news but felt slightly irritated at having to guess at Cressy's intentions for the future. She was aware of the general wish to be kept informed, but reckoned that the town could wait until she had persuaded her father to accept the decision she'd come to. She finally broached the subject one afternoon when he was allowed up and they were sitting in a pleasant day ward together.

"I'm not going back to London, except to clear out my room and say goodbye to the agency. If you can bear the idea, I'm going to learn how to run a bookshop." Her father's troubled face forced her to be flippant. "If you're about to say you don't need me, I shall be mortally hurt."

"I'm afraid I can't truthfully say anything of the sort, but you can't give up your life in London for good, my love. We shall have to find some other solution."

She shook her head and he recognised the signs of his daughter with her mind made up. In the past, nothing – persuasion, cajolery, command – had made an iota of difference to her insistence on doing what she thought was right; he had no hope that things would be any different now.

She stretched out a hand to cover his. "Listen, please. I can see you agonising over the great sacrifice you think I'm about to make. The truth is that I've wanted to come home for ages. I've been away long enough to know that I'll never make a Londoner. Mama will have her hands full keeping an eye on you, Christopher can't do more than look after Dartmouth and get the new shop started here. That leaves Totnes for me, with your guidance and instruction."

His thin fingers gripped her own. "Cressida love, I can't allow it. Apart from a job which I know you enjoy, what about all your friends in London?"

"Pleasant, but not essential. In fact, by a strange twist of fate, the people I should miss most of all will probably be back in the West Country themselves before long. Have you come across them . . . a family by the name of Credland?"

"I knew William Credland slightly – a tough business man, but very well regarded. I seem to remember that he made a stir by marrying again after his wife died. Nothing very unusual about that, but the surprise was his choice of a foreign girl much younger than himself. I don't know what happened to her when he died – went back to her own country, probably."

Cressy shook her head. "No, she didn't. I can report that she finds Belgium boring, and isn't very keen on Plymouth, either! You'd understand why if you met her – she's a true cosmopolitan, a warm and amusing woman who thrives as long as the people around her are loving. In the company of her bullying stepson she's like a goldfish deprived of water. Her own son, Colin, is different, fortunately – as sweet to her as Giles Credland is unkind."

She saw her father's mouth twitch. "If I'm right in thinking sweet Colin is also coming to Plymouth, I may feel less guilty about keeping you here!"

"I should have come anyway, but having you not feel guilty is a bonus." Cressy waited a moment, then took her next fence all standing. "I've got another idea as well! You must have something to do that will keep you from feeling bored. Your mind is stuffed with

35

local knowledge, and there's a fund of material in the notebooks and photographs you've been collecting for years. What about converting all that into a series of illustrated books for children? Devon's history is the history of this country in a way that's scarcely true of any other county, and apart from that, there's the moor itself, the marvellous churches, the natural history . . . there's even a publisher no further away than Newton Abbot who'd probably jump at the idea."

He was silent for so long that the eagerness in her face dwindled into doubt. "You don't like the idea . . . think it's stupid?"

"I don't *like*, I *love* it," he said after a moment's thought, then smiled. "In fact, I don't know why I didn't dream it up for myself."

She went home content but when it was Helen's turn to visit him he couldn't help asking whether they shouldn't try to drive Cressida back to London.

"She wouldn't go," his wife said definitely. "I know living in London's given her a sophisticated air she didn't have before, and she goes out of her way to mislead Derrycombe by pretending that she loves being there. But she's been longing to come home. In any case, she's only half-convinced that I shall make a proper job of looking after you!"

"Did she mention someone called Colin Credland?"

Helen nodded. "He was touched on, briefly! There was a good deal more about his mother, and another member of the family – Colin's half-brother, I think. On the strength of crossing swords with him once, Cressy seemed to think he was the man she's most prepared to hate."

Roland Marlow smiled at his wife. "Did she tell you the rest of it – that I'm to become a writing gent, to take my mind off all the things I'm not going to be allowed to do?"

"It's all arranged. You're going to be the Great Panjandrum, sitting in your armchair, issuing orders, and occasionally throwing us a word of praise!" Her face quivered into grief suddenly, and her eyes filled with tears. "Not the life you'd have chosen, my dearest, but will you try to put up with it for our sake?"

He lifted her hand and dropped a kiss in the palm of it. "I'm blessed among men, and I can put up with anything."

36

Chapter Four

WHEN Cressida went to the Manor with the news that she was going to stay in Derrycombe, Lucy was out, but finally tracked down to St Fritha's, practising hymns for Sunday's service. Her expression matched the sound – downright mournful, both of them – but she managed to smile when Cressy told her so.

"So would you be mournful ... 'though I walk through the valley of the shadow of death' *again* ... the Vicar can't seem to remember that there are other psalms."

"Teach me to play the organ and I'll take turns with you alternate Sundays."

Lucy considered this for a moment. "That means you're home for good?" When Cressy nodded she smiled at her with great sweetness.

"Poor Cress ... I'm sorry. It's sad for your parents too, of course, but it must be very hard to come back when you'd actually managed to survive going away. Why are you smiling – don't you mind terribly?"

"Except for the reason, I don't mind at all. I'd have come anyway in the end – might have been here already if Andrew hadn't obliged me to go on proving something pointless!" A gleam of spring sunlight slanted down through the high windows of the chancel, illuminating her face. It had the clear-cut delicacy of a cameo, but Lucy registered the fact without envy.

"You look very ... experienced, Cress. Are you?"

"I'm not sure I know what that means – the reckless sampling of this and that? If so, I shall disappoint you! I've learned quite a lot in the three years in London, but otherwise Miss Marlow remains much the same!"

"I know nothing at all," Lucy said with sudden painful regret. "I never shall know . . ." She had accepted her place in the Pollack procession, was already more or less resigned to an order of things that seemed immutable.

"It's not too late to learn," she said gently. "If you want to get away, the room in the flat I shared is still available."

Lucy's long face flushed. "It'll sound boastful, but I think I'm needed here. I've come to realise that."

Cressida felt a wave of affection for a girl who made such modest claims for herself, then registered something that her friend had just said.

"Realised how? Has something changed?"

Lucy nodded. "I think something *is* changing, at least," she said thoughtfully. "You know almost as well as I do what life's been like at home: formal and busy and cold! My mother used to unnerve me because I assumed that what I sensed in her was the disappointment she felt in me. It made me worse, of course, because the more I yearned to change her opinion of me, the stupider I became."

"What happened? Did you find you weren't the cause of her disappointment after all?"

"Yes, and it came about almost by accident one day. I had to play the organ for a wedding in church – big occasion, all the local gentry present to hear me murdering Lohengrin rather more than usual! Afterwards my mother rent me for it . . . 'that a daughter of hers should have been such a foul musician', and a good deal more in a tirade that was quite unlike my self-controlled mother. Sheer surprise must account for the fact that instead of agreeing with her, I saw red – lost my temper for the first time in my life and shouted that if she didn't like the way I did it, she could bloody well play the organ herself."

Cressy stared, fascinated by this disclosure. "Was she *very* flabbergasted?"

"Yes, but also made aware how much she'd hurt me, and *that* suddenly prompted her to explain. She'd been a brilliant music student herself, and she fell in love with one who was more brilliant still. I dare say he'd have made a hopeless husband, but my tartar of a grandmother scotched the affair anyway. Mama was married off to Bart, whom the Countess considered reasonably suitable, and my poor mother never touched the piano again. Love *and* music lost in return for a marriage she didn't want."

Cressy thought it explained a lot about a self-controlled woman too strong-minded to give in to grief, but not inclined either to come to terms with second-best. Life at the Manor might have been different had she been able to.

"What happened after poor Lady E explained; did she regret it and go all stiff again?"

Lucy shook her head. "That's the strangest thing of all; I'd swear she's relieved to have told me. It's very sad, but at least she knows what it feels like to fall in love; I know nothing about life in the raw at all. Young Doreen Endacott knows more than I'll ever know and she's barely seventeen."

It was true, and perhaps even tragic in its way, but suddenly Cressy had to struggle not to laugh. "D'reen knew about life in the raw at seven, much less seventeen, and so would you have done if you'd had Doll Endacott for a mother!"

She fought with herself a moment longer, but the thought of Doll in place of Lady Evelyn was too much for her. A moment later it was too much for Lucy as well, and they collapsed in the childhood habit of shared laughter. 'Mrs' Endacott, ampler now than when she'd first come to Derrycombe, had been wont to explain that in her youth she'd followed the Fleet. It seemed more likely that the Fleet had followed her, and Doreen, Danny, and several other children had been the result. Broadly speaking, she was respectable now, and worked for people, like Helen Marlow, kind-hearted enough to put up with her slapdash cheerfulness. Doreen was proving herself a worthy daughter, already swelling visibly and seeing nothing wrong with procreation. Derrycombe would have preferred Doll and her brood to settle somewhere else, but in the end familiarity proved stronger than contempt; the town accepted them, and only warned its hot-blooded sons not to compete with visiting fishermen and travelling salesmen.

Cressy finally wiped her eyes and managed to speak without collapsing again. "I don't think you're quite cut out for Endacott life, but there must be a happy medium. As a start, I'm going to drag you to Plymouth to get your hair cut, and after that we'll make Oxfam a present of most of your wardrobe. The metamorphosis of Miss Lucy Pollack is about to begin!"

"I think I might like that. Cress, I'm truly sorry about your father, but it's lovely to have you back again. We don't seem to laugh much at home; even Andrew's got very grim. Perhaps you can do something with him as well?"

Cressy shook her head. "He's not what you'd call malleable. In any case, it's a long time since we were friends."

* * *

Before Roland Marlow was allowed home from hospital Cressy paid a final, hurried visit to London. She rang Marguérite's number several times but it remained unanswered until a strange voice announced itself as the new tenant. Neither Marguérite nor Colin had been in touch with her since she left for Derrycombe, and she was both saddened and disappointed by the fact. Colin had walked into her life with such laughing gaiety that she'd laid aside caution much too soon. It was absurd to miss so sharply a man so briefly known, but what did time have to do with such things? 'The heart has reasons that reason knows not of.' There was even more to regret than the loss of happiness for herself. Beneath his surface lightness she'd had small glimpses of a different man – vulnerable and far from confident. She would have liked to help him find peace of mind, but couldn't share his search unless he invited her to. Setting off once more from Paddington, she wrote *finis* in her mind to the chapter in her life that had contained Colin Credland.

The train back to Totnes was punctual and a demon taxi-driver delivered her to the gate of Lantern Cottage half an hour earlier than she'd told Helen to expect her. She pushed open the drawing-room door and found her mother happily pouring tea for a visitor. Astonishment held her rooted to the floor for a moment, then she walked into the arms of the man she'd spent the journey mentally saying goodbye to. Colin's smile lit up the cold, damp afternoon, reminding her that lightness of heart was the element in which

40

he most usually seemed to live. Helen registered the expression on her daughter's face and abandoned once and for all the idea of Andrew Pollack as a son-in-law. Here was the man Cressida would settle for.

"You've obviously introduced yourselves," Cressy said happily. "Dear Colin, I imagined you still in Paris."

"Dearest Cressida, I was in Froment's factory at Orleans until two days ago. I got back to Paris to find Marguérite recovering from a sharp dose of flu, which is the reason why you haven't heard from her. She gave me the news about your father. I didn't telephone. I wanted to wait until I could come myself, in case there's something I can do to help."

His face was full of the tenderness that she had found as bewitching as his laughter; now, it offered the lovely assurance that her anxieties were his as well, as much to be shared as moments of pleasure. She hadn't been mistaken after all, and Marguérite's star conjunctions hadn't lied about the future.

She dragged her mind away from the thought and smiled at him. "There's nothing to do except wait until we fetch my father home tomorrow, and can feel complete again. Where is Marguérite now? I rang the number in London but a strange voice answered."

"I've brought her down to Plymouth. She's in a hotel there, feeling thoroughly miserable – partly because she isn't quite well yet, but mostly because she's bored to death. She longed to come with me this afternoon, but was afraid she might have flu germs still hanging around." He turned to Helen with the hint of formality that only now and then reminded Cressy of his foreign mother. "May I bring her to meet you when your husband is home again?"

"We'll look forward to it, but now you must excuse me because it's my turn to visit him. Don't rush away. Cressida's cooking supper, so it will be much better than if I were doing it!"

When she'd driven away Cressy felt self-consciously aware of the joy she'd shown at seeing him.

"We'd love to give you supper," she said quickly, "but don't feel obliged to stay if you've got something to do in Plymouth."

"There's nothing I want to do except to kiss you properly and hear you say that you missed me at least half as much as I missed you. Did you, my dearest Cressy?"

He spoke so seriously that happiness flowered inside her. "I hated London without you," she confessed, "... hated London *more* without you."

"Good, though perhaps not good enough for a man who wants you to say that you're in the same state of breathless, fingers-crossed happiness that *he's* in. Say it, please, Cressida."

There was no laughter in his voice now, and she was moved almost to tears by the discovery that he was in the grip of some new emotion that no previous experience had taught him how to handle.

"It's ridiculous when we've known each other such a little while," she admitted unsteadily, "but yes, my state is much the same as yours!"

"Not ridiculous – inevitable and right. I knew it the moment I had to leave you behind in London."

His arms enfolded her and his mouth found hers; gentle at first, his kisses demanded more and more urgently a response she was helpless not to give. When he finally released her but framed her face gently in his hands, she felt bereft to be that far away from him.

"I've remembered that you've got to cook the supper," he said with a little smile. "We must stop while we still – while *I* – still can!"

Cressy did her best to look as if she would be capable of concentrating on the making of a rabbit pie. "How did your work with Froment go?"

"Rather well . . . we finished up with a very good deal, and even my dear half-brother couldn't find anything to complain about."

She was silent for a moment, then remembered what he'd said about Marguérite. "Colin, what's to be done about your mother? She can't be left to shrivel up in the shadow of your hateful relative. Why doesn't she just decide where she wants to live, and tell him to jump in the River Tamar if he happens not to like it. He's not her keeper."

Colin's mouth twisted with a kind of bitter wryness. "In a certain sense it's exactly what he is. I have a job with Credland's and a certain number of shares – though not enough to block anything

Giles makes up his mind to do. Marguérite gets an allowance, of course, and in fairness to William I'm bound to say that it would be more than adequate for most women. Not for my darling mother! She's immoderately generous whenever her heart is touched, and wildly extravagant as well. It's not a curable condition; she simply has no idea of what dull and prudent people insist on calling 'the value of money'!"

"You mean she can't afford to live as and where she pleases?"

"Just that. Left alone in London or Paris, she's capable of blowing a month's allowance in a single day. I help as much as I can, but even so she's had to ask Giles to bail her out from time to time. He refuses to do it any more, and now she's frightened. That's why I brought her down here; I daren't leave her in London."

Cressy could detect no trace of resentment in his voice, and wondered how many other sons would have borne so lovingly the responsibility he was faced with.

"Can Giles really not afford to go on helping?" she asked diffidently.

Colin gave the little shrug that reminded her of his mother. "He's a rich man, but it gives him the chance to pay off old scores."

"Because Marguérite married his father? It's archaic!"

"She committed a worse sin than that by giving William another son – two strikes against her, you see."

Cressy chewed her lip, resisting the temptation to waste time in hating a man she found despicable. "She spends money because she's bored. Hotel rooms and rented apartments are no way to spend the rest of her life; she needs a proper home again, to give her something to do, and a chance to make some friends. Do you agree so far?"

"How could I not? You'd convince a man with a wooden leg that he could dance the rumba! Proceed, oh wise one."

"Well, the thing she loves doing most of all is redecorating houses ... she's always mentally rearranging the tasteless mess other people make of their homes. Why don't we find her a house she can transform – somewhere near Plymouth, so that you can keep an eye on her? The trick is to find the right spot for her."

"Why not Derrycombe . . . she adores you, and you could keep an eye on her too."

Cressy considered the idea. "No reason at all," she decided finally, "except that she might think she was being banished to some kind of rural purgatory."

"She might get bored with it in the end, but by then she could sell a much improved house at a decent profit, and she'd be more accustomed to doing without William than she is now. Let's try it, my darling. Be a dear good girl and find us the perfect dilapidated house for her to work on!"

Suddenly her smile was brilliant. "As it happens, I think I might even be able to do *that*, but it takes real nobility of character to tell you about it because it's a house I've always wanted to live in myself!"

*   *   *

She and Helen fetched Roland home next day, and Cressy was made painfully aware again of the way in which life flung joy and sadness into the same melting pot. She wanted to sing and dance whenever she allowed the thought of Colin to invade her mind; wanted to rail to Heaven at the sight of her father slowly walking round his garden, inspecting what had happened to it in his absence.

"I can hear your teeth grinding from here," he said beside her. "Don't fret on my account, love. If you'll promise not to, I'll try not to feel guilty about keeping you at home. Is it a bargain?"

"Yes . . . we've got you back – that's the main thing."

"Good. Now come and admire my polyanthus. They're more beautiful than ever this year, and if you look closely you can just see tiny leaves beginning to unfurl themselves on the willow tree." He turned to face her, his own expression full of love and understanding. "Let's admit that my pleasures are going to be different from now on . . . rather more small-scale than they were. But they'll be all the more intense. If you can understand that, you'll know that there's no need to break your heart over what's happened."

"You mean that by being obliged to 'stand and stare' you'll see more?" she asked slowly.

44

"Just that." He tucked his hand in hers and led her on again, and she kept to herself the bitter truth that he'd been a man who'd liked to do things as well as observe them.

* * *

Colin and Marguérite were among the first people to call and Cressy was content to see that parents and visitors had no difficulty in liking each other. Marguérite eyed her hostess's coral-coloured outfit approvingly. "What a pleasure to look at you! I'm so tired of the sight of English women encased in heather-mixture tweeds."

Not expecting her guest's direct approach, Helen looked surprised for a moment, while Marguérite blushed like a child caught out in a misdemeanour.

"Colin will tell you I never remember *not* to make personal remarks here in England . . . forgive me, please."

It was Roland who answered her. "Don't apologise, it was a charming compliment. I doubt if Helen has worn tweeds in her life, heather-mixture or otherwise, but her wardrobe's viewed somewhat askance here because of it. I don't know why; she's a constant pleasure to *my* eye."

It was all Marguérite needed to take him to her heart: that rarity among Englishmen, a husband who was ready to compliment his wife in public – in fact ready to compliment her at all. The visit was such a success that the Marlows watched their guests set off with Cressy after lunch hoping that they wouldn't be put off by the derelict appearance of the house that had belonged to Admiral Blake.

When they arrived, it looked undeniably forlorn, having stood empty since the Admiral's death. Once-white walls were now a dismal grey, and paint was peeling off every door and window-frame. The garden around the house was an unkempt meadow, and even the gulls hunched miserably along the roof looked like querulous pensioners. But still the house spoke to Cressy, and she could scarcely bear to look at Marguérite, knowing that she would find it hard to forgive a friend who didn't perceive the beauty beneath the shabbiness of what was being offered to her.

" 'Scope for improvement,' " Colin quoted in her ear. "For once the estate agent's brochure doesn't lie!"

Inside, though nothing could spoil the lovely proportions of rooms and windows, the dirt and dilapidation were even worse. Marguérite wandered from room to room, saying nothing until she came to the Admiral's tower, and looked out on the estuary and the bay sparkling in the afternoon sunlight. At last she delivered her verdict.

"Clever Cressy to know that it was exactly what I wanted. I may not live long enough to see it finished, but we *must* buy it," she said to Colin.

"We may not have enough money," he reminded her with the gentleness he always used towards her. "You can't spend a fortune we haven't got."

For once he hadn't understood and she looked disappointed in him. "Dearest, I don't want a fortune. It needs to be made elegant in a simple way."

Having a clear idea of what even simple elegance might cost in his mother's hands, he murmured something about surveys and reports, but she refused to listen. In imagination the house was already hers, and by the time they drove back to Plymouth she had almost decided on the colour of the drawing-room walls.

*   *   *

There was no news from her for several days but, apart from praying that surveyors and Giles Credland between them wouldn't destroy the happiness she saw in store, Cressy was obliged to concentrate on her own affairs.

She was familiar with the Totnes shop, knew the layout of the stock, and the general routine; but all the work that went on behind the scenes had to be learned from scratch – the interviews with publishers' reps, the ordering and cataloguing of books and, worst of all, the keeping of accounts and management of staff. Unless she was competent to do it all, she couldn't call herself a bookseller. She was generous in her praise of assistants who'd struggled to carry on by themselves in her father's absence, consulted Christopher Goodhew whenever she got into difficulties, and drove home each evening to assure Roland and Helen that there was nothing to worry about.

But being cooped up indoors was a strain, and when the afternoon of an early-closing day suddenly turned fine after a week of solid rain, she went off walking on her own. After a long ramble round the point she turned inland, climbing up into the grounds of the Admiral's House through a gap in the fence. Rain and mild spring weather had turned the overgrown garden into a wildly beautiful jungle, and she was disentangling herself from the embrace of a rampant bramble when a voice spoke behind her.

"You're trespassing."

The brusque but still beautiful tones told her who was there, but its owner made no attempt to help free her. She was angry as well as scratched before she could finally turn and face him.

"I doubt if I'm trespassing any more than you appear to be."

"Wrong . . . this is Credland property – as from noon today."

"Then I'm surprised you haven't already got the fence electrified by now."

"Give me time, Miss – Marlow, isn't it?"

Cressy nodded, still thinking of what he'd just said. "Do you mean Marguérite's got the house already? Oh, I'm glad. She wanted it so much."

"The house, ruin – let's call it by its proper name – is mine, not my stepmother's. I suppose the previous owner was a friend of yours, and you had it in mind all along, knowing that Marguérite wouldn't be able to resist something so totally unsuitable?"

She held on to her temper with an effort that was heroic. "Very well, the house is yours. Are you going to allow Marguérite to restore it and live in it?"

"For as long as she wants to, which won't be very long in my opinion."

He was standing at his ease, hands thrust into the pockets of shabby corduroy trousers. Dressed so, with a rollneck sweater that had also seen better days, he looked even larger than when Cressy had seen him in city clothes. On territory which suited him better than an over-furnished drawing-room, and which had the added advantage of being his, he was completely in control. She felt again

Sally Stewart

the futile longing to attack him, with anything that would redress
the balance of power that was so obviously his, but it was he who
spoke first.

"I suggested in London that Colin should be allowed off your
hook, but you knew you only had to come back here and wait for
him. You must have been laughing yourself sick."

"It had its amusing side," she agreed politely, pleased that he
didn't know the real reason for her return to Derrycombe; it
seemed to put him at a slight disadvantage. He moved towards
her with the extreme lightness which big men sometimes possess,
and it took an effort of will not to retreat.

"Don't interfere in our affairs, if you please. They're enough of a
mess already, God knows, without you trying to make them worse
for whatever odd pleasure it gives you."

In the lonely isolation of the garden the idea occurred to her
that for the first time in her life she was afraid of another human
being. Common sense insisted that he wasn't a psychopath or a fool,
and wouldn't actually assault her; but huge strength and extreme
shortness of temper didn't go well together. She prayed her voice
didn't tremble when she answered him.

"My only concern is to help Marguérite, not make her relationship
with you more intolerable than it already is. Now, if I'm allowed to
I'll walk home along the road – as far as I know, that's still in the
public domain."

Even then he didn't hurry to move away and she hated him for the
deliberate insistence on his own strength and her weakness against
it. When she was free to walk to the front gate he followed her –
to make sure, she supposed, that she left his property.

"A word of warning," he said abruptly, obliging her to turn and
face him. "I tried to give it to you once before but you wouldn't
listen. Your view of my stepmother isn't complete."

"If you're about to offer me *your* view again, don't bother.
The worst I know about her is that because she's lonely and
unhappy most of the time she isn't very good about managing
money."

Unbelievable as it seemed, she could have sworn for a moment
that sardonic humour lightened his heavy features; then the gleam

48

of amusement, if that was what it had been, was gone again, leaving her thinking that she'd imagined it.

"It's one way of putting it," he agreed. "Well, since you've summed up Marguérite so neatly, I hope you'll do at least as well with my half-brother – but perhaps you find it harder to be clear-sighted where he's concerned."

Damn it, he *was* laughing at her, this ox of a man who trampled over them all with complete indifference. When she was on the far side of the gate it seemed safe to risk a parting shot.

"Fencing isn't your sport. I suggest you stick to laying about you with a cudgel in future."

It gave her the last word, but she walked away sad. Marguérite's future looked as uncertain as before, and the wrong person now owned the Admiral's House.

Chapter Five

WHEN Marguérite telephoned the following day, she sounded very excited.

"Cressida . . . isn't it marvellous . . . we've got that darling house. I may need just a *little* help to begin with – names of local workmen, and suchlike – but I promise not to go on being a nuisance . . . darling, are you still there? You haven't said a word."

"I haven't been able to so far! It's lovely news. Is Colin pleased, too?"

The bright voice at the other end faltered for a moment. "Perhaps not quite as pleased as I am: he hates it when we have to consult Giles about money and things."

It occurred to Cressida that Marguérite perhaps hadn't even registered the fact that the house didn't belong to her; in which case her own brush with its owner had better not be mentioned. "If you need help, my mother's the fount of all local wisdom," she said instead. "Anyone for miles around who can build, paint, or sew gets roped in to help her in the theatre."

But when Colin next drove over to Derrycombe she confessed to him that she'd been found trespassing in the Admiral's garden.

"Giles was unpleasant, I expect."

"Well, yes. Does he hate women on principle or did something happen to sour him at an impressionable age?"

She saw a reminiscent grin touch Colin's mouth. "There *was* a girl he'd earmarked as an obedient wife – Angela Harcourt-Smith as a matter of fact. It seemed only an act of common humanity at the time to detach her from him."

Given Giles's looks and lack of charm, the contest had been an unequal one, and Cressy felt an unexpected tinge of sympathy for a man who couldn't help being aware that he made no appeal to women. And Angela, too, had been no safer in the long run, because her rescuer's kindness had stopped short of putting up with her when he found her a bore.

"Giles said the house was his," Cressy reported, by way of changing the conversation.

"He would, of course. When the Plymouth house was sold a trust was set up – necessary, I'm afraid, or Marguérite would have run through the money in no time. But such trusts aren't easy to break, if they can be broken at all. So Giles announced that he would buy the house himself – lordly sod!"

"But trying to be helpful, perhaps?" Cressy ventured.

"Not at all – making sure we know who's boss."

He smiled as he said it, but she was chilled by another glimpse of an alien world in which currents of distrust and hatred swept away familiar landmarks. The feather touch of fear brushed along her nerves, making her wish for a moment that she hadn't been instrumental in bringing the Credlands to Derrycombe.

"My sweet, don't look so worried," Colin said with a sudden return to gentleness. "Marguérite will happily forget that Giles owns the house, and I doubt if I shall run amok and murder him! Meanwhile, tomorrow's Saturday, thank God – release from the prison house! Let's run away and spend it by ourselves."

She was obliged to shake her head. "The idea's lovely, but I promised to play tennis with Lucy Pollack tomorrow. I can't let her down. I've neglected her too much recently."

"Perdition take her, whoever she may be. It's much more important not to let *me* down."

"Old friends are important too," she corrected him, "and Lucy's not a girl for hating – you'd agree if you knew her. In fact, why not get to know her? Come and play tennis too."

It was only when they were driving up the hill the following afternoon that something long buried in her memory surfaced to trouble her. Colin heard the little gasp she gave, and turned to smile at her.

"Something wrong? My aged flannels won't do?"

"You look elegance itself, as always, but I've just remembered an ancient quarrel between Sir Nicholas and your father. Lucy may not even have known about it, but if her parents are at home the name of Credland may put a certain strain on Manor hospitality!"

Instead of making it an excuse to call the visit off, he seemed to relish the idea more than before. "I hope the Squire and his lady *are* at home . . . a real test of my social flair, wouldn't you say?"

For once she didn't smile back at him, but when they got to the Manor it seemed that his social flair was not going to be put to the test after all – Bart and Lady Evelyn were not there. Colin set out to please Lucy, and in no time at all she forgot to feel shy of him. They'd played two games and honours were even when Andrew sauntered out of the house and asked to meet the Manor guest. To Cressida's surprise, and even more to his sister's, he suggested completing the foursome.

"Lucy and I know each other's game . . . fairer if we split up," he said firmly.

She looked unnerved by the suggestion, but it was soon obvious that Colin's kindness equalled his social flair. He was an ideal partner for her, quick to praise, and generous enough not to poach balls that she could deal with herself. She blossomed under this unusual treatment and, intrigued by what was happening at the other end, Cressy paid insufficient attention to her own game. At the end of it she sensed that Andrew thought she'd let the others beat them. She'd never liked him less or valued Colin more.

When Sir Nicholas and his wife reappeared they were drinking cider in the conservatory that a Victorian ancestor more concerned with comfort than aesthetics had defiantly tacked on to the back of the house. Lucy, still flushed and triumphant, introduced her partner with pride. Lady Evelyn smiled at him, remembering little of the Credland dispute that had so infuriated her husband.

"It must be your mother who is bravely tackling the old house down on the point," she said. "I hope she realises that the whole of Derrycombe will take the keenest interest in what she's doing!"

Colin smiled at her. "She'll enjoy that. The only danger is that she may drive the workmen to despair, because she knows exactly what she wants. If they tell her a particular colour doesn't exist, she seizes pots of paint and mixes it herself."

While he talked to Lady Evelyn, Andrew stared at Cressy. "So you finally lost your quirky house?" he murmured.

She hadn't expected him to remember that long-ago conversation when they'd discussed the Admiral's House; since he had remembered it, she supposed he could also recollect the rest of the same painful occasion. "Yes, I've lost it," she agreed after a moment. "But it's found someone who'll cherish it, so I don't really mind."

Then it was Bart's turn to venture on awkward ground. "Are you with the family firm in Plymouth?" he asked Colin.

"Dogsbody-cum-roving salesman. Not the inventive genius my father was, I'm afraid."

"You must still have a genius of some kind; a company like yours needs outstanding talent if it's to stay ahead of the competition."

"My half-brother Giles runs Credland's now," Colin said briefly. "He's an engineer by training – quite a good one, we're led to believe."

If the tribute wasn't enthusiastic, at least he'd controlled his animosity for once, and Cressy smiled at him approvingly, but he turned to speak to his hostess.

"The Manor is very beautiful. Would you allow me to bring my mother to see it? She is always interested in other people's houses but this one would bowl her over."

Cressy wondered why she'd had a moment's anxiety about letting him come. Colin bent on making himself agreeable was irresistible; if offered to a group of hungry cannibals, he would have no difficulty in persuading them to eat someone else. The distaff side of the Pollacks were going down like ninepins and even Bart was visibly thawing. Leaving aside Cain and Abel, had any two brothers ever been so different? She felt proud of Colin for triumphing over an old quarrel, but knew a qualm when he deliberately took the risk of referring to it. He was a born gambler, she realised, unable to resist the lure of danger.

"I believe my father crossed swords with you once, sir. I'm sorry if that makes me *persona non grata* here!"

It was within a hair's breadth of being impudent, and Cressy watched the Squire for signs that he'd taken offence, but he merely gave a little shrug. "Nothing to do with you, nor was it your father

I had dealings with. Giles Credland blocked something I wanted to do in Plymouth. Can't say I was happy about it at the time, but he had as much right to fight for what he wanted as I did."

Driving away from the Manor, Cressy smiled at Colin.

"You behaved beautifully – especially to my friend Lucy. I've never seen her so happy and sure of herself."

"Calculated, all of it," he said with sudden honesty. "I told you I was going to see if I could make them accept a Credland!"

She stared at him, faintly disturbed, and reluctant to believe that she was to take him seriously.

"Don't look at me like that, Cressida, and for God's sake don't ever expect too much of me. If my dear brother hasn't already warned you about that, he will certainly do so."

Her face broke into its irradiating smile. "He tried one day, but wasn't allowed to get very far."

"I was afraid of that," Colin said sombrely. Then he kissed the end of her nose, put the car in gear, and ended the conversation.

*   *   *

As spring gave way to summer the changing season was reflected in the holiday visitors who swarmed off the small river steamers that chugged upstream from Dartmouth, and had to stop at Totnes because the Dart wasn't navigable thereafter. The town shopkeepers welcomed the fact, but Cressy often wondered what the other citizens thought of the crowds clogging the narrow streets. There seemed to be an accepted route along which they swarmed – the climb up Fore Street from the quay, and an obligatory photograph or two of the remains of city wall and Norman castle. Then it was time for coffee or tea, and the trudge back to the quay, often interrupted by a call at Marlow's bookshop on the way.

She had to remind herself that she was a shopkeeper too, there to entice customers into her shop, not wish that they would go away. The window displays had to be eye-catching and beautiful. Books about the West Country were flanked by good water-colours by local artists, cookery books peeped seductively from among the china and glass she'd filched from Helen's cupboards at home, and when children's books were on display she added a backdrop of painted cardboard cut-outs of the characters that inhabit everybody's childhood: Pooh, Rupert, Badger, and all the rest. She enjoyed the work, copied her father's patience with customers who didn't know what they wanted, and listened to those who came for someone to talk to rather than for something to buy. But running a business was arduous, and it was hard as the weeks went by to match Colin's resilience or share his ambition to sample every pub and restaurant in the county. Saturdays, especially, became a bone of contention between them because she refused to accept his suggestion that the shop could then be left to her assistants.

"You're the boss, for God's sake," he said irritably one day. "*You* make the rules."

"I follow my father's rules, and they don't include foisting Saturday work on other people when I'm not prepared to do it myself."

"The puritan work ethic! I knew we'd stumble over it sooner or later. Tell me that we can't enjoy ourselves on the Sabbath either and it will be the end of a beautiful friendship!"

He smiled as he said it, but she knew that his patience was wearing thin. As far as he was concerned, she might just as well have been still working in London as chained six days a week to a bookshop in Totnes.

*   *   *

The Admiral's House was in the hands of the builders, and Marguérite drove herself over from Plymouth every day to inspect progress, change her mind, sack her workmen and then immediately reinstate them with an apology so charming that they forgave her and went back to work. She took to dropping in at Lantern Cottage in the course of these visits, and although Helen began by worrying about the effect of such a mercurial guest, it soon became clear that she did Roland no harm. In fact he observed her with the disinterested pleasure of a lepidopterist who'd netted a particularly exotic butterfly.

One morning she arrived looking so downcast that he assumed some minor hitch. "You've just decided that your entire colour scheme is a mistake and you've got to start again."

"My colour scheme is perfect," she said, distracted for a moment even from the matter at hand. "No, it's far worse than that . . . worse than anything I could have imagined."

"A tidal wave we haven't heard about has washed the house out to sea?" This was Helen, plunging wildly.

Marguerite shook her head. "You'll never guess. Giles is beginning to like my house – to covet it!"

Roland tried to look grave. "Dear Marguérite, is it really such a bad thing that he should take an interest in it?"

"Bad? It's absolutely disastrous; the next thing will be that he'll want to *live* there. Already, he keeps turning up at weekends, with the excuse that the garden's a wilderness. I know it is, but I can find a gardener when I have time to think about such things. I don't want Giles out there, stripped to the waist, labouring like a coal-heaver and telling himself that he can do what he likes in his own garden."

"Tell him it's *your* garden."

They watched her eyes fill with tears. "It isn't, that's the trouble. The house belongs to him. He's probably only waiting until it's ready to tell me he wants to live in it himself, and I shall die of disappointment."

"It's big enough to share," Helen suggested, hoping to give comfort. "Perhaps that's what he's waiting to suggest."

"Then dying would be preferable," Marguérite answered simply.

There was a little silence in the room, and Ronald found that he no longer wanted to laugh. Even allowing something for foreign exaggeration, despair haunted her face; it was impossible to pretend that the Credlands were a normal family, made up of people who rubbed each other up the wrong way occasionally.

"He'll get tired of labouring as soon as the novelty wears off," Roland suggested finally. "Living here and working in Plymouth may not be totally impractical, but it borders on that for a man who works a twelve-hour day. Why not believe what he says, that he just wants to see the grounds back in order?"

Marguérite looked slightly less tragic, and Helen diverted her by raising the matter of the house-warming party that was to announce to Derrycombe the rebirth of the Admiral's House.

Before it took place Cressida had the serious disagreement with Colin that she'd sensed was coming. It dragged into the open the fact she'd refused to allow herself to face – that at the moment her life was not her own. Like an inexpert trapeze artiste hoisted into space, she simply kept launching herself at the next bar that hurtled towards her, hoping against hope that her hands would close round it in time. She was torn between the opposing fears that her father would die if she turned her back on him or that she would lose Colin if she didn't. Working for Giles chafed him enough, without the added irritation of finding her always trapped in the web of other people's needs. At the end of an unsuccessful evening which they *had* spent together the threatening storm finally broke about her head.

"You sound jaded, and I feel worse," Colin said when they were on their way home. "We both need a little dissipation. Unfortunately we haven't the time to go to Paris but Dr Credland prescribes a long weekend in London. How about it, Cressy?"

She wished the prescription had been forty-eight hours' uninterrupted sleep, but struggled against tiredness to consider the significance of what he was suggesting. She knew that it was time to abandon sedateness and commit herself by sleeping with him; she wasn't dismayed by the suggestion itself, only by its timing.

"Dr Credland's prescription sounds lovely, but would he be kind enough to ask me again in a month's time?" she suggested with a tired smile. "The shop's still inundated with Saturday visitors and I can't leave the others to cope just yet."

The mulish set of his mouth prepared her for what was coming next. "I'm asking you *now*."

"Then I'm afraid the answer's still no. Please, dear Colin, bear with me a bit longer."

Her regret was genuine, but tiredness blinkered her to everything but the stubborn conviction that she couldn't for the moment interfere with the remorseless routine in which her life was fixed. Her working day had begun eighteen hours earlier, and the thought of sleep was as enticing as a carrot dangled under a donkey's nose. She wanted more than anything in the world just to go home, tried with an effort that made her jaws ache to suppress a yawn, and didn't quite succeed.

58

"Stupid of me not to realise why you refuse . . . I'm boring you."
His cold voice and glinting, unamused smile made a stranger of him.
She wanted to shout that she had more right to be tired than he
had to be unreasonable, but she knew that anger would only make
matters worse. Instead she put out her hand to touch his in a little
pleading gesture.

"Don't be cross. You couldn't be boring if you tried, and I'd
come with you gladly if I could. I promise I *will* come as soon
as I can."

"Not good enough, Cressida. It's time to decide whether *we're*
more important than all the other commitments you cling to so
tenderly. I'm tired of being fitted in to the odd hours you can spare;
you must make up your mind."

He was right, but surely unreasonable in insisting that she must
make up her mind *now*. The feeling that she was being given an
unfair ultimatum made her speak more coolly than she intended.

"I know we can't go on as we are, but it's too late tonight even
for small decisions about weekends, much less big ones about the
future."

"Then *I'll* make up your mind for you." She was dragged across
the seat of the car into his arms, and a moment later his mouth was
hard and hurtful on her own. His hands began to explore her body
insistently but without the tenderness that would have made her
respond. There was nothing to respond to in a demand for mere
physical surrender. She could only try to resist him by being as
totally passive in his arms as she could manage, and in the end the
onslaught ended as abruptly as it had begun. She was thrust away,
and he sat with his head buried in his arms on the steering-wheel.
Exhaustion and regret washed over her, but she was aware as well
of his own desolating sense of failure. She stared out of the window,
not surprised to find that the world outside was achingly beautiful;
it always seemed to be so when human affairs went terribly awry.
Moonlight laid a silver track across the quiet sea below them, and a
sprinkling of stars gleamed like sequins on dark velvet. She turned to
look at him again, and stretched out her hand to touch his cheek.

"Come outside . . . it's so beautiful."

He lifted his head to stare at her. "Aren't you being rash? A frustrated lover is hardly the man to entice into taking a moonlit stroll."

"You once promised that you'd never do anything to hurt me," she reminded him gravely.

A rueful smile touched his mouth. "Trust you to confront me with it now! I wonder why I love you so much."

They stood for a while on the cliff-top, staring at the silver ribbon unrolling across the water to where dark water merged with the darker sky. With his arm about her shoulders, she sensed the sadness that had replaced his previous fever. If it would have helped, she'd have made a gift of herself now, but the timing was still wrong . . . the moment when he'd wanted her had come and gone. Instead, he began to talk quietly.

"Half the time I long for a crystal ball that would show me the future; at other times, when demons gibber on the margins of my mind, I'm thankful I don't know. That's why I need *you* so desperately, Cressy; someone sane and loving. I can't spend the rest of my life watching Giles playing the part of Lord God Almighty, but my dear, expensive mother complicates the business of breaking away. Promise me you won't get tired of the mess we're in, and shuffle me off for some rich, straightforward suitor like Andrew Pollack."

She reached up to kiss his cheek. "No difficulty about promising that; even if Andrew hadn't shuffled *me* off a long time ago."

"It's not the impression I get. Of course he wants you . . . you're beautiful." His fingers gently traced the outline of her mouth, as if he was trying to commit it to memory. "It's peaceful here . . . lovely. I think if I asked you now you'd let me make love to you, but you're too tired, my dearest dear, and I shall take you home instead."

His tenderness, and the wistful yearning that lay beneath it for the peace of mind he hadn't discovered yet, made her want to weep.

"Colin . . . forgive me for making things worse for you when my intention was to try to make them better," she said unsteadily. "For the moment you can't abandon Marguérite, and I'm afraid to abandon my father. It's difficult but not desperate as long as we don't lose each other."

He nodded and led her back to the car, but she realised that he hadn't said whether he agreed with her or not.

Chapter Six

GILES Credland felt even more irritated than usual with his stepmother. At the best of times she was a feckless, tiresome woman whose wayward charm had never made the slightest appeal to him; now, she'd seen the possibilities of a dilapidated house that he wanted for himself. The fact that it belonged to him only made matters worse – he must allow her to live in it if she wanted to. This attraction to a heap of bricks and mortar had taken him by surprise. He'd grown up in a large Victorian villa in the middle of Plymouth, comfortable but irretrievably ugly. He'd felt no affection for it and only resented Marguérite's insistence that it should be sold when his father died, because what had been good enough for Jane Credland should have been good enough for *her*.

Beauty in the perfect design and functioning of a piece of machinery he'd always been able to perceive, but it simply hadn't occurred to him that a house could achieve the same feeling of 'rightness'. Now, prowling among the chaos of the workmen's paraphernalia, he wasn't blind to the paradox that beauty of the serenest kind was gradually emerging from Marguérite's hail of commands and counter-instructions.

She had no time to spare for the wilderness outside and, he suspected, very little interest in it either. Flowers, when needed for decoration, came easily from a florist's shop, and she saw no pleasure in the toil of planting things, or in the delay of waiting for them to grow. It suited him very well, because he could continue to think of the garden, at least, as his. Gardeners he knew he didn't want; his garden was not to be domesticated, or reduced to municipal neatness, full of mathematically planned displays. But how to set about converting the jungle around him into a fitting foreground to the glorious backdrop of estuary, sea and sky, this his years of living in a service flat overlooking the Hoe hadn't taught him.

His weekend work in the garden rarely coincided with Marguérite's own visits, but one day they happened to be at the house together and a shared picnic lunch seemed inevitable.

"You'll hate the idea but I shall give a house-warming party as soon as I move in," she said defiantly. "I want everyone to know that I shall be living here."

It cost her something to say it, in case he should finally announce his intention to exclude her from what she'd just created, but he merely asked a question instead.

"What about Colin? I haven't seen him around, but does he plan to live here too?"

The sardonic note that always edged his voice whenever he spoke of his half-brother made her nervous, but she did her best to explain calmly. "He's made friends in the neighbourhood, and there always seems to be something going on."

"He already had a 'friend' here, of course. I suppose Cressida Marlow absorbs all his spare time?"

Marguérite looked vague. "Well, yes . . . but when Cressy's busy he goes to the Manor . . . he's become very popular there."

"That must have strained even *his* social knackiness! The worthy baronet has no reason to like the Credlands."

"He has no reason to like *you*," she said bravely. "That doesn't stop the Pollacks liking Colin and me."

"Well said . . . in fact, your trick, I think!"

He conceded it with a gleam of amusement that she barely recognised as such. For the first time, it occurred to her that, when not frowning, he reminded her a little of William. She remembered her tactics in the past, and a glimmer of doubt came to trouble her. Afraid of not getting what she'd wanted, she'd often been indirect; if the small deceits that had seemed justified at the time had angered him, perhaps she was partly to blame.

"Have your party if that's what you want," he said now with unusual mildness. "Personally, I like the house as it is . . . empty of other people, and sounding only of the wind in the trees and the sea on the rocks down below." The surprise in her face wasn't lost on him and he went on to complete her bafflement, "I like what you've done here, by the way. The outside won't do it justice for a long time yet. The gardener is willing, but very ignorant I'm afraid."

She found her voice, and tasted the rare pleasure of being able to give her stepson advice. "You should consult Cressy's father, Roland Marlow, at Lantern Cottage. He leads an invalid's life now after a heart attack but, apart from Evelyn Pollack, he's the gardening expert in Derrycombe."

Giles nodded without committing himself, having no wish to meet Roland Marlow if it meant seeing his daughter again. But in the course of a brisk walk after lunch, he rounded the end of the quay and found in front of him the name of 'Lantern Cottage' worked into an attractive wrought-iron gate. In the garden beyond a tall, thin-faced man seemed to be hesitating.

"You weren't thinking of coming in, by any chance?" he asked pleasantly. "If so, the moment's well-timed. There's a kitten stuck in our tree, and I'm afraid my tree-climbing days are over. I'm Roland Marlow, by the way."

"Giles Credland. You know my stepmother and Colin, I think. I'll be glad to shin up the tree for you."

The kitten mewed piteously, but resisted rescue all the same, and was finally brought down at the cost of a long scratch across Giles's hand, and some damage to his temper.

"Sorry about that," Roland pointed at the scratch. "You'd think they'd be intelligent enough to know when they're being helped. I can offer you sticking-plaster or a soothing glass of beer!"

Over the beer Giles opted for, Roland explained why the women of the house were out. "Cressida and my friend Christopher Goodhew are getting our new bookshop in Derrycombe ready for opening. My wife, though not entirely happy about leaving me on my own, is helping them."

"My stepmother said something about a heart attack . . . I'm sorry. It must be damnably frustrating to have to watch other people doing the things you'd rather do yourself."

"Yes," Roland agreed simply, "but it also makes unfair demands on my wife and daughter. Helen toils cheerfully for me out here although she's not at heart a gardener, and Cressida pretends that she asks nothing more of life than to run my bookshop in Totnes."

He was aware of Giles' eyes fixed on him, blue eyes oddly at variance with the swarthy ugliness of the face they were set in. "Is that why she left London? I once put a rather different interpretation on it and she didn't correct me."

His host resisted the temptation to ask what the wrong impression had been and tactfully changed the subject.

"Are you going to be living at the Admiral's House too? We shall all go on calling it that, by the way, through sheer force of habit."

"I like the old name, and the house too, but it's my stepmother who will be living there."

"And Derrycombe itself, do you like that?"

Giles took time to consider a reply. "Yes, but I can see it thanking God every Sunday that it's the way it is: no trash, no tourists, and above all nothing rudely industrial!"

A grin warmed his harsh features, making Roland wonder why Cressida had taken in such dislike a man who wasn't to be hated just for not having Colin's easy charm. She was often cussed, of course, but not prone to unfair prejudice when it came to making up her mind about people.

"I suppose we *are* in danger of becoming a museum-piece," he conceded thoughtfully. "A bit of fishing still goes on, and the Squire absorbs youngsters on the estate when he can, but there are many who don't want farming jobs nowadays and they have to find work away from Derrycombe. Perhaps we shouldn't have set our faces quite so firmly against trade and tourism."

Giles shook his head. "Anything but tourism . . . it's the kiss of death."

"A diehard preservationist talking?"

"Not at all. I don't want anything preserved that can't sustain itself honestly. The bogus charade of once self-respecting boatmen who pretend to be the Cornish equivalent of Venetian gondoliers fills me with rage. There are places along the coast that are travesties of the honest-to-god fishing ports they once were; and the descendants of men who crawled along putrid tunnels searching for tin now pride themselves on being macho barmen and purveyors of chips and ice-cream."

The contempt in his voice was laced with something that sounded like angry pain, making Roland reflect that the conversation wasn't the bland small-talk that most of his visitors considered suitable for an invalid. It was as refreshing as a breath of wind in his lungs on the top of High Tor.

"You obviously hate the sight of coaches lined up from the Lizard to Land's End," he pointed out. "I'm not keen on them either, when they infest Dartmoor throughout the summer. But visitors bring money and, with the failure of everything except the china clay industry, Cornwall must need revenue even more chronically than Devon does."

"I know all about Cornwall's poverty. Pandering to hordes of holiday-makers, or becoming the geriatric home of the rest of the country's pensioners may be one way back to wealth, but it's the wrong way. Prosperity should come from exploiting its traditional skills and resources, which include the inherited temperament of true Cornish people. Thank God for the climate, which may eventually drive the others away!" Suddenly he smiled at his host. "Sorry . . . you shouldn't encourage me to ride my hobby-horse!"

"It's a hobby-horse we share, although what's happening to Devon concerns me more dearly. It was my greatest pleasure in life to take Cressida walking on a once-empty moor; empty, that is, to anyone who couldn't see what was there. She learnt to trace the history of the place as well as I can, and still loves it more than anywhere else she knows."

He wondered what he'd said to disconcert his visitor again. "When I met her for the first time – in London – she didn't look like a girl whose happiness was in wandering over Dartmoor," Giles slowly explained. "It occurs to me now that she rather enjoys setting traps and watching me fall into them."

He sounded irritated, and Roland couldn't blame him; it was just the sort of thing Cressy might do if she thought he needed teaching a lesson. Before he could apologise for the fact, Giles spoke again. "You must miss what you're no longer allowed to enjoy."

"Yes, but I'm learning to sublimate desire by writing the history of Devon for children, at the instigation of my daughter."

"She sounds a bossy piece, if you'll forgive me for saying so."

It produced a shout of laughter, but then Roland shook his head. "She's not always as biddable as she might be, but on the whole we like her the way she is."

Giles looked unconvinced but abandoned the subject. "I don't know how mobile you're allowed to be, but if I drove you to the house could you tell me how to change a wilderness into a garden?"

"Striding up and down hills is beyond me now, but I can certainly walk round your grounds, and no gardener is proof against an invitation to advise!"

They arranged a tour of inspection for the following weekend, which Helen welcomed when she heard about it, but Cressy did not.

"He got round you by helping with the kitten, but he's still an arrogant boor," she said definitely. "Worse than that, he's deliberately cruel, playing with poor Marguérite like a cat with a mouse. She's terrified that he'll suddenly want the house for himself."

"I got the impression that he hadn't any thought of her *not* living there."

"Then why doesn't he tell her so? What could be more cruel than leaving her in doubt?"

Roland held up his hands in surrender. "Does it offend you very much if I offer a little advice on his garden? If so, I'll cancel the arrangement."

"Now you're being silly," she said with great dignity. "You must do as you like about Giles Credland."

All the same she had no intention of being at home when Giles called to collect her father, and was careful to be playing tennis at the Manor when he arrived the following Sunday. Even that wasn't without its irritations because Andrew now seemed determined to be present whenever she arrived with Colin, and it was also becoming obvious that Colin spent more time at the Manor than she did herself. The fact worried her only on Lucy's account and she thought it was

66

time to say so. But while the two men rewhitened the lines on the tennis court, there was something else to say first.

"You're looking a treat," she told her friend warmly. It was true; Lucy's mouse-brown hair was now cut short to curl softly round her ears, and a broken fringe prettily concealed her high forehead. Cressy was about to add that it was exactly what she'd been recommending for years when Lucy's reply silenced her.

"It was all Colin's doing. He insisted on taking me into Plymouth yesterday to a place Marguérite recommended. Then he helped me choose a new dress for her house-warming party. Imagine Andrew or my father doing such a thing! Wild horses wouldn't drag them inside a women's shop. But the strange thing is that Colin isn't the least bit effeminate; he just seems to understand that we sometimes need a bit of encouragement."

Cressida stared at her flushed face, wondering whether another rescue mission was also about to go awry. Angela had bored him and he'd abandoned her. Perhaps she hadn't minded, but Lucy was different; affections once given were given for good, and her fragile confidence in herself wouldn't survive being shelved too abruptly.

"You're very quiet," she said anxiously. "You don't mind, do you, Cress? I'm not trying to poach, and it wouldn't be any good even if I were. I shan't ever be a dazzler like you, but Colin's kind enough to make me feel that I'm not beyond hope, that's all."

"You've never been beyond hope – only in need of a little help." She hesitated over what to say next. "Colin gets lonely when I have to be at the shop, and I'm grateful to you for keeping him company. I know I'm not being fair to him, but I have the feeling that my father's safe as long as I'm helping Helen keep an eye on him. That's one problem; another is that there's just too much to do."

"Colin and I often talk about you," Lucy reported without resentment. "You need help, Cress, and I've got an idea to put to you. Would you and your father let me take over all the school work for you?" She waited but no comment came. "You don't like the idea? It's true I don't know much about books, but I thought I could learn, and I am quite good with children. You always used to say I could manage the little devils in the Sunday School class!"

It was the most positive speech Lucy had ever made. If that, like the new hair-style, was Colin's doing, Cressy couldn't regret his effect on her; he might cause her unhappiness in the long run, but at least she would know that she was properly alive.

"I can't see anything wrong with the idea at all," she said slowly, "provided you can sell it here. I'm not sure Lady Evelyn's going to relish the thought of you driving around the county with a car-load of books."

"I told you, it's not so difficult to make her understand things these days," Lucy said with a touch of pride. "She knows I'm bored silly with what I do – I'm a left-over from three generations ago, and if I don't break out soon I'll end up another Gwyneth Morgan: mother-ridden, moustached, and mildly mad!"

Cressy tried to gasp that since Gwyneth was on the shady side of forty, there was still a little way to go, but a fit of helpless laughter overtook her. Lucy promptly collapsed as well, and Andrew couldn't help grinning at the sight of them doubled up with merriment at the end of the tennis-court, like the children they'd been not so very long ago. When Cressy finally mopped her eyes, she reverted to serious matters again. "I'll talk to my father as soon as I get home. The decision's his, but I can't help feeling that you've just got yourself a job."

For the rest of the morning only half her mind was on the game, and Colin chided her for it on the way home. She explained that she'd been thinking about Lucy's suggestion and his face brightened again.

"The idea took, then? I hoped I'd planted the seed. All you have to do now, sweetheart, is make sure it sprouts. I refuse to have you tied to that bloody shop much longer."

She thought it wasn't the moment to remind him that the shop would still be there even if Lucy took over the school work. He pulled her into his arms, and didn't make the mistake this time of being rough; his mouth was tender on hers, and she wanted to agree that the only thing that mattered was this sea of delight on which they could float together if only they had time. When he let her go his smile was brilliant with the certainty of having won.

"You're agreeing with me at last that we can't waste any more time. It ought to be Paris in the spring but there's nothing wrong with September. As soon as Marguérite's party is out of the way. We shall *splurge*, my darling, in the most exciting city on earth. If that doesn't get the taste of provincial Plymouth out of our mouths, nothing will."

Cressy surfaced slowly out of the depths of bemused happiness, promising herself that she wouldn't say she liked provincial life. But something else had to be said. "Dearest Colin, could it be just a little later than that? September means a new school term and there'll be Lucy to get started. It's also the birthday month of both my parents, and there's a family habit of a joint celebration—"

"—and then Helen's drama society will start rehearsing *Puss in Boots*, and there'll be only ninety-one shopping days to Christmas," he ended savagely. "Why not just say that you don't want to come to bed with me, in Paris or anywhere else? Tell the truth, Cressida, because I'm sick to death of half-baked excuses."

His voice was like a lash laid across her skin. She wanted to shout that he wasn't the only one who suffered, that she was not only tired but desperately torn, and that the knowledge of his frustrations only added to her own. But their last quarrel was still vivid in her mind; another one now would damage them, perhaps beyond repair.

"I don't offer you excuses," she said unsteadily, "only reasons that you aren't able to accept. You jeer at me for being a puritan, but even to please you I can't pretend that I think responsibilities don't matter. That doesn't mean I don't ache for you to love me, and even the fear that my father might slip away from us if my back is turned isn't enough now to prevent me going away with you as soon as I can." It was, she thought, the greatest commitment she could offer him.

"I retract the word 'excuses'," he said finally. "But before long, Cressida mine, you're going to have to make a choice: is it going to be you and me, or you and the other attachments that keep tying you to Derrycombe? Even for you I can't play second fiddle indefinitely."

They drove in silence after that and she didn't see him again until the evening of his mother's party. The Marlows were augmented by Christopher Goodhew, now settled in his own flat above the Derrycombe bookshop, and the four of them set out for the

Admiral's House with Helen happily predicting that Derrycombe's social life was going to be transformed by Marguérite's continental touch. Dressed herself in a risky but successful mixture of pink and coral-coloured chiffon, she was conscious of doing her bit to enliven Derrycombe, and she didn't miss the Squire's blink when he caught sight of her.

"Glad to see your father's well enough to be here," Bart said to Cressy. "Helen, too, bless her . . . never seen her look quite so tremendous!"

She grinned at the choice of word. "Mama and Marguérite enjoy seeing if they can outdo each other. I know when I'm beaten and don't try to compete."

Sir Nicholas looked at her standing beside him, tall and slender and elegant in a simple tunic of white silk. "You look perfect to me," he admitted unexpectedly.

Appreciation was welcome, wherever it came from, but she waited for the moment when Colin would be free to join her after welcoming guests with Marguérite. By the time the buffet supper was over, it was painfully clear that the moment wasn't going to come. He'd attached himself to Lucy instead, and she was transformed both by that fact and by the beautiful jonquil-yellow dress they'd chosen together.

Cressy told herself that she would not feel anxious on her friend's account, or angry on her own, and got through the endless evening with a bright, false smile pinned to her mouth. She was trying to look interested in Gwyneth Morgan's description of her mother's latest ailment when Giles Credland loomed up in front of them. Gwyneth was put aside with a brusque apology and Cressy shepherded towards an empty space by one of the long open windows.

"I might have been enjoying myself for all you knew," she muttered as soon as they were out of earshot.

"In that case you were concealing it remarkably well. I never saw a woman more obviously praying for someone to come and rescue her."

Cressy refused to admit that it might have been so and tried another tack. "Knight errantry . . . not your usual line, surely?"

"No; I had an ulterior motive." It wasn't entirely true. He'd seen the desolation behind her smile and felt a strong inclination to kick

his half-brother through the garden into Start Bay. Mixed with that
not unusual feeling was irritation with the girl at his side. No one
who looked as self-possessed and sophisticated as Cressida Marlow
did should be, in fact, so vulnerable.

"I've been looking for a chance to get an apology off my chest,"
Giles said abruptly. "Your father told me the real reason why you
left London. I'm sorry I jumped to the conclusion that it had to
do with Colin coming back to Plymouth."

"Kind of you to say so, but I hope you haven't been losing any
sleep over something that doesn't matter."

"Meaning that you don't give a damn what I think. Why should
you, indeed?"

He was quick to get the point, she conceded privately. Nothing
had to be spelled out for Giles Credland, and it gave a certain
zest to conversations with him that she didn't find elsewhere in
Derrycombe now that Admiral Blake was dead.

"My dear brother seems to be exerting himself," Giles said next.
"Quite the delightful host; he's even got her ladyship smiling."

She wouldn't allow him to be tactful. "Why not say what you
mean – that he's got Lucy Pollack smiling too?"

Giles looked bored, and she couldn't blame him; other people's
muddled love-affairs were boring, especially to a man with no
human weakness of his own.

"You seem determined not to accept the idea that Colin's life is
governed by self-interest," he said with calm detachment. "Viewed
in certain terms at least, the worthy baronet's daughter must be
quite a catch!"

"You, viewed in any terms at all, are despicable." She all but
shouted the words at him, saw Gwyneth turn round to stare, and
had to make do with a furious murmur. "Everything warm and
human shrivels up and dies as soon as it collides with you. No
wonder Colin described you as a lump of Cornish granite."

"If that was all he said, he was being unusually restrained. He's
freer with his tongue among some of his colleagues, family loyalty
not being one of his strong points."

"Well, it doesn't exactly leap to the eye in *you*," she said between
gritted teeth. "You've had something loathsome to say about Colin

71

or Marguérite each time we've met. If it's all the same to you, I'd just as soon avoid you altogether in future."

"I'll ring a leper's bell," he suggested affably. "Would that suit?"

"Admirably!" She stalked away and, determined that she might as well martyr herself in a good cause, kept Gwyneth Morgan company for the rest of the interminable evening.

Chapter Seven

A TACTFUL silence was preserved at Lantern Cottage on the subject of the party. Colin telephoned, but only to say that he would be away for a week in the north, attending an important trade fair for Credland's. It left his mother alone at the Admiral's House, and Cressy felt obliged to pay her an evening visit. She was accustomed by now to Marguérite's swift changes of mood, but it didn't occur to her that party gaiety would have given way so soon to the conviction that happiness was over.

"You're wondering what you're going to do with yourself now that the house is finished," Cressy said gently.

Marguérite was half-apologetic, half-sad. "I do love it, *chérie*, and even Giles admits that I've made it beautiful, but sitting here by myself I couldn't help thinking of the winter. I'm not sure I shall be able to bear it then, with nothing to listen to but the wind and the sound of the sea outside. Giles says that's how he likes it – well, he's half-Cornish, of course!"

The conclusion was so doleful but definite that Cressy couldn't help smiling. "I don't think it has much to do with hailing from across the Tamar; I like the house wind-and-sea-loud, too."

"It didn't seem lonely when it was full of workmen, and there was always something to think about; but suddenly all the excitement is over."

"You're missing Colin; the house will seem much less empty when he gets back."

Marguérite hesitated for a moment, then bravely tackled the subject of the party. "I'm afraid you must have made him cross, dearest – he always retaliates. William never bore malice, so I

73

suppose it's a fault he inherits from me, but it won't last long. My dear son soon gets over things."

"He wanted me to take a holiday with him in Paris, and wouldn't agree to wait a few more weeks." It begged a more important question, but Cressy felt disinclined to discuss the future, even with Marguérite.

"And now you think he's behaving like a spoilt child, sulking because he can't have what he wants immediately?"

Cressy gave a little nod. "I thought he might have tried a little harder to understand."

"Darling, *you* have to understand something too," Marguérite insisted. "Colin has been in Giles's shadow all his life, always in second place, always made to feel that what he wanted didn't count. He adores you, but if you're putting him in second place as well, he'll pretend not to mind by paying attention to someone else. At least he was thoughtful enough not to worry you too much by picking on boring, blameless Lucy Pollack!"

Cressy blinked at the notion that his behaviour could, even by maternal partiality, have been called thoughtful. Every so often Marguérite said or did something that underlined how differently they viewed things; it was a fact to be accepted along with the warmth and charm that were also part of her make-up. But the memory of Lucy's radiant face at the party still haunted Cressy's mind.

"Spare a thought for Lucy," she said at last. "Not only is she not boring, but she's also liable to get hurt."

A shrug put Lucy and the subject aside, and she knew it would be useless to persist.

"We've strayed off the point," she remembered instead; "we were talking about *you*. Life would seem much less boring here if you made more friends, began joining things."

"The Women's Institute, the Guild of Church Needlewomen, the Flower-Arrangers' Circle . . .? Darling, I don't want to be difficult, but I can't feel that they sound much like me!"

It might be true, but Cressy found herself irritated by such a carping spirit. "Well, we must find something that *does* interest you. What about starting an interior decorating society? Better still, start your own consultancy service and get people to pay you for what you love doing!"

She made the suggestion half-jokingly, but it held promise, and she felt disappointed when Marguérite rejected this as well.

"I should be much too expensive. Other people always want to do things cheaply. I should either spend all their money or walk out in a rage."

It sounded all too true, and Cressy sighed and made her last throw. "Well, a companion here then, so that there would be someone else living in the house even if Colin had to go away."

At last a dazzling smile lit the forlorn face opposite her. "Dearest, the perfect answer! You must move in here yourself, then Colin would be sure to be here too. You know you love it."

She didn't say that in acquiring a companion she would also be acquiring a daughter-in-law, and Cressy doubted whether so trivial a detail as marriage even occurred to her. It was tempting to point out that London or Parisian ways wouldn't quite do for Derrycombe but the words died on her lips because she remembered that Colin had never mentioned marriage either. Perhaps 'commitment' didn't mean to him what it meant to an irredeemably small-town girl.

She walked home eventually, having cheered up Marguérite at the cost of depressing herself. It was something to be reckoned with, this indifference to inflicting hurt which seemed to be a part of the Credland make-up. In Giles's case it was a positive relish for crashing into people headlong, but neither Marguérite nor Colin had seen anything wrong in making use of Lucy. She found it an uncomfortable thought, but honesty insisted on a worse one: the fault was as much hers as Colin's. He'd warned her at the beginning of their friendship that he wasn't a patient man. It sounded fine to claim that love must wait while she minded her father's shop and helped him write his Devon books; but this high-minded sense of duty, called by its other name of spiritual pride, had a more hollow ring. Her father had probably been as aware of it as Colin was, and only the kindest of hearts had prevented him from telling her so. It was time to accept the fact, and to accept one more painful home-truth while she was about it: Miss Helping Hands had overreached herself in the matter of Marguérite as well; she wasn't going to fit contentedly into Derrycombe after all, and the whole idea of settling her in the Admiral's House had been nothing but an expensive disaster. A woman who couldn't cope with life alone didn't need a house, Cressy decided, what she needed was a husband.

The problem of her own future with Colin was something she must solve herself, but there was nothing to stop her seeking help with Marguérite. Her mother knew every unmarried male in the locality, and she could probably even make a shrewd guess as to which of them could afford an extravagant wife who would alternately enrage and enchant them. Cressy was about to embark on the subject at breakfast next morning when the conversation took a different turn.

Roland Marlow looked up from the newspaper he was skimming through to smile at her when she sat down. "James dropped in last night for a game of chess. He was disappointed not to see you."

Cressy shook her head. "If you and my darling godfather were swiping each other's pawns off the board like flies, I very much doubt if I was missed!"

"Well, he brought a titbit of news. The auction of the Fishmarket and the Harbour Master's house down on the quay is arousing unexpected interest."

"I thought it was a foregone conclusion. In fact I'm sure Lucy said that Bart already had an architect working on plans to convert both buildings. He's going to turn them into desirable residences!"

"The sooner, the better," Helen agreed. "Those empty buildings have been an eyesore for years. Derrycombe is never going to have a mackerel fleet again, so they might as well be used for something else; and if Nicholas Pollack has anything to do with them, the conversions will be beautiful."

"I'm sure they will, but what occurs to James and me is that they will also be exceedingly expensive," her husband pointed out. "No local people will be able to afford them, and they'll be bought by more strangers from outside. I know we shouldn't object to Midland gents taking well-earned retirement here, but I can't help wanting to see Devon people living in Derrycombe."

"When you said the auction was arousing interest did you mean that someone else is involved?" Cressy asked.

"Well, between these four walls, Giles Credland has been inspecting the premises carefully, according to James."

"Because he's in the conversion business too?"

"Yes, though perhaps not in the same way as the Squire. However, we shall have to wait and see. He's not a man to make us a present of his intentions, and until the auction takes place we shan't know whether he's going to bid or not. But it means that he has an advantage over the Squire, who's made no secret of his plans."

Cressy left her parents still talking about it and set off to drive to the shop. Half-way along the quay she spotted Ben Davy waiting for the Totnes bus and stopped to pick him up.

"Mornin', m'dear." He climbed in and settled himself with a satisfied sigh. "I was jest wonderin' whether it'd be my lucky day and you'd happen along." He waved vigorously in case the people they passed should fail to see him in Cressy's car, and then got down to serious conversation. "Not a bad mornin' for early September, showers and sunshine – just what my beans was askin' for."

Cressy grinned at the serene conviction in his voice. The good Lord in Heaven no doubt had one or two other things to see to as well, but he knew better than to neglect the needs of Ben's Giant Longpods, which must collect their prize at the late-summer show as usual. She pointed to a quartet of gulls looking at their reflection in the shallow water of low tide in the estuary. "I never look at them without remembering what you used to tell me when I was small . . . that they were inhabited by the souls of dead fishermen. I believed you!"

"O'course . . . you should believe anythin' I tells you, Cressy love." He'd politely refrained from lighting his pipe, but now removed it from his mouth to stab the air in the direction of the derelict buildings across the river. "There's talk of the old Fishmarket bein' done over . . . not afore time, I reckon."

"Yes, but the question seems to be how it's to be done over. Do we want it looking nice, so that people from outside will pay a lot of money to come and live here, or not 'nice' at all and kept for working use?"

Ben's faded blue eyes almost disappeared in a silent grin that screwed up his face. "It weren't never *nice*, properly speakin', always reeked o' mackerel! I reckon we've got enough outsiders, Cressy. What town needs is somethin' to keep its own kind here. How many young chaps and maidens can ye call to mind who stay when schoolin's done? Away they go ... Plymouth or Exeter ... even London if they're real adventuresome like you!"

"Do other people share your view?" she asked curiously.

"Depends who ye ask, I reckon. Shopkeepers like the carriage trade, stands to reason; and I 'spect the gentry'd see Derrycombe stay the way it is – law-abidin' and peaceful. So what the likes of me think don't matter."

She turned her head to grin at him. "Ben dear, you *know* you practically run Derrycombe from the Snug at the Smuggler's Arms!"

He thought about this for a moment. "Well, let's say runnin's done by me *an'* Squire."

When they got to Totnes she set him down at the bottom of Fore Street and said goodbye, but the conversation lingered in her mind during the course of a busy day. The summer rush was almost over but already, it seemed, Christmas ordering had to be thought about, and there were still the final touches to be put to the exhibition which would be taken round the schools. Her father had chosen Dartmouth as the subject of the present display, and their only regret was that it should have quite so much history behind it. A place that had been the starting-point for expeditions reaching from the medieval Crusades to the invasion of Normandy in 1944 gave them more material than they knew what to do with. But Christopher had painted a stirring backcloth to these great events, Roland Marlow contributed beautifully costumed figures cut out of cardboard, and Cressy's job was to supply the books that told their story.

Her father had insisted that the school work could most sensibly be run from the new shop in Derrycombe. Cressy had agreed, but found Christopher surprisingly resistant to the idea of letting Lucy do it. In the end she'd accused him bluntly of inverted snobbery and had the wind taken out of her sails when he immediately agreed.

"She trails clouds of Manor glory, all the same," he insisted thoughtfully. "Can't help it, that's the background she's stuck with. If I should ever need to tick her off about something, she'd look down her long Pollack nose, and I'd see ghostly earls and countesses asking themselves what the devil a jumped-up parvenu like young Goodhew thinks he's doing putting Lucy Pollack in her place!"

Cressy had smiled at the idea, but stuck to her guns. "Give it a try, please. We need help, and she's so very keen."

Lucy's first arrival at the shop threatened awkwardness all round. She made an unlucky reference to her bicycle, which reminded Christopher of the morning he'd driven her home, but constraint didn't last. Before the morning was out Christopher had forgotten about the Manor and the long line of earls, and even ceased to wonder what had changed a dowdy prim-faced spinster into this smiling girl, dressed like the rest of them in jeans and cotton shirt.

The Totnes shop closed at half-past five, but Cressy rarely left for another hour after that. The evening of her journey in with Ben she stayed even later than usual, but when she finally locked the door to go home, turned round to find herself staring at Colin.

"I've been waiting for you to come out," he said simply. "My poor little love, you look tired to death, and I'd like to fly you away to a Greek island where you could sleep in the sun. Instead of that, you must drive yourself home and I must set off for London. But I had to see you first. Where shall we go – the nearest pub?"

"Let's walk down to the river; I've been cooped up indoors all day."

"I should have thought of that. It was almost the first thing I learned about you – your insatiable need to be near water!"

She didn't know what had changed, or why; but the cool stranger of Marguérite's party had disappeared. His eyes were full of love again, and the teasing tenderness in his voice was like balm on a wound she hadn't dared admit to for fear it would hurt more than she could bear.

"It's been a long week without you." She confessed it with the candour that set her apart, he thought, from other women.

"It's been intolerable, and made worse by the fact that I knew

79

I'd been a bloody fool. Cressy, could you try to forget about that party? Tell yourself it didn't happen at all?"

Happiness brought her face to life again, wiping away the fatigue of a moment ago. Doubt and anxiety were blown away and, with them, the tattered rags of her banner of spiritual pride. Not even to be the most lovingly dutiful daughter in creation, or the most devoted seller of books, could she go on doing without him.

"The party is forgotten," she agreed obligingly. Then her smiling face clouded again. "Forgotten except for one thing. Colin, Lucy got drawn into our difference of opinion. We mustn't let that happen again – she's too vulnerable to being hurt."

"There aren't going to be any more differences of opinion. We're going to heap all our money on a number marked 'marriage' and rake in a lifetime's happiness when it comes up." Her hand, held in his as they walked along, was carried to his lips and lightly kissed. "At least, I pray that's what we're going to do, but there's something to be explained first."

His face suddenly looked so grave that she was frightened into being flippant. "You've got a wife already, only you'd forgotten to mention her so far?"

"That isn't the problem . . . it's this: I'm on my way to Brussels first of all, to pick my way through the jungle of EEC legislation. But after that, dear love, my job is to set up an office for Credland's in Paris. We should have done it years ago, but I'm the only one who can do it and Giles has finally had to admit the fact. There's nothing I should like better than living in Paris, but I know what you feel about your father and Derrycombe. I'm asking you to cut yourself in half, I realise that."

It was the exact truth, and life was at its usual game of mixing joy and sadness. She'd known all along that she would have to make a choice, but this choice was worse than she'd allowed for. Only it wasn't a choice at all; this time she must put Colin first. She was about to say so when he spoke again.

"I'm not asking you to make up your mind now. In fact I wouldn't dare, in case you said no. But if you'd just think about it, dear girl, while I dash around the Continent and get things organised in Paris . . . is that asking too much?"

His blue eyes were full of an anxious pleading she had never seen before; peace of mind was in view at last and all she had to do was reach it down for him.

"It isn't too much . . . Paris isn't too much . . . nothing is," she said with serene conviction. "My father and Derrycombe will be here waiting for us whenever we can come back to visit them."

Colin's face was suddenly transformed. "Cressy love, I'd sing, break into a dance with you – if we weren't in the middle of respectable Totnes! All I can do instead is walk you to your car, and say goodbye to you with heroic self-restraint."

"Well, with my reputation as a staid bookseller to consider, I'm much obliged to you!" She was torn between tears and laughter, light-headed with happiness and, confusingly, sad beyond measure. "Dearest Colin, how dare Giles Credland not appreciate you properly? I'd like to be a giant for five minutes. I'd pick him up in one hand and *shake* him into admitting that you're as necessary to Credland's as he is!"

Colin smiled and kissed the end of her nose, respectable Totnes notwithstanding. "Sweetheart, be on my side by all means; but I no longer care what he thinks of me. In fact the more he undervalues me, the more I can despise him for being stupid!"

Cressida agreed reluctantly, then thought of something else. "What are we going to do about Marguérite? I can hardly bear to admit it when it was my idea in the first place, but we should never have encouraged her to go to the Admiral's House; she's bored and lonely there already."

"I know, she's said as much to me on the telephone. Long-term I'm not sure what the answer is, but all I can do for the moment is to take her with me. She can stay in Paris while I'm in Brussels; I shan't be too far away there to keep an eye on her."

"William left you quite a responsibility, I think," Cressy said gravely. "She drew a pig of a stepson in Giles, but she got a son in a million in you."

Five minutes later they were standing beside her car and it was time to go their separate ways. Colin stared down at her, as if trying to commit her face, feature by feature, to memory.

"I promise I won't pester you, sweetheart; come when you can . . . but come soon!"

Cressy nodded, suddenly blinded by tears. "Just as soon as I can organise things here, and brush up a French verb or too."

He kissed her mouth, and stood waiting while she got into the car and mopped her eyes. When she drove away he was still standing there, and she was tempted to weep again because he looked so unbearably lonely.

Chapter Eight

ANDREW took his place in the crowded auction rooms of Jessop and Olliphant, wishing that Bart had been able to come himself – he was an old hand at this sort of thing. But his father was in the north of the county, acting as an executor to the estate of an aged Camelhay who'd died leaving the hoarded muddles of a lifetime to be sorted out by someone else.

Andrew nodded to everyone he knew, and relaxed in the knowledge that almost none of them could have the slightest interest in acquiring the Fishmarket – they were there simply for a morning's entertainment. The only one to keep an eye on was wily Dan Pengelly, a local builder, who was rumoured to have ambitions to tear down the buildings and redevelop the site. Bart's intention was to keep the present facade intact, so that skilful conversion inside would leave the harmonious huddle of buildings along the quay outwardly undisturbed. Andrew felt pleasantly sure that right was on the side of the Pollacks, as usual. They would pay a fair market price, and out of their investment would come something that would make Derrycombe more, not less, attractive. Dan, given a free hand, would run up a line of horrible villas and make a fortune out of them.

There were various other items to come under the hammer first but Cressy's godfather, James Jessop, was conducting the proceedings himself this morning, which meant that things went at a briskly professional pace. The audience began to fear that the entertainment would be over too soon, but James was surely keeping the exciting bit till last and then they'd see a bit of spirited haggling. Finally they got to it. James delivered a brief but comprehensive description of the Fishmarket and adjoining Harbour Master's house, lingered for a moment regretfully on the fact that their original purpose had disappeared, and then asked for the first bid to be made – all bids, James said severely, to be understood as being in thousands.

Andrew waited for Dan to make the first move, but heard a voice he didn't recognise offer twenty. At James' request for an improvement, Dan responded by shouting twenty-five.

"Thirty." This was the unknown bidder answering a lift of the auctioneer's eyebrow, and Andrew decided it was time for him to intervene.

"Thirty-two," he called. "Thirty-five," said Dan, immediately followed by "Forty," from the voice at the back. A ripple of excitement went round the room. This was something like – this merry ding-dong was what they'd come for.

Old James was enjoying himself, and so was everyone else who wasn't, figuratively speaking, throwing money across the platform like confetti at a wedding.

"I'm offered forty," called James, "is there any advance on forty?"

"Forty-five," said Andrew firmly, confident that at least it weighed Dan Pengelly out of the race.

"Fifty." This time Andrew managed to locate the bidder – Giles Credland stood propping up the wall at the far end of the room, one hand carelessly thrust into his jacket pocket, the other raised to mark where the bid had come from. Andrew felt the palms of his hands grow wet. Bart hadn't bargained for Credland, and the bidding was approaching the ceiling he'd stipulated.

"Any advance on fifty?" asked James.

"Fifty-two."

"Mr Pollack is offering—"

"Fifty-five," said Giles, in a silence that spoke of a hundred or more souls all holding their breath for what might happen next.

James paused considerately, to give Andrew time to make up his mind. Oh God, what to do? Bart would have a fit at the price, but it was unthinkable to lose, and the last thing they wanted was that sod Credland with another foothold in Derrycombe.

Andrew took a deep breath. "Fifty-seven."

The audience gasped. Young Squire was airborne now, all traces kicked over. Pity the excitement was done, but it had been fun while it lasted, and they'd known all along Squire would win.

"Sixty," called Giles calmly.

Uproar! James banged on the table, calling the meeting to order. "Less noise, please, ladies and gentlemen; I cannot hear the bid." He frowned down at Ben, who was muttering something in the front row, and then looked across at Andrew.

"I'm offered sixty thousand pounds for the Fishmarket and the Harbour Master's house . . . is there any advance on sixty thousand pounds? Going . . . going . . . gone!"

His gavel banged on the table in front of him. The auction was over. Andrew scarcely heard the buzz of conversation, being concerned only with wondering what Bart would have done. But people were looking at him to see how he took defeat, and it was necessary before he could get out of the damned place to say something to Giles Credland.

"Congratulations," he muttered with difficulty. "If you're going to develop that site I hope you won't do anything that makes a mess of the centre of the town. A lot of us think Derrycombe matters, and we like it the way it is."

"I like Derrycombe too, but I don't suppose what I plan to do will win universal favour. It's hard to please everybody even if one wants to."

Andrew rose to the bait. "But *you* don't usually want to."

"That seems to be my deplorable reputation," Giles agreed blandly.

He nodded and Andrew tried not to feel dismissed by a man who had the advantage in every way – in age, size, experience, and some indefinable air of authority which left him nothing to say. He drove back to the Manor disgruntled and depressed, and found only Lucy there waiting to hear the result of the auction.

"Before you say something tactless and cheerful, we didn't win," Andrew said sourly. Then the expression on her face made him apologise. "Sorry, no reason to snap at you. I'm just riled because Giles Credland outbid me. Dad won't be pleased, but that bastard would have gone on pushing up the price for ever. Then he stood there, gloating over me."

She was silent for so long that he stared at her. "We don't seem to do very well against the Credlands," she murmured at last. "I was in the shop when Colin phoned Cressy from Paris; whatever misunderstanding they had is over. Silly of me to have imagined—" She broke off, unable to confess to what she *had* imagined, and walked out of the room.

Andrew watched her go. 'Not doing very well' against the Credlands scarcely began to describe their showing against a family that seemed to walk away with everything the Pollacks wanted. He loathed, abominated them.

James Jessop brought the result of the auction to Lantern Cottage. He was too discreet to say so, but Cressy had the impression that the outcome had pleased him. She didn't say so either, but couldn't agree with him; the less Giles Credland had to do with Derrycombe, the better.

"Did he say what he was going to do with the place?" Roland wanted to know.

"Didn't bother to say anything at all. Handed over his cheque, thanked me for conducting the affair efficiently – which he seemed not to have expected – and disappeared. I don't blame him – the *Chronicle*'s pushy young reporter was hanging around, waiting to ask questions. Andrew was representing the Squire, by the way, but it wouldn't have made any difference; Credland intended to win. I wonder why?"

"I think he has his own idea of what places like Derrycombe need," Roland said slowly. "It may not be the Squire's idea, but we ought to give it a fair hearing. The last thing we want is to have the town forming itself into two opposing camps. Nothing good comes of a fight. Confirmed scrappers like to claim that it clears the air, but I don't even believe that."

Cressy smiled at a sentence that summed up her father's philosophy and left them still talking. It was time to go to the Manor, to do a little air-clearing of her own.

Andrew, not seen since the night of Marguérite's party and scarcely spoken to even then, was in the courtyard. She wasn't aware that he watched her walking towards him, with the long-legged stride that reminded him of the girl who'd been his friend. Rage at his own

86

helplessness rose in him like a fever. 'As flies to wanton boys, are we to the gods; They kill us for their sport.' It was exactly how he felt: powerless to correct Fate's error, or its malice in the way it ordered things. Cressy should have been here with him, not firmly in the Credland camp, attached to a man he disliked, who was in turn part of a family he hated. The anger he'd had to conceal at the auction finally overflowed, but now it had very little to do with the morning's outcome.

"Come to shed crocodile tears for the Pollacks, Cressy?"

The bitter hostility in his voice made her face go pale, but she forced herself to answer him calmly.

"I don't think I understand you. Why should I want to do that?"

"You probably know Giles Credland outbid us at the auction this morning; his brother gets his fun in a different way, but the result's the same: Lucy is another Pollack left with egg on her face and the feeling that the rest of Derrycombe is having a good laugh at her expense. Time was when you were supposed to be a friend of hers."

"I *am* her friend," Cressy answered steadily, "and I don't believe anyone in Derrycombe would want to laugh at her. If she's been hurt I'm truly sorry."

"Perhaps you'd like to tell her so?"

"It's what I came to do, what I *will* do if you'll stop looming in front of me like Horatius defending the bridge. As for the auction, my godfather had the running of it, which means that it was properly and fairly conducted. I suppose Giles Credland bid higher than you but that doesn't constitute a crime. Even the Pollacks don't have some God-given right to get everything they want."

Andrew's mouth twisted at the irony of it. Did the world at large envy them at the Manor, see only the outward appearance of a life that was more than adequately comfortable and more than usually secure? If so, the world at large was wrong, as usual. Bart, being a simple man, was probably the most content of them, but Andrew suspected there were times when even he couldn't convince himself that all was right with the Pollack world.

"I'm not sure any of us would claim that we've got what we

wanted," he commented in a different tone of voice. "Quite right too, you'll probably say, because it's time someone else had a look in. But I can't help wishing it didn't have to be the bloody Credlands."

She acknowledged the change in him by lowering her own sword-point. It had never been possible to hate Andrew for long, and even now her flashes of irritation couldn't outlast the sadness of being at odds with him.

"I wish we could all have what we wanted, but life doesn't seem to be arranged that way," she said gently.

"You are getting what you want, I understand. Lucy seems to think you're going to marry Colin Credland. It will probably provoke a storm, but I'll say it anyway, Cressy: I wish you'd chosen some other man."

"Because it makes Lucy unhappy?"

"No, because I think he'll make *you* unhappy in the long run."

It was said with a gravity that made resentment impossible. "You don't know him well enough to say that," she pointed out after a moment's silence. "In fact you don't know him at all, or anything about the odd, unhappy life that he's had to contend with. You've inherited a dislike of the Credlands because your father clashed with Giles years ago; that's not difficult to do, and Colin clashes with him most of all. He won't be happy until he's free of his brother altogether." Suddenly it was a relief to share with Andrew the news she hadn't given to anyone else. "I haven't broadcast the fact yet, but we shall probably live in Paris; Colin is opening a Credland's office there."

"Will that make you happy? You couldn't even settle down in London because your roots were here. I don't give much for your chances if you allow yourself to be dragged abroad."

Andrew was having his usual effect on her: the more categorically he told her she couldn't, wouldn't, or shouldn't do a thing, the more certainly it became the thing she was going to do.

"I told you life wasn't perfectly arranged," she said, "but home is where the heart is; with Colin, I shall be able to make do, wherever we are."

He stared at her, then gave a rueful little shake of the head that acknowledged defeat. "Odd how we go on making the same mistakes. Wouldn't you think by now I'd have learnt how *not* to deal with you!"

Suddenly she wanted to weep for the fact that life was not only imperfectly but strangely arranged. Andrew was woven into almost every thread of her past life, and the man she was going to share the rest of it with was, comparatively, a stranger. She felt like a worm that had been cut in half – Cressida Marlow and Mrs Colin Credland – two separate creatures existing independently of each other.

"I came to see Lucy," she remembered suddenly. "Is she in the house?"

"You'll find her somewhere inside."

She was on her way across the courtyard when his voice halted her.

"Cressy, forget what I said about crocodile tears, please. Lucy says I'm an ill-tempered pig, and for once I think she's probably right."

The smile that lit her face chased away sadness and strain. "I dare say brothers are like eavesdroppers: never hear good of themselves!"

The conversation with Lucy threatened to be even more painful but she'd underestimated a girl who not only lacked guile but took it almost for granted that life wouldn't hand her what she wanted.

"Sorry if I was in the way when Colin telephoned, Cress. I should have made myself scarce sooner."

"Why? We were talking shop and not expecting personal calls. I suspect Colin thinks we only play at selling books!"

"Dad and Andrew too," Lucy agreed. "They're male chauvinists to a man. Let the little women keep themselves occupied and out of mischief, as long as they don't think they're engaged in anything that matters!"

Cressy grinned, but fleetingly. "From you that sounded unusually bitter. Is it how you feel?"

"Not about Colin, if that's what's worrying you. Even at the party anyone but me would have known at once what it meant – that you and he had had a misunderstanding of some kind. I was a bit confused for a while, but there was no reason to be. Colin has been kind, but the kindness hadn't anything much to do with *me*. It's his special gift to make a woman feel that she matters, offered to anyone free of charge! But the rest of us haven't the slightest excuse not to know that it's you he loves."

"You've special gifts of your own, it seems to me," Cressy said slowly, "generosity of spirit being the most precious of them."

Lucy accepted the tribute with a blush and made haste to deflect the conversation away from herself. "Are you going to marry him, Cress? I can see the problems, but if it's what you want to do, you mustn't let anything stop you."

"It wasn't Andrew's opinion a moment ago. He obviously looks on me as some sort of traitor for joining the Credland camp. So if the school exhibition work is going to make life difficult for you, you must chuck it in."

"I'm going to offer to do more, not chuck it in," Lucy said tranquilly. "Colin won't want his wife working as hard as you do, if he's prepared for her to work at all."

It occurred to Cressida that even a little while ago they would have been much more likely to talk about Lucy's problems than her own. Now, the girl who'd always been a lame dog had become an equal. Having a job to do and doing it well enough to win Christopher's good opinion had had something to do with the emancipation of Lucy Pollack, but Cressy thought Andrew had been wrong about Colin's effect on his sister. Lucy had been stunted all along simply by the fear of not being what was expected of her – plain when she should have been handsome, timid instead of brave, happy to be at the back when a Pollack was required to be out in front, leading the rest. Now she knew that, given the right encouragement, she could be any of these things. The lack was in the people around her, not in herself after all, and the knowledge removed the doubt that had been so crippling.

"The future's even more complicated than you might suppose," Cressy said after a long pause. "Colin probably gives the impression of being a man who'd rather laugh at life any day than take it seriously. It's only one side of the coin; the other is darkened by his hatred of Giles Credland – freely returned, I may say. To be happy, Colin must get away from him, and the chance has arisen at last, but it will mean living in Paris."

Lucy stared at her. "Will you mind? Do your parents know?"

"Not yet, but I must tell them soon – when I've had time to think what to do about the Totnes shop."

She spoke calmly but her face was filled with pain. Lucy had thought herself miserable about Colin, but if the sadness in Cressy's eyes was what came of being in love, she decided that the writers of romantic fiction lied and it was better to do without it altogether.

"Well, when you talk to your father, remember that I'd like to help," she said again. "My family have accepted now that I'm not a true Pollack at all, having this ridiculous attachment to books! It wouldn't scandalise them unduly if I worked full-time for Christopher. Things could have been worse from their point of view; I pointed out to Dad the other day that I might have got hooked on working in a betting-shop!"

Cressy's troubled face broke into a delighted grin. "Did it make him feel any happier about having his only daughter going into trade?"

"I doubt it, but at least he roared with laughter. Time was when I couldn't raise a smile in him. I think I've come on a bit, don't you?"

Cressy agreed that it was so, and went home eventually feeling that it was she who'd been comforted by the visit, not Lucy. It was a relief, above all, to be certain at last of what she was going to do, and when the ordeal of telling her parents was behind her, she could begin to look forward to the future. Already, her present life seemed half-unreal. The plans that had to be made for the Christmas season seemed to have very little to do with her, and later in the day when she listened to Helen's pessimistic commentary on the progress of the new pantomime production, she had the feeling that it belonged to a life she had already left behind.

Chapter Nine

VERY early on a Sunday morning was a good time to have the world to herself – thinking time, for which she needed to escape from other people. She sheltered from the wind among the rocks jumbled at the foot of the headland and regretted the empty house behind her. With Marguérite and Colin likely to remain away, and its owner a man who spent his working life in Plymouth, Cressy sadly foresaw a time when it would become neglected again. Better to turn her back on it and look at Start Bay, now a mass of grey-green water piled up into long menacing ridges by the force of a high wind. It was a familiar but fascinating sight and she watched while each wave held itself suspended for the moment of maximum power before being consumed in a frothing fountain of white on the rocks just below her vantage-point.

Her glance followed a handful of gulls riding on the back of the wind to something she might otherwise have missed: the blob of colour, black and yellow, away to her left was a rowing-boat being taken out with the fast-ebbing tide. Not the morning for a rowing-boat, in fact, madness for it to be so near the mouth of the river in such conditions. She stood up, with some hopeless idea of shouting a warning, saw two small figures trying to wave, and in horrific slow motion, watched the boat capsize as the first wave caught it. A moment later the huge figure of Giles Credland came hurtling towards her from the direction of his own grounds behind her.

"Two children out there in a rowing-boat – they lost an oar, and have just overturned. Pray God they have the sense to hang on. Here's the key to my boat, moored in the inlet. Run and find a man who can bring it out to me."

93

He was stripping off shoes, sweater and trousers as he shouted at her, and stopped for only one more parting shot because she didn't leave at once. "Don't argue – just find someone to bring that bloody boat."

Without waiting to see him run into the water, she heaved herself up over the rocks to the path that skirted the grounds of the house above the sea wall. A single glance over her shoulder showed the upturned boat drifting out into the bay, and a black dot moving steadily towards it, lifted by one wave, and buried by the next. He was immensely strong, and not a man who knew when he was beaten, but . . . *children* out there. She ran on again with sobbing breath and a stitch in her side no worse than the sharpness of her own despair.

The inlet was just ahead of her now, and there was the boat in mid-stream, with its dinghy attached to the line which ran between the boat and the shore. It was five minutes' desperate work to pull the dinghy in to the bank and to haul herself in it out to the boat, but she was in the cockpit at last, fumbling for the ignition switch and the starter button. The engine stuttered once, then roared into life, and she gave a little sob of thankfulness as she cast off from the mooring buoy and the boat gathered speed. She turned out of the inlet into the main stream, and there the wind funnelling straight in from the bay seemed to hold them motionless, but she opened the throttle and they made headway again.

Spray drenched the glass screen in front of her, the wipers swept it away, but there was nothing to be seen, only a waste of heaving grey water crested with white. Dear God, where were they? She slackened speed, peered desperately through the glass, and caught a flash of yellow on her port side. *Fool* not to have remembered that they would be drifting that way with the wind from the south-west. She spun the wheel, felt the boat yaw sickeningly as the next wave hit it broadside on, and didn't even notice the water that poured into the cockpit, drenching her. They were round, and now the wind was slightly astern. Three minutes later she was alongside the upturned rowing-boat, and, thank God in heaven, the children were sprawled across the top with Giles, treading water, holding them clamped to it. She throttled the engine right back, trying to hold the boat steady

as near to them as possible. Tim Gurney – she might have known, of
course, that it would be Tim – scrambled upright, held his younger
brother balanced while Cressy heaved him in-board. Then with two
of them to pull, it was easier to get Tim over the rail as well. Giles
struggled to right the rowing-boat, grabbed its painter and threw
it to Cressy, who secured it to a cleat at the stern of his own boat;
then he shouted to them to stand clear. It was difficult, even with
his huge strength, but at last he hauled himself over the side and
stood in the crowded cockpit, water streaming off his body and
running down his face from the black hair plastered to his head
like an animal's pelt.

She was thankful to see him move automatically towards the
controls. Now that reaction was setting in it would have been all
too easy to misjudge the turn into the estuary, or do some other
damn-fool thing.

"Blankets down below," he said briefly.

She wrapped them round the shivering children, Nicholas whim-
pering quietly, Tim white-faced at the thought of retribution ahead
but half-convinced, now terror was over, that the excitement had
been worth it. Cressy glanced at her watch; still not yet eight o'clock,
and less than an hour since she'd set out from Lantern Cottage. They
were in the comparative shelter of the estuary now and she could hear
St Fritha's bells being rung for Early Communion. Giles steered the
boat towards the first flight of steps climbing the sea wall, and there
was Jim Gurney, among the little knot of people already gathered
there. He was at the foot of the steps by the time the boat had
been nosed gently against the wall.

"These two are all right, and so's the boat, but it's minus its
oars," said Giles.

Jim Gurney scarcely heard what he said. Nicholas was lifted into
his arms, and his grey face broke into a smile.

"I saw the boat gone, but didn't know where to start looking.
I'm – greatly obliged to you, Mr Credland; I was mortal afraid
we'd lost them."

"No need for a larruping," Giles said casually. "They've had
fright enough out there to teach them a lesson, and they behaved
very well, kept their heads like veterans." Suddenly he smiled, too.

95

"By way of penance, they could walk down to the rocks later on and collect the clothes I had to leave there!"

Cressy occupied herself with re-folding blankets, conscious of feeling drained and tired. The sensible thing would be to climb out of the boat herself and walk home, but before she could say so Giles had started the engine again and with a wave to all three Gurneys was coasting across the river towards his own inlet.

"Now I shall have even further to walk," she heard herself say crossly.

"I thought of giving you breakfast first, then you won't feel so irritable. I expect you're hungry."

It was the truth, she realised, but it suddenly occurred to her as well that they could both have been naked for all their sodden clothes concealed. Giles should have looked ridiculous, standing there in shirt and underpants from which water still trickled down his legs, but she hadn't the smallest desire to laugh at him.

She couldn't relinquish ill-temper – it seemed the only prop she had to cling to; but against all expectation it only made him smile. Amusement warmed his pale-blue eyes, and for the first time she could see a fleeting likeness to Colin. William Credland must have had just such eyes to have given them to both his sons.

"A hot shower, dry clothes and an enormous breakfast – then you'll be yourself again," he promised, as he might have reassured a wayward child.

She trailed after him up the path, too tired to insist that she would rather go home. Marguérite's luxurious bathroom was offered to her, and at that moment its lure was impossible to resist. She peeled off cold, wet clothes, hung briefs and bra over the hot pipes, and lowered herself, feeling faintly ridiculous, into an elegant sunken bath that seemed made for Elizabeth Taylor playing the part of Cleopatra. By the time she climbed out again her nylon underclothes were dry, and she wandered into the adjoining bedroom wondering what she could borrow of Marguérite's to put over them. Clothes were already laid out on the bed: cream-coloured jeans she recognised as Colin's, and not much too big because he was slightly built for a man, a blue cashmere sweater that came from the same source, and a cotton shirt belonging to Marguérite. There was nothing to be done about her half-dry hair, but she purloined some cream found on the dressing-table, and smoothed it into skin that felt unpleasantly stiff after being doused in salt water and then steamed. She went downstairs, looking decorous again, and surprised to realise that she would also have liked to look a little more glamorous. It would have been a weapon, and she needed whatever help she could get against Giles Credland.

He was already in the kitchen, laying china and cutlery on the pine table. When his eyes flicked over her she regretted her reach-me-down appearance even more. It was the wrong moment to be aware of him as a man for the first time in his company, and to feel even a little inexperienced and shy.

"Regretting the fact that you're here?" he asked calmly. "This morning's excitement made me forget where we got to in our last conversation. Say if the strain of sharing breakfast with me is too much for you and I'll take you home instead."

She had forgotten the conversation too; in their brief struggle out in the bay there had been no time to remember that she'd been going to ignore him in future. There was also the undoubted fact that she *was* very hungry.

"We could call a truce until after breakfast," she suggested cautiously.

He might have smiled again except that, as usual, he found her contradictions irritating. She appealed to his brother and ought, therefore, to have been easy to label and despise. But it was hard to label a girl who still looked beautiful with a shiny face and borrowed clothes that were too large for her; and contempt was out of the question when she'd just shown herself resourceful and brave.

"I told you to find a man," he remembered with a small spurt of resentment.

"So you did, but there didn't seem to be time." Now that he was back to his usual disagreeable form, she felt composed again; in any case there was no need to let shyness get the better of her because it was clear that his mind was dominated by the single thought of food. Released from awkwardness, she could behave naturally again.

"Thanks for what you did this morning . . . without you both those children would have drowned and Jim and Edie Gurney would never have got over it."

"If we're ladling out compliments, I thought you did rather well yourself."

She found herself wishing that the half-ironic comment had been sincere, but his impassive face offered no clue to what he was really thinking.

"What does larruping mean?" she asked suddenly.

"It's Cornish for a good wallop. If our quaint vernacular entertains you, we'd have said it was nibby-gibby out there this morning."

"Touch and go?"

He nodded, and her amusement died in the memory of the moment when she'd thought the bay was empty.

"Language lesson adjourned . . . it's time to eat. My cooking isn't of the fancy kind, but I can manage anything that will go into a frying-pan."

"Since I can manage a bit more than that, why not leave breakfast to me? I ought to telephone home first, though; I set out for an early-morning walk what seems to have been a lifetime ago."

"They already know at the cottage where you are; I rang Helen before I came downstairs."

It wasn't any surprise that he should be so competent a man, but she hadn't expected to find him thoughtful as well. They ate their way through the huge platter of sausages, bacon and eggs that she eventually brought to the table in a silence that was almost friendly. That in itself was more than she had expected, but when only the coffee-pot remained to be emptied, he began to converse as well. She used the word deliberately in her mind to mark the change from past exchanges, which had always been battles.

"I expect you know your father's been teaching me to become a gardener? With a little more time I fancy he could teach me other things as well."

Her eyes watching him across the table were suddenly full of fear. "Time for *him*, you mean? I get the feeling that he and my mother have found some way of coming to terms with the question mark that now seems to hang over his life, but I can't manage that kind of acceptance. I want to shout at Heaven's door that we can't do without him for a long time yet, even while I know that Heaven can't hear."

Flood Tide

She hadn't admitted as much before to anyone else, and wondered what had possessed her to make the forlorn little confession now.

"I wasn't hinting at a short life for your father," Giles said with unexpected gentleness, "only regretting that I haven't the time to profit by his wisdom. I don't regret a life given over to Credland's, but I can't help seeing the difference between him and myself. He's an all-round man, complete, able to see life steadily and see it whole. I'm a bit like a tree that's only put out branches in one direction."

"You'd have liked the Admiral, too," Cressy said suddenly. "Not everybody did, but *he* was a complete man as well – brave and forthright."

"And you loved him," Giles surprised her by suggesting. "I like his house – the tower was a master-stroke."

"I'm afraid Marguérite doesn't like it," she confessed with regret. "Perhaps we should have guessed, but she seemed so excited about it that I convinced myself she'd finally found what she was looking for."

"Which is what, in your opinion?"

"Contentment, I suppose . . . something more to fill her life than a round of meaningless pleasure."

A raised black eyebrow almost provoked her again but she was determined, if possible, to part company with him just once without figuratively coming to blows.

"What are you going to do with the old Fishmarket?" she asked instead. "Something philanthropic? A garden of rest . . . sheltered housing for Derrycombe's aged citizens?"

Her voice challenged him to admit that he had nothing so public-spirited in mind, and he didn't disappoint her.

"Philanthropy makes no appeal, and I'm much more inclined to let the ageing citizens feel responsible for themselves. My concern is with the future – that's to say with youngsters like Tim Gurney, who have more spirit than sense, and no outlet here for a sense of adventure that leads them to escapades like the one we got embroiled in this morning. The Fishmarket is going to become a workshop where they can be taught skills that enable them to create something. But the first intake will be boys from the back

99

streets of Plymouth, the raff and scaff who hang about at street corners at the moment, getting into trouble because they don't know what else to do with themselves."

Cressy stared curiously at him. "I thought you said philanthropy made no appeal?"

"It doesn't. I shall expect to get skilled hands for Credland's out of the scheme."

"When does the rest of Derrycombe know what you have in mind?"

"As soon as Tom Snape publishes my application for planning permission at the Town Hall. Local opposition, are you thinking?"

"I'm afraid so. Quite a lot of people want to keep the town just the way it is, which certainly does not include welcoming the raff and scaff of Plymouth back streets. The fathers of boys like Tim will welcome your idea, and a few more *might* if you limited the intake to Derrycombe children."

"There aren't enough of the right age at the moment; in any case it has to be on my terms, not Derrycombe's."

"And that comes as no surprise," she said as if talking to herself.

A brief grin acknowledged the hit before he surprised her in earnest by a sudden change of topic.

"Why the name of Cressida?"

"My father's choice. It might have been worse. My mother was hooked on the works of Gilbert and Sullivan at the time and very much wanted Iolanthe!"

His eyes lingered on the dark hair falling over her forehead again now that it had dried.

"I always imagined Troilus' lady-love to be divinely fair . . . I suppose because Shakespeare speaks of her somewhere as 'Cressida of the bright hair.' "

She feared that her mouth dropped open, knew that it had when his eyes glinted with amusement, but did her best to recover. "A lop-sided tree, indeed! I suppose I shall find next that you play the violin like Paganini, and toss off elegant water-colours in your spare time!"

"No, reading is all I can lay claim to; your first impression of me as a boorish philistine isn't very wide of the mark."

He'd read her thoughts with an accuracy that made her blush, and was now amused by the fact; it needed more practice than she'd had recently to cope with a sparring-partner of this calibre.

"Are you going to marry Colin?" he asked next.

"Yes." She said it proudly, glad of certainty that didn't leave her at a disadvantage with a man who'd probably come into the world knowing his own mind.

"May I ask when?"

"It depends how soon I can settle things here and join him in Paris."

"Is Paris as attractive as all that? I have the impression that you belong here – that you're a sea creature."

Cressy gave a little smile. "Now it's my turn to quote the Bard. 'There is a tide in the affairs of men, Which, taken at the flood, leads on to fortune'!"

"And in the case of women, according to Lord Byron, 'leads on to – God knows where'! Why not wait a while, see how Colin makes out – see *if* he makes out – before you commit yourself?"

The past half-hour had been so unexpectedly pleasant that she was assailed now by a sense of treachery towards Colin. This man's rescue of the children should never have made her forget that he was of different clay from themselves. For him, commitment to another human being was a sign of stupidity or weakness. He still was, always would be, their enemy.

"What you mean is, wait for him to fail," she said in a voice shaking with rage. "You *want* him to."

"Before you slay me with indignation or try to soften me with tears, let me remind you that we've had this conversation before. You know nothing except the half-truths fed to you by Colin and my stepmother, and that's all you want to know; so the subject might as well be deemed closed."

"Just as well," she managed to agree, "since truth and generosity and family feeling are meaningless words to you. People mean nothing to you either unless, like the Plymouth children you intend to bring here, they offer no threat to your own precious self-sufficiency. I find I don't hate you after all; I feel very sorry for you."

"I doubt if you do, and I should take exception to it if you did, because I can't abide mawkish sentimentality! We've done quite well . . . haven't been at each other's throats for fully an hour, but it's obviously time you went home now. Shall I drive you?"

"No thanks, a walk will restore me to the good humour I manage to enjoy with everyone but you."

She collected the rest of her clothes and left the Admiral's House – for the last time, she thought. But she'd over-estimated the benefit of the walk back to Lantern Cottage. Far from being soothed, she grew steadily more depressed. For a little while she'd seen Giles Credland in a different light. He had strength and courage and even kindness to offer when he felt inclined, but they – Marguérite, Colin, and herself – would always be excluded. For as long as Colin remained part of Credland's, their happiness would be tainted by him. Paris had seemed too far away, but the truth was that it wasn't nearly far enough.

Chapter Ten

THE rescue in the bay was the talk of Derrycombe. Even Sir Nicholas, met in Totnes one morning, was moved to inform Cressy that a man he had no cause to like had done very well.

"Hear you were involved too . . . brave of you, my dear. I hope young Tim got the trimming he deserved from his father."

'Larruping', she corrected him silently; it was strange that the peaceable Squire should want Tim punished when the lump of Cornish granite had hoped for just the opposite.

"It's kind of you to let us appropriate Lucy," she said out loud. "I don't know how we'd manage without her."

"Seems to enjoy it," said Sir Nicholas, sounding astonished that it should be so. Cressy couldn't stifle a smile, but he didn't take offence and they parted company on the best of terms.

Giles' moment of local esteem lasted no longer than it took for knowledge of his Fishmarket plans to run like wildfire through the town. She reported this to Colin in one of their evening telephone conversations.

"Why sound surprised, my darling?" he wanted to know. "It's my brother's special talent to set everybody around him by the ears."

"I'm not surprised at all, but this time I can't help feeling that it's the town that's being unreasonable. He's proposing something that will benefit a lot of youngsters who haven't much hope otherwise. In the long run it might even benefit the town itself, but above all Derrycombe likes to be left in peace. Self-interest seems to blind people to everything else."

"Nothing new about that, either. But Derrycombe might as well resign itself. If Giles is hell-bent on doing something, it will take the battalions of the damned ranged against him to win."

Cressy ran her mind over the likely opposition. "You could almost say it's what he's got! However, it all hinges on the public meeting. If his scheme's outvoted there, the Council will refuse the planning permission he needs."

"I'd like to see it happen. Just once I'd rejoice to see him beaten."

The usual note of venom sounded in his voice and she abandoned as pointless the idea of suggesting that Giles beaten might one day mean Credland's beaten as well.

"I'd rather hear about you," she said after a moment. "Is everything going well – what about the premises you thought you'd found?"

"Things are going reasonably well, I suppose, but there seems to be a hell of a lot to think about, and I could do with some help. But Giles hasn't offered it and I'm damned if I'll ask."

He sounded tired, faintly discouraged, and unusually disinclined to talk.

"What about Marguérite?" she asked next. "Is she all right?"

"Yes, but lonely . . . missing you, probably, like me. I know I promised you a breathing-space, and I won't try to rush you on my own account, but could you possibly pay *her* a visit, Cressy, even if it's only a long weekend?"

His concern for his mother touched her, as always. Most men by now might have considered Marguérite more of a responsibility than she was worth. Colin continued to love and take care of her, but it was obvious that he did need help. He mustn't fail, as Giles expected him to, and she must offer herself now, not when the difficulties were over.

"Dear Colin, I'll come very soon – in time to spend Christmas with you, and then to start helping straight afterwards."

She heard his sigh of relief over the telephone wire. "In that case I can even look forward to the dreaded festive season, sweetheart . . . normally, I loathe it!"

She put the telephone down at last, trying not to think of the Christmas rush in the shop and all that must be got through before she could leave for Paris. The most important task of all was to tell her parents, but she was still looking for the right moment to launch such a conversation when the evening of Giles's public meeting arrived. Roland preferred to have an account of it brought back to him, but Helen and Cressy set out together for the Town Hall.

Long before the proceedings were due to begin, every seat in the room was taken and latecomers were obliged to stand three-deep round the sides. The platform at the far end almost sank under the combined weight of councils, both parish and town, and in some cases both functions were embodied in the same citizens, visibly inflated by this dual responsibility. The Squire was prominent as usual and Tom Snape, the Town Clerk nominally in charge, was flustered by the size and excitability of the audience. To make matters worse, he had a sneaking sympathy for Giles Credland's proposal even though he knew it was his duty to be impartial. The officials from the County Planning Department in Exeter were there in force to give Authority's view, and he gravely doubted their impartiality, seeing that they'd been wined and dined at the Manor before being brought down to the Town Hall. Finally everybody who could be crammed in was in, and there was no excuse not to start. Tom stood up and banged the table in front of him; Derrycombe's public meeting was about to begin.

Giles, called upon first to describe his plans in case anyone present hadn't understood the written application on view at the Town Hall, rose and made a leisurely survey of the room. Watching him, Cressy thought there was something to be said for sheer size. Either by accident or because it amused him to do so, he'd found a seat in the middle of his most rabid opponents. She wouldn't have been surprised to see him scoop up Gwyneth Morgan under one arm and Deirdre Drew-Browne under the other and hold them suspended in mid-air while he talked. If he felt the temptation, he resisted it and contented himself with addressing the Chairman. Lucy, taken unawares by the beautifully resonant tones that filled the room without effort, whispered to Cressy beside her, "No difficulty as far as the women are concerned. With that voice he could persuade them to renounce universal suffrage if he set his mind to it." There was no impassioned appeal, however; he was brief and businesslike, and merely nodded when Mr Snape offered him the chance to address the meeting again when other speakers had been heard.

The Exeter officials took many more words to explain that there was no actual bureaucratic objection to what Mr Credland proposed, and the Town Clerk apologised in his heart for doubting the incorruptibility of those set in authority over him. Then he bravely called for opinions from the floor, and pandemonium broke out. When order had been more or less restored and Tom had insisted that only one person at a time could be heard, it was Gwyneth's enfeebled mother, suddenly restored to health and vigour, who remained on her feet, determined to have the first word. She would have liked the last one as well, but was finally forced to yield the floor to Colonel Carstairs, Mrs Drew-Browne, Dan Pengelly and half a dozen others, whose rambling objections were finally summed up with magisterial authority by the Squire. Laying aside natural inclination, he said, the citizens of Derrycombe had also a clear duty to resist a proposal so destructive of the peace and beauty of their town. No possible good could come of it, and it would simply insert into its comparatively law-abiding children all the criminal elements that the back streets of Plymouth contained. He deplored – they all did, the Squire amended sorrowfully – the fact that such elements should exist; but it was for Plymouth to deal with its own problems. He preserved a dignified silence on what his own plans had been for the Fishmarket, and sat down to fervent applause from his supporters.

"Giles has lost," Helen murmured on the other side of Cressy. "Nobody's going to dare vote for him after that."

The Town Clerk was thinking the same, but the steel had entered Tom Snape's gentle soul. He'd promised Mr Credland a fair hearing and that was what he was going to have. There were noisy objections when he invited Giles to speak again, but Giles merely sauntered to the foot of the platform where he could command a view of the audience in front of him. Cressy had the impression that he'd finally decided to take the meeting by the scruff of its neck and shake it into agreeing with him.

"He isn't beaten yet . . . in fact I doubt if he's ever beaten," she murmured to her mother, and then fell silent because he began to speak.

"Ladies and gentlemen, you've listened to Sir Nicholas and others

106

assuring you that my scheme will destroy Derrycombe. My intention
is, in fact, to try to keep it alive. The town has been fortunate so far
– wisely guided, perhaps – in turning its back on the quick profit
and slow death that the tourist industry entails. I know of small
towns and ports in Cornwall that allowed themselves to fall into
the holiday business trap to escape the poverty that followed the
collapse of traditional industries. They took the easy way out instead
of finding better ways of staying alive. Only a few years were needed
to drag them into a more destructive mess. Naturally tough, proud
people were taken over lock, stock and barrel, and once-beautiful,
peaceful places became transistor-ridden playgrounds awash with
Coca-Cola cans and ice-cream cartons. *That* is the holiday industry."
He spoke slowly, giving his words time to sink in. Cressy felt sorry for
the Squire; more than most of those present, and bitterly opposed to
Giles as he was, he must be agreeing with every word.

"For the moment Derrycombe is spared this degradation and it
is still adequately alive, but it is becoming a town of ageing people."
His gaze wandered over the white and grey heads dotted around the
room, but he went on to say with a perfectly straight face, "I'm
not suggesting the mass extermination of anyone past the age of
sixty-five, only that we should do something to keep young people
in the town as well. As things are, they can't learn a trade here, find
a job, or even pass the time except by drinking themselves silly in the
Smuggler's Arms. They drift away, in fact whole families drift away,
and the vacuum is filled by elderly strangers from outside, knowing
nothing of Derrycombe's past and caring little for its future. My
workshop will give boys leaving school the practical skills they
haven't been taught, and my company will give them the prospect
of a job when the time comes. They can even start enterprises of
their own. There's room enough for anyone with a good idea and
the gumption to make it work. The price to Derrycombe will be a
little more noise, perhaps a little more disorder, because until there
are local recruits enough to fill the places I shall bring boys here from
Plymouth. The Squire refers to them as criminal elements; they're
not, but they will become so unless they're given a chance. Your
choice is a little less peace, or a little more life. A corpse is peaceful,
I believe, but it can't be said to have much of a future."

He sat down in a silence that suggested everyone present had already stopped breathing. Mr Snape rose nervously. "Would anyone care to support Mr Credland by proposing that the scheme should be allowed to go ahead?"

Nothing happened for a moment, then Ben Davy erupted from his little coterie of friends in the front row.

"I'm for it," he roared. "Reckon Mr Credland's right: future's what we'm needin' to think about. Squire does 'is best, but farmin's changed and there bain't enough jobs. Fishin's gone . . . what else is there unless we start summat new?"

He sat down to murmurs of approval from his neighbours, but Tom looked unhappy still.

"Yes, Ben, but I need a proper proposal for the record."

"Pernickety old fool, Tom Snape," Nat Selby was heard to say loudly to his friend. "What's ee think yew jest done?" But Ben didn't mind getting to his feet again.

"All right, Tom . . . I *propose* Mr Credland goes ahead . . . will that do?"

The Town Clerk nodded and there was silence while it was written down. "Will someone now second Mr Davy's proposal," he asked.

Profounder silence this time, everyone now gripped by a determination to let someone else do the talking. Cressy looked across the room at Jim Gurney, saw his eyes desperately fixed on the ground, and pitied his predicament. He owed Giles Credland an enormous debt, but the Squire had employed him all his working life and paid him well; it was an obligation of another kind, and when all was said and done Sir Nicholas was a Derrycombe man.

"I must have a seconder," Tom prompted them desperately. He peered at Nat who, unable to find words for a public announcement, searched the next row for someone who looked as if he might speak, and came at last to Cressy. She wasn't aware of thought, or of a decision taken, only of suddenly finding herself on her feet.

"Mr Snape, I was one of the young people who found it necessary to leave Derrycombe. I was lucky enough to be able to come back, but most of those who go, go for good. I think we should give

Mr Credland's scheme a fair chance, and I now second Ben's proposal."

The audience had gone very quiet, aware that it had just been listening to the youth of the town speaking. She sat down and heard Helen murmuring beside her, "Darling, did you have to? Yes, I can see that you did!"

Ben was shouting to his friends, "She's a good little maid!" but she knew that many others didn't think so. Derrycombe's favourite daughter had fallen from grace with a vengeance. Lady Evelyn's icy stare was only part of the general coldness flowing around her; she'd betrayed them and they would never forgive her.

Mr Snape hurried on to the business of voting, those in favour of the proposal first. The count, surprising him more than anyone else, came to one hundred and ninety-two. Those against could only muster one hundred and four. Hubbub broke out again, but Cressy sat quiet in the middle of it, feeling rather sick. She saw the Pollacks leave, and only Lucy turned round to smile at her with what seemed reckless bravery.

Giles stood in the middle of a knot of people now anxious to explain why they'd begun by seeming hostile to the scheme. The expression on his face was withdrawn and slightly bored, and she wished he wouldn't make it so damned obvious that he didn't care what they thought. As Colin had said, he would somehow do whatever he set his mind to, and even having to explain his reasons publicly was something he privately resented.

She walked home with Helen, silent and strangely dispirited. In a week or two it would be Christmas, and the weather had no right to be so unseasonably mild and wet. She blamed it for the fact that the problems confronting her seemed to require more energy and resolution than she possessed. She excused herself and went to bed as soon as they got back to the cottage, leaving Helen to provide an account of the meeting.

"Cressida's upset – what happened?" Roland asked immediately.

"She threw her cap into the ring. All the speeches were going against Giles, led by Hilda Morgan on the subject of Our Heritage! At least we need never try to think of her as an invalid again; she isn't Welsh for nothing when it comes to talking, and she's got the stamina of a Sherman tank!"

"Cressida, my love," he reminded her.

"Yes, well, Tom Snape was waiting for someone to get up and second Ben's proposal on behalf of the application. Everyone seemed glued to their seats – not even Jim Gurney made a move, though the poor man was dreadfully torn. In the end Cressy got up herself."

"The Pollacks were there, of course?"

"Of course, all of them except Lucy looking at my darling daughter as if she'd suddenly grown two heads. But when the vote was taken it turned out that Giles had won. If he was surprised he didn't show it, but Bart was utterly dumbfounded."

Roland thought of Cressida's face as it had looked a moment ago, strained and very tired. "Thank God I've settled it," he said slowly.

"Settled what?"

"The future. I've been waiting because she seemed uncertain; now I realise that I was being cruelly unfair. The decision should have been mine, not hers."

Helen stared at him. "Could you stop talking in riddles and tell me what it is you've settled?"

"I asked Christopher to find another manager for the Dartmouth shop. Glutton for work that he is, even he can't run them all."

"All? You mean you're organising Cressy out of a job? She'll think you're sacking her."

"She won't think anything so silly," he said with a rare hint of irritability. "She should have told us long ago to organise our affairs without her. Colin Credland won't wait for ever, and it would break her heart to lose him."

*   *   *

Helen was still thinking over this conversation when Giles Credland called the next morning. She congratulated him on the outcome of the meeting, wondering whether he would comment on Cressy's part in it. He didn't, but went straight to the point as usual.

"I know you can't spare a thought from *Puss in Boots* till after

110

Christmas, but then will you help me convert the Harbour Master's house into a youth hostel? It's a job that seems to need a woman's touch."

Helen looked doubtfully at him. "Surely the woman you need is Marguérite?"

"She's exactly the woman I don't need. Apart from the fact that she seems to have taken root in Paris, I'm not asking for sunken baths and silk-lined curtains! All I want is for the place to be comfortable, homely, and practical to run."

"That I think I can manage," Helen agreed. "You're going ahead immediately – not waiting for planning permission to come through?"

"It's a foregone conclusion now, though without Ben Davy and Cressida things might have gone the other way. Kind of her to weigh in, but it won't have done her reputation any good in the town."

"Perhaps it doesn't matter; we don't think she'll be here much longer." Helen hesitated a moment, then tackled an awkward subject with the bluntness that reminded him of her daughter. "It's a topic to be skirted round between us, isn't it – Cressy and Colin? I hope it needn't stop us being friends as well."

Giles smiled at her with sudden affection. "I can't think of any reason why it should. I shan't be invited to be Colin's best man, but if you're kind enough to ask me to the wedding, I shall behave with my usual grace and charm!"

Later in the day Cressy found the opening she was looking for. Helen, anxious to improve her daughter's opinion of Giles, reported his concern for her reputation in the town. The moment for confession had come, and Cressy took a deep breath.

"My reputation doesn't matter, but I dare say it will irk the town even more to discover I've helped wish on them something I don't have to live with myself. Darlings, will you mind very much if I leave you soon? I'd hoped not to have to rush away, but Colin needs help. I said I'd go in time to spend Christmas with him and Marguérite, and afterwards I can share some of his work in Paris. We shall be living there because of his new job, and it's just as well; Giles will always make sure there's no room in the company for him here." There was a moment's silence which impelled her to

111

rush on, "You admire Giles, I know, so perhaps you blame Colin for not getting on with his half-brother."

"Cressida, my love, hold your horses," her father said firmly. "We don't have the right to blame either of them, and the fact that Colin and Giles are incompatible has nothing to do with us. We admire Giles, and shall soon learn to love Colin."

At last she smiled. "How can we manage at Marlow's?"

"I've been thinking about that, having an idea of what was in the wind. I sounded Christopher out a little while ago. He can manage Totnes and the shop here, with some extra help, and he's got a cousin more than ready to try his hand at running things in Dartmouth."

Cressy's smile went slightly awry because she was struggling with a strong desire to burst into tears. "Easy! And there was I thinking myself indispensable and agonising about going!"

"Of course you're indispensable to *us*," her father said quietly, "but as far as Marlow's is concerned, you should have been allowed to get on with your own life months ago, my love."

He hadn't rebuked her but she felt ashamed, all the same, of something that had probably sounded like pique.

"Lucy was keen to help more," she remembered suddenly. "I may have made that difficult for her now, but she's become very redoubtable . . . takes Lady Evelyn in her stride! She even told Bart he should be grateful she likes dealing with books – it might have been a betting-shop that took her fancy!"

It provoked a roar of laughter, but when they'd sobered up again Cressy reverted to the beginning of the conversation. "Christmas away from home seems all wrong, but Marguérite is lonely and Colin's got too much to do to have to worry about her as well."

"Couldn't they come here?" Helen suggested hopefully.

"I think Marguérite prefers Paris, and Colin prefers not to be anywhere near Giles, so it's better if I go there."

Roland registered the strain in his daughter's face and forced himself to smile at her. "Of course you must go, my dear; go where your future is, and forget about Derrycombe."

He was making it easy for her; she was at liberty to arrange her life in any way she pleased, and it should have been unalloyed happiness. But she was prepared now for the fact that happiness was never unalloyed.

*   *   *

A fortnight later Christopher's cousin was installed at Dartmouth and he'd accepted Lucy as his own full-time assistant at Totnes. She tried to pretend that he only looked sad sometimes because he was tired and worked too hard; if it would help him she would work herself into the ground, but she couldn't bring back Cressy for him. It would have been a relief if she could have blamed her friend, but Cressy didn't go out of her way to steal people's hearts . . . and if Andrew was anything to go by, they never managed to get over loving her.

Chapter Eleven

CRESSY'S departure for London years ago had been tempered by the almost certain knowledge that she would come back; *this* was separation. The winter landscape unfolded outside the train window but she saw nothing of it. Even a brave attempt to grapple with French irregular verbs, of which the language seemed to have far too many, couldn't keep her thoughts from following Helen home, mile by familiar mile along the road back to Derrycombe. It wasn't until she walked out into the exit hall at Charles de Gaulle Airport in Paris and found Marguérite waiting for her that the first faint stir of excitement began to lift her unhappiness.

"Dearest, I thought you'd never come. Colin's had to go to Brussels again, but he'll be back any day. I promised him faithfully I'd be here to welcome you."

Marguérite was muffled up in furs against the cold, looking every inch the elegant Parisienne; if boredom and loneliness had afflicted her in Devon they weren't apparent now.

"You look like something out of *Anna Karenina* and I feel like a provincial dowd!" Cressy said candidly.

"Not a dowd, exactly, but you look tired, my lamb. You must have a little rest before we plunge into gaiety. Shall you mind a sofa-bed in my tiny flat until Colin gets back?"

"I don't mind anything at all," Cressy said obligingly. "I'm ready to come to grips with whatever Paris offers me!"

Marguérite's chiming laugh made people turn and stare. "Oh, Cressy . . . we've missed you so. Everything will be perfect now that you're here."

Her flat was indeed small but its locality, she explained, was all-important. A narrow street just off the Boulevard St Germain was the 'right' quartier to be in, and a little crampedness inside mattered not at all. Cressy had no view on the matter of which arrondissement was acceptable and which not, but she liked what she saw from the long windows of Marguérite's flat. The sitting-room was on the third floor of a tall old house, looking out over roof-tops conveniently lower than they were themselves; from it she could look towards the river over an enchanted city now lit against the early winter dusk. She stood on the minute balcony staring at the view until Marguérite protested about the cold and she had reluctantly to come inside.

They decided not to eat out and Cressida volunteered to cook. The refrigerator yielded eggs and cheese to make a soufflé, but very little else, and it was obvious that her hostess wasn't in the habit of catering for herself. Wine, Marguérite said proudly, she did have, and Cressy drank her share, trying not to think that they could have done with a little less wine and a little more food.

When coffee was made and she'd refused the brandy Marguérite offered her, she thought it was time to ask her first question.

"I know Paris is beautiful and exciting, but don't you miss that enchanting house at home?"

"What has the winter been like?"

"Windy and rather wet so far!"

"Then, dearest, I don't miss it at all. On a summer afternoon, maybe; it's lovely then. But I get depressed by oilskins and wellingtons, and I cannot sit listening to nothing but the wind, and the sea gulls quarrelling on the roof!"

Cressida wondered if she remembered her excitement when they first looked at the house, and her feverish insistence that it was exactly what she needed. It had all been a sad mistake, but there seemed no point in saying so now.

"If you're never going back, what will become of it?" she asked instead. "I'd hate to see it die of neglect again."

"Darling, Giles will live in it himself," Marguérite said blithely. "It's his in any case, and he was *willing* me not to want to stay, so I don't feel bad about it. My stepson likes his own company, which is fortunate since no one else enjoys it."

Cressy smiled but felt obliged to be honest. "My parents like him . . . in fact my father, especially, considers him a friend."

Marguérite gave a little shrug that said the ways of people even as delightful as the Marlows were sometimes more than she could comprehend. Cressy abandoned the subject and broached another question.

"Let's forget Giles and talk about your own dear son. He's sounded very tired on the telephone recently. It seems infamous to expect him to get a new office started here single-handed, but it will be a feather in his cap that not even Giles can deny."

Marguérite gave her usual fatalistic shrug. "Giles can always deny anything, even the fact that poor Colin works very hard. But at least we've escaped from dreary Plymouth."

Half-laughing, half-serious, Cressy protested. "It *isn't* dreary . . . you mustn't say such a thing to someone who hails from Devon!"

"Oh, Devon . . . Drake and that highly improbable game of bowls! I doubt if it ever happened, *chérie*; but even if it did, history has nothing to do with making Plymouth a civilised place to live in."

Cressy knew that it was pointless to argue. Marguérite's estimate of what constituted a civilised place depended on the restaurants, theatres and shops she was only likely to find in a capital city, and even local patriotism carried to excess could scarcely make a case for Plymouth against Paris. Rather than try, Cressy preferred to pin her hostess down to a matter that seemed more important.

"Has Colin ever thought seriously about leaving Credland's? I know it ought to be his birthright, but I can't see that he's ever going to be happy tied to Giles's chariot-wheels."

Marguérite looked vague. "I really don't know, *chérie*. Sometimes he seems to be hinting at other plans, but I can't imagine what he would do away from Credland's. You'll have to ask him. Tell me about Derrycombe instead."

Though doubting her interest in a place she'd yearned to escape from, Cressy realised that the future didn't interest her either – only the present moment mattered to Marguérite.

The rest Marguérite had promised didn't extend beyond a night's not very comfortable sleep in an airless little room which overlooked the well between their own building and the back of the one behind. There was coffee for breakfast, but otherwise only the stale remnants of a bag of croissants presumably bought days ago and subsequently forgotten. Cressy managed to eat one, but told her hostess firmly that they were going out the moment the shops opened.

Marguérite's eyes sparkled. "Lovely, dearest! What shall we buy? I know several little boutiques that sell really gorgeous clothes for a fraction of the couture prices."

"What I had in mind was gorgeous food . . . meat, bread, butter, fruit, vegetables . . . things to make meals with!"

"But, Cressy, why? In Paris there's a café in every street, and a good restaurant in every other one. We don't need to eat here. In any case, Colin will insist on taking us out as soon as he arrives."

"But I shall die of hunger before then. Let's at least stock the refrigerator, then if he's sick of hotel life we can feed him here."

Marguérite accepted the idea with her usual willingness to fall in with whatever anyone more resolute than herself suggested. She even agreed that the croissants left something to be desired. They shopped for food, lunched out on onion soup because Marguérite said she put on weight if she ate more than one meal a day, and Cressy trailed round boutiques with her all the afternoon, hungrily planning in her mind the enormous dinner she was going to cook and eat that evening.

They were recovering from the exertions of the day and sipping sherry when the doorbell rang. Cressida went to open the door and found Colin standing there, smiling at her.

"I couldn't wait a moment longer," he said simply. "Knowing you were here, Brussels couldn't be tolerated for another minute. I stood up the worthy chap who was supposed to be giving me lunch and roared down the autoroute instead. Sweetheart . . . I can't tell you how lovely it is to see you."

His hands gripped hers hard, but he made no other attempt to touch her; it seemed to be enough that she was there, within reach. The restraint of his welcome touched her more than exuberance would have done. Nothing was hidden by this quiet but heartfelt greeting. He was truly content to have her there, and she was truly content to have come.

"It's seemed a long time," she agreed, smiling at him. "My fault, I know. I should have come sooner."

His eyes searched her face, and then very gently he kissed her mouth. "Dear love, how tired you look. But now I'm going to take care of you."

They walked into the sitting-room together and Marguérite swooped on him with joy. "*Mon amour* . . . you said tomorrow! How rash – we might have gone out already. Never mind, now we can go out to dinner together."

She looked so delighted at the idea that Cressida almost cancelled what she'd been about to suggest; but Colin had just driven several hundred miles, so she made her suggestion anyway, as tactfully as she could.

"It's almost a year since we first met over the dinner I cooked for you in London. Couldn't we celebrate in the same way? There's masses of food."

"Much nicer," he agreed at once. "Maman and I will be scullions while you do the difficult bits."

His mother accepted the change of plan as happily as if they'd offered her dinner at Maxim's. All she needed for happiness, Cressida realised again, was simply to be with the people who loved her. Only loneliness dulled her spirit, while hostility shrivelled her into despair.

They celebrated the anniversary in high spirits and high style, but Cressy was aware that something more important lay beneath Colin's surface gaiety. He was also celebrating the fact that she'd finally chosen to step over the wall that separated her from whatever life they now made for themselves. She'd come voluntarily and there was no place left for doubts and reservations, or for the code of behaviour implanted by a Derrycombe upbringing. She had burned her own little boat and must sail henceforth in Colin's. The tenderness in his eyes when he looked at her confirmed what he was thinking, and told her that love was held in check only until the right and perfect moment presented itself.

The following morning, offered any choice she cared to make, Cressy requested a visit to Versailles. Marguérite declined a share in the expedition and, on the eve of Christmas, they had the whole vast place almost to themselves. They braved the sunlit but freezing grounds as well, but when she shivered suddenly he was quick to pull her into his arms.

"You're cold, *ma mie*. Shall we consider Versailles 'done' and go and find some friendly restaurant to thaw out in?"

She smiled at him but her eyes lingered again on the grey pile in front of them, set with such perfect grace and precision above its ascending parterres, lakes and terraces.

"It wasn't the temperature making me shiver. There are ghosts here . . . don't you feel them?"

Colin looked faintly puzzled. "It's atmospheric, I grant you, sweetheart, but you needn't be haunted by anything that happened here a long time ago. Any old shades lingering around are either trampled underfoot by the hordes of summer visitors, or sent packing by the worthy bureaucrats from the Ministère des Beaux Arts!"

"Perhaps that's why I can feel them so vividly *now* . . . they re-emerge when it's unvisited in winter and jostle each other in this cold clear air."

He kissed the end of her nose, and then her mouth. "You're too susceptible. What's going to happen when I take you to somewhere really haunted, like Delphi or Mycenae?"

"I don't know, but places don't have to be exotic; I'm just as moved by the remains of a Bronze Age settlement on Dartmoor, or a ruined engine-house like Botallack perched on a cliff-top in Cornwall – anywhere where people have lived intensely and left some trace of themselves in the air."

He nodded, but she had the impression that he was relieved when she put seriousness aside and announced that she was hungry again. "It's something to do with the ever-present aroma of French cooking also haunting the air! I was never this ravenous at home."

They spent the afternoon with Marguérite, but after dinner in a charming neighbourhood brasserie he didn't make the mistake of asking her not to go back to his mother's flat, simply took it for granted that there was only one way for the evening to end. What he now called home was a room in a small hotel in the rue Jacob, and waiting for her there was an extravagantly luxurious overnight case equipped with everything she might possibly need. Colin saw her stare at it thoughtfully, and then smile at him.

"Was I taking too much for granted, sweetheart?"

"No, you've been wonderfully patient, and I've taken too long to leave my hang-ups behind and get here." His answering kiss was the tenderest promise of the delight to come. Virginity, by now something she felt to be almost an embarrassment, was finally lost without awkwardness and without regret because he was so tender and skilful a lover.

Later, lying peacefully in his arms, Cressy murmured, "I've got a lot to learn . . . will you go on being patient with me?"

"It won't be difficult – my pupil shows exceptional promise, and I happen to love her very much!"

She awoke while it was still dark, and the room was only faintly lit by the glow of a street-lamp outside the uncurtained window. Colin slept deeply by her side, and for a moment of coldly lucid terror she couldn't think what she was doing there. His face was unfamiliar in sleep, and his body, turned away from her, no longer seemed to recognise her as part of itself. She was a stranger in a strange land, lost except for the memory of shared delight. It was something, but not enough to help her now. She needed him to wake and find her, but a small voice whispered that he hadn't understood about the ghosts at Versailles; there might be other things he didn't understand. Memories assailed her . . . Andrew's voice of long ago telling her that preserving happiness was just a matter of stuffing more coins into her piggy bank of contentment . . . her father explaining that joy was not a wasting asset. For the first time in her life she knew him to be wrong; she could see happiness in her mind's eye, and measure it like sand dribbling through an hour-glass. Tears scalded her cheeks, soaking the uncomfortable French bolster. But she finally wept herself to sleep again and woke a second time to find Colin coming into the room with a tray of coffee.

"There's room service of a kind, provided you don't mind going downstairs to fetch it! Good morning, sweetheart, do you feel as happy as I do?" It was possible now to put aside the terrors of the night and smile at him.

"Very happy . . . luxuriously content! But I can't help wondering a little about the future. Can we talk about it soon?"

He put down the tray, and sat on the edge of the bed. His hands travelled over the softness of her skin, and he wanted to make love to her again, but her eyes were fixed gravely on him and he kissed her mouth gently instead.

"The future holds nothing but good, but yes, we will talk about it soon. First things first, though. Shall we go back to bed, or have breakfast with Marguérite, or find a café somewhere?"

"Breakfast with her, I think. On her own she doesn't bother to eat, then wonders why she gets tired and depressed."

Far from wondering why her guest hadn't returned the night before, Marguérite seemed to think she'd behaved exactly as she should; at last Cressy was one of them, with Derrycombe and the rest of unlamented Devon forgotten.

If it wasn't entirely forgotten, Cressida did her best to conceal the fact, and she kept to herself the longings that assailed her for the simple rituals of Christmas at home. Her plea for a Christmas morning visit to Notre Dame took Colin by surprise, but he accepted the idea readily enough, and even found himself enjoying the music and the winter sunlight slanting brilliantly-coloured shafts down through the dark forest of Gothic pillars.

During the days that followed they walked far and wide, and Cressy was glad to be seeing Paris for the first time in mid-winter. Cold it might be, but at this season of the year it belonged entirely to itself, not to the rest of the visiting world. She was entranced by view after view etched on the cold, clear air, and found it easy to be enthusiastic whenever it was time to telephone Lantern Cottage.

It was easier, in fact, to talk about the city itself than about the life she was leading, which uncomfortably straddled Marguérite's cramped flat and Colin's room at night. Feeling rootless and displaced, she hoped that the round of café life they'd settled into wasn't to be the basis of things to come. She managed to seem cheerful and content by reminding herself that she and Colin were taking a well-earned holiday. When he was ready he would tell her how far he'd got with the new office and how she could begin to help him. The future would become clear in his own good time.

The brightness of Christmas gave way to days of sleety drizzle that ruled out explorations on foot. Finally, desperate at being confined indoors, she dragged them out one afternoon for a brisk walk in the Bois. The outing wasn't a success, and she didn't protest when Colin supported his mother's plaintive view that only madmen and the true-born English found pleasure in such exercise. When they got home she offered them tea and buttered toast by way of a peace-offering and was in the minute kitchen preparing it when she heard the doorbell ring.

Five minutes later she walked into the sitting-room, and all but dropped the laden tray in her hands. Never very spacious, it was now consumed by the huge figure of Giles Credland, who propped up the only available piece of free wall.

It was history repeating itself, a case of *déjà-vu*. She found herself remembering with absolute clarity not the last time she'd seen him, surrounded by people in the Town Hall at Derrycombe, but the very first time, engulfing an ornate chair in Marguérite's flat in London. He looked no more amiable now, and acknowledged her arrival with a nod that merely said he wasn't surprised to find her there.

Marguérite said nothing at all, and Cressy felt obliged to break a silence that was becoming awkward, even though the only remark she could think of sounded absurd.

"Tea for you? We're just about to have some."

"No, thank you." His cold voice ruled out the faint hope that he was making a purely social call, or an enquiry about Christmas at home as her next conversational gambit. She decided that the burden of finding something else to say didn't rest with her and, having supplied the others with tea, sat down as far away from him as possible.

Giles glanced at her withdrawn face, wishing with a vehemence he found surprising that she wasn't caught up in their lives. His opinion of her had fluctuated a good deal, but he was left with a conviction that Roland Marlow should have found some way of chaining her to Derrycombe.

"Shall we discuss the weather next, or get down to brass tacks?" he asked suddenly.

"Brass tacks are much more in your line, so let us have them by all means," Colin agreed. "I'll begin by asking what brings you to Paris? If it's my rate of progress or lack of it, you should have guessed that everything shuts down here over Christmas."

Cressida watched the fragile cup tremble in a huge hand and expected to see it shatter under the strain, but the rage she sensed in Giles was searingly cold, and completely under control.

"I'm not here because of the new office, even though I'd hoped it might be in operation by now. I was summoned by Jules Froment. He's excitable at the best of times, but this morning he was almost incoherent with anger. Our joint project, nearing completion, as you well know, after months of investment, headaches, and combined effort, has – according to him – been pre-empted by our chief competitor. Buchard has something already out that is almost identical in every detail, and it's being vigorously marketed. Froment is convinced Buchard couldn't have dreamed it up himself, so too much was given away about it, accidentally or deliberately, either by his people or by someone at Credland's."

"And by 'someone' I suppose he means me? More likely, *you* mean me."

"You've been our only representative over here. With French chauvinism well to the fore as usual, Jules insists that his own people are blameless; none of them, apparently, would be seen dead helping the opposition to a fraudulent advantage."

A faint smile touched Colin's mouth, which Cressy thought fool-hardily reckless in the circumstances. She waited for an explosion of fury, but Giles still remained superhumanly controlled. "It's a grave complaint Froment's making; don't think we can brush it aside with a laugh and a shrug of the shoulders."

Afraid that Colin might still risk a light-hearted reply that would bring the world crashing about their heads, Cressy decided that it was time to take a hand in the conversation. First, to make her own position absolutely clear, she got up and moved across the room to sit beside him.

"It's *infamous* to suggest that Colin might be to blame, if that's what you're doing." Her voice almost broke under its own weight of anger but she swallowed and struggled on. "Even if Froment's staff are as blameless as he likes to imagine, which is open to doubt, has he never heard of coincidental invention? History's littered with cases of simultaneous discoveries being made in places much further apart than the width of the Channel."

Giles turned a cold blue glare on her. "I'm afraid you don't understand. The design of the new machine was a logical extension of things we'd been working on. To anyone else it's revolutionary . . . unthinkable for them to have landed on without going through *our* preliminary stages first, and we know that Buchard certainly hasn't done that."

"Then let Froment examine his own leaks more carefully," she insisted doggedly.

Giles gave her up and turned to his half-brother. "Any other suggestions?"

Colin shrugged his shoulders in the gesture inherited from Marguérite. "I was instructed to raise interest in the damned machine, if you remember, and it could hardly be done by not mentioning it at all. It's possible that some brilliant engineer at Buchard's could have put two and two together and made six out of them, but that's a risk you and Froment seemed willing enough to take at the time. Now that you've come unstuck, you're changing your tune."

Giles shook his head. "It's the same old tune – that you and I have never liked or trusted one another. At the least, your discretion is now suspect, and I have no confidence in your fitness to represent Credland's abroad. You loathe being tied to Plymouth, so it's time to do something we should have done years ago. My father's will allows you to sell your interest, and I propose to buy out your share-holding – the value to be fixed by an independent assessor. There will also be a generous lump sum payment as compensation for the loss of your job; after that we go our separate ways."

The terms calmly announced made Cressy go cold; under an apparently unemotional front so much twisted irrational hatred lay concealed.

"What if I refuse the offer?" Colin asked.

"Then I must waste time I can ill afford in getting to the bottom of the Buchard affair. Who knows? I might have to offer you a handsome apology."

125

"Since the effort would probably kill you, the idea has a certain charm; but on balance I agree with you about parting company. Subject to seeing the actual figures, I accept the terms."

Rejection handled in this high style became a victory, Cressy thought proudly. However bitter his hurt, and however great the injustice being done to him, he was up-staging Giles.

"May I ask what you propose to do about Marguérite?" he asked next. "Is she concerned in the new arrangements as well?"

"Her connection with Credland's is out of my hands. Unlike the terms affecting you, the arrangements made by my father have to stand until her death."

"Which no doubt you hope will be soon," she suddenly cried in a trembling voice.

"I anticipate that you will live to such a ripe old age that you'll probably outlast me," he assured her calmly. "It would be helpful, though, to know whether you still have any interest in living in the house at Derrycombe?"

"None at all. You may have that windblown, sea-ridden place to yourself, and I hope that it very soon drives you mad! I shall stay here with Colin and Cressy."

Giles stared for a moment at the white-faced girl sitting silently beside his brother. She looked as he'd first seen her, dressed with a simple but instinctive sense of elegance he recognised without knowing how it was achieved. He liked the spareness of her altogether – face, slender body, and unornamented clothes. Above all, he liked the way her eyes met his limpidly clear as the waters of the Tamar leaping down from the heights of Dartmoor, revealing without subterfuge whatever was in her mind. What was in her mind now was simple loathing of himself. Except for one friendly breakfast shared together, their meetings had been a series of head-on clashes, but he was suddenly visited by the extraordinary idea that he wanted to pick her up like a child and take her home.

"When you next see my parents, please give them my love," she said quietly. "I shall let them know, of course, when our – our plans are fixed, but tell them that life here is more exciting than I could ever have imagined." Her hand tucked itself into Colin's, deliberately making clear the new relationship between them.

"Exciting? I think they'd rather you said happy."

"That too, of course." The conversation was too painful to continue and she stood up abruptly to end it. "Excuse me if I leave you . . . it's time to start cooking supper."

When she returned the room seemed empty because he'd gone, but Colin and Marguérite were smiling at one another.

"Life begins again, my dear ones," he announced. "To have seen the last of brother Giles calls for vintage champagne, but we shall have to make do with something less festive."

Cressy knew that it still wasn't the moment to ask questions. For a little while yet she must pretend that all she wanted was to watch Colin pour wine, cook steak and *pommes frites* for them, and possess her anxious soul in patience.

Chapter Twelve

IT WAS far from being spring, but sitting on a bench out of the sharp wind in the Tuileries gardens, Cressy pretended to herself that the winter was almost past. She looked also, nowadays, for any sign or portent that the winter coldness lying around her heart might disappear as the season itself changed. She'd chosen her bench with care, and for once had it to herself. There was no lonely soul on the seat beside her, craving another human being to talk to. There was time to think about the general unsatisfactoriness of life, and the conversation she'd had with Colin that morning.

Looking back, Giles Credland's visit had been the pivot on which subsequent disenchantments had begun to swing. For a little while afterwards Colin had continued to be the most perfect of companions – their days spent discovering Paris in the cold winter sunlight, their nights in shared loving in their little room in the rue Jacob. He was as generous as Marguérite, constantly on the look-out for some small gift that would give her pleasure, and happy to take her wherever she asked to go. Only when she'd suggested from time to time that they couldn't spend the rest of their lives in idle enjoyment had he brushed the objection aside with a smile that didn't quite conceal irritability. But this morning she could wait no longer; at the risk of almost certainly annoying him she'd insisted on knowing what he was going to do now that his job at Credland's was over.

"It's not that we aren't having a lovely time," she hastened to explain. "I just feel that it can't, shouldn't, last for ever."

He smiled at her over the cup of coffee she'd poured for him.

"The puritan work ethic raising its ugly head again, darling? It's a pity you weren't cut out to be a lotus-eater ... it makes a sad difference between us."

"I like play but I enjoy work as well. There's also the fact that we must be galloping through money and can't live on air."

"We have heaps of money, but if it will set your earnest little mind at rest, I'll confess that I've got another job lined up; I'm starting with Buchard at the beginning of next month."

It was odd that he hadn't mentioned it before, but she found herself even more startled by his choice – Buchard of all people! It took a moment or two to realise that of course he must stay in the line of country he knew, and that since he was unlikely in the circumstances to offer his services to Jules Froment, Buchard was the only other serious possibility.

"Shall you be doing things in reverse?" she asked. "Waving the *tricolore* in England on behalf of Buchard's products?"

"Certainly not; my days of waving anybody's flag are over, thank God, likewise my days of being *anywhere* on sufferance. I'm joining the company as a fully-fledged director."

He smiled as he said it, but she wondered if he would ever recover from the damage done by his brother. Giles Credland had some virtues, but if he went to a lonely grave, it was no more than he deserved.

"Well, I'm impressed by the directorship," she admitted with only a little teasing, "but since your own future looks so settled and prosperous, let's talk about Marguérite. Does she really want nothing better than that poky little flat she's renting? I know the Admiral's House turned out to be a mistake, but we weren't wrong about the principle – she still needs a permanent home of her own, and presumably if we're going to stay over here, so will she."

"Heaven preserve me from a worrying woman!" Then he relented and pulled her into his arms to kiss her. "You're quite right, and I don't thank you nearly enough for the way you look after my mother. We'll abandon pleasure and devote ourselves to organising her chaotic life."

She hovered on the edge of saying that they might also organise their own, but he hadn't so far raised the subject of marriage and she was nervous of being laughed at for a small-town ambition to be made 'respectable'. Colin had led a footloose life and must be allowed to come gradually to the idea that a hearth and home of his own weren't things to despise as being suburban and dull.

Thinking about it now on her bench in the gardens, she felt more hopeful. The question of his future was settled, and if they could find somewhere more permanent to live than a hotel room she would lose the sensation she sometimes had of being on a kind of lover's probation.

They spent the next fortnight concentrating on Marguérite's affairs, beginning with the time-consuming job of persuading her trustees in England, in the course of numerous telephone conversations, that she must be allowed to realise money to buy an apartment in France. They combed the arrondissements for one in which she agreed she might be prepared to live, and finally found a pleasant apartment at a price she could almost afford. Matters hadn't been finally settled when Colin had to abandon them to take up his appointment at Buchard's, and Cressy was left to struggle alone with the trustees, French lawyers, and Marguérite herself, who cared not at all about the legalities involved and only wanted to begin furnishing an apartment she didn't yet own.

From then on the daily pattern of life began to change. Colin, the confirmed lotus-eater, became absorbed in his new job, sometimes not even coming home in time to dine with them. When he was there, he and Marguérite dropped into the habit of speaking the French he was using all day. Cressy could understand it well enough now, but concentration left her tired, and gave her the uncomfortable feeling of being excluded from what they were thinking rather than saying. Seeing less of Colin, she saw more of Marguérite's circle of so-called friends, and found them uncongenial. They were clever, brittle people in whose company Marguérite herself became less familiar, and less delightful.

Telephone calls to Lantern Cottage had to be carefully edited to iron out strain, but it was a growing worry about money that finally provoked her first sharp disagreement with Colin. It went against the grain to ask him to finance her, but since arriving in Paris she'd bought most of the food they ate at home and she was running out of funds. She approached the subject one morning by suggesting that it was time to find herself a job.

"You've got one already – taking care of me and keeping Marguérite out of trouble . . . task enough for anyone."

"There's that as well, of course," she agreed, smiling at him, "but what I meant was a job that earns me money."

"You don't need money – we have plenty."

"*I* have none left, and there's also the question of finding something to do with myself. I came to Paris thinking I was going to help you. I can't spend all and every day visiting exhibitions, drinking coffee in cafés with Marguérite's friends, and poring over fabric samples with her. I need a proper job to do."

"Such as what? Cooking?" he suggested coolly.

She tried not to be nettled by his tone. "It was what I was trained for, and good food's appreciated here."

"Nevertheless, you will not hire yourself out as a cook, *chérie*."

"You mean Jacqueline Buchard wouldn't approve?"

Cressy had already dined with the Buchard family, and although Colin was now apparently devoted to them, she hadn't liked Armand Buchard and found every hackle she possessed rising in the company of his wife. Jacqueline carried Parisian chic into the realm of art; that and her quick cold wit seemed to reduce Colin to a slavish admiration that Cressy felt no inclination to share.

"Jacqueline would be right not to approve," he said flatly. "I have a certain position to maintain for Buchard's, and so do you as my wife – more or less."

Lover or mistress would have been more accurate, and she thought it would have sounded better than a more-or-less wife, but she held on to the coat-tails of fast-disappearing temper and made another suggestion. "Books, then. I know something about them – or would a bookshop offend Buchard sensibilities as well?"

"Don't be snide, *chérie*. If you must live in a lather of activity, why not offer your services to some charity or other? God knows there are enough of *them* looking for free labour."

But he was warned by the flash of anger in her eyes and abandoned his position immediately. "Darling . . . I've been thoughtless, and I'm sorry. You seemed to have money and it didn't occur to me that it might be running out. I'll open an account for you tomorrow. As soon as Marguérite's settled we must think where we want to live ourselves. Won't that give you more than enough to do for the time being?"

She accepted the truce at once, disarmed by the return of tenderness in his voice, and by the assurance of something she hadn't been sure of – that he did want a home as much as she wanted one herself. A job could obviously wait until she'd got an apartment organised, and in the meanwhile she would pocket pride and accept the money he gave her.

The disagreement was over, if not quite forgotten, but it led her to desert Marguérite and set out for a walk on her own. Instinct took her towards the river, as usual, and she stood for a long time on the Pont Royal, watching the Seine making steadily for the sea. Even Paris, which she thought of as a feminine city compared with London's massive bulk, weighed heavily on her now, and her heart went with the river. There, where it lost itself in the Channel, would be the sound of sea birds crying, the fresh sharp smell of tidal water, and a horizon bounded only by the sky. A wave of homesickness rose and overwhelmed her, obliterating everything but the knowledge that she was stranded in an alien place. A passer-by stared at her with impersonal curiosity, and she touched her face to find it wet with tears. When she could trust herself to see the traffic again, she finally walked back to what now passed for home.

Colin was exuberantly cheerful that evening, determined that they must drown the memory of the morning's quarrel by going out to dine. She did her best to smile brightly and look interested in the fellow-diners whose names he seemed to know, but the long empty day had made her feel tired, and she couldn't compete with the tide of lassitude inexorably creeping over her.

"Darling, you're not exactly stimulating company – perhaps you'd rather be back at the flat, comparing recipes for potage with Annette Duclos?"

His steely smile warned her to be careful, but Annette was the only woman among Marguérite's friends whom she actually liked and she refused to allow him to belittle her.

"I like talking to Annette – she's a culinary wizard and I intend to learn as much as I can from her for your benefit. But I do also know when I'm being spoiled by being taken out to dine so lavishly. I'm only sleepy because I had too much fresh air this morning. Forgive me, please."

When he smiled more naturally the awkward moment was past, but the evening had become a failure for both of them. His love-making that night was more selfish than usual, and Cressy sensed that male self-assertion was needed to wipe away the memory of a day that had begun and ended unsatisfactorily.

Ease and intimacy seemed to have been restored by the time she discovered from Marguérite that it was Colin's twenty-eighth birthday. She would have preferred a celebration by themselves, but they were required to attend a formal dinner party the Buchards were giving. The president of some important EEC committee was being fêted and hints of possible contracts hung on the air, tantalising as perfume.

Told that she was required to look her best, Cressy had her hair trimmed by a fashionable coiffeur whose prices perhaps only proved that a lot of women with more money than sense patronised him. Still, her hair did have a certain something about it afterwards. She made up her face more carefully than usual, and wore a beaded top and skirt that had been a present from Marguérite. Colin approved the final result and they set off amicably for the Buchards' palatial apartment.

She thought the EEC dignitary hardly worth the bother. He was a small self-important man, and she pitied Colin the thankless task of entertaining his dull Dutch wife during a long and elaborate dinner. She wasn't much happier with the partner she'd drawn herself – Pierre Lenoir, another Buchard director – overweight, in her view, and much too pleased with himself. His knee tried to nudge hers beneath the table, and receiving no encouragement in this, he amused himself with slanderous comments about Jules Froment.

"You don't seem to relish competition," she was finally tempted to point out. "I take it that Froment – perhaps Credland and Froment combined – give you a certain amount of trouble?"

"No trouble at all. Don't forget Colin is with us now, bringing a lot of useful inside information."

She stared at the smiling face beside her, liking it less and less.

"His present loyalties lie with Buchard's, of course, but I doubt if he feels obliged to discuss Credland's affairs with you – in fact I'm sure he doesn't."

Pierre Lenoir almost purred into her ear. "My dear Cressida, how do you suppose we learnt about the new Credland–Froment machine? Colin must have told you that he gave us the blueprints months ago. Without that information we couldn't have . . . what's the English expression . . .?"

"Stolen from them?" she suggested coldly.

Her blanched face told him that she hadn't known. Better if she still hadn't, perhaps, except that he didn't mind if she and Colin had a fight on their hands about it. For himself, he preferred a woman who understood how businesses had to be run. He turned eventually to the more co-operative partner on his other side, and Cressy stared at her plate, wondering whether she would ever be able to eat *bœuf en croûte* again without remembering this moment and feeling sick. She drank the water in her glass in a desperate attempt to combat rising nausea, and prayed to God to help her get through the rest of the evening without disgrace. She must try *not* to think of Colin explaining to Giles that some Buchard engineer had put two and two together and arrived at the Credland invention; must *not* look at Colin across the table, now keeping Jacqueline Buchard amused. He was seated between his hostess and the guest of honour's wife, singled out, she'd thought, beyond what he probably expected. Wrong, she now corrected herself; he'd have expected no less as his reward for betraying Credland's.

She could force down no more food, but continued to sit at table, played with a coffee cup afterwards, and talked to whomever bothered to talk to her. The purgatorial evening ended at last, and when they drove home a merciful heaven saw to it that Colin had drunk enough wine to send him to sleep immediately. She lay awake beside him, waiting for the dawn and the day that would have to decide their future.

She dozed at last, and woke later than usual to the discovery that he'd already made himself coffee and left her to sleep. She regretted his considerateness: a whole day had to be killed now before she could talk to him. She spent it, as arranged, mostly

135

with Marguérite, but couldn't have said afterwards where they went or what they talked about. Exhaustedly, she waited for the moment when Colin called in to collect her.

She was grateful that he was punctual for once because long anticipation of the scene ahead was making her feel sick again. He smiled at her when he came in.

"You were lost to the world when I left this morning." Something about the pallor of her face made him stare at her again. "Not feeling well, *chérie*? You're very wan-looking."

Marguérite smiled at him. "You let her drink too much wine last night . . . she admitted to a hang-over this morning."

"I did *not* drink too much wine." Cressida hadn't intended her conversation with Colin to take place in front of Marguérite, but suddenly the tension locked up inside her had to be released. "My 'hang-over' had a different cause. I sat next to Pierre Lenoir last night," she said to Colin, "but perhaps you were too busy to notice."

"I was busy, but I did notice. You didn't seem to be enjoying yourself. Not the sort of man you like, perhaps, but surely not unpleasant enough to make you feel ill?"

"Wrong . . . he practically destroyed me. According to him, you deliberately gave Buchard the blueprints of Giles' new invention, so that they could rush it into production and come out first with something they'd stolen from Credland's."

"And you believed him?"

The question stopped her in her tracks, and she was aware in that moment of the most terrible thing of all: it hadn't occurred to her to doubt the truth of what Lenoir had said.

Colin misread her silence. "Don't suffer any pangs of remorse, my darling. I did exactly what Pierre said, and remarkably useful it's been. We're making a huge amount of money out of that design!"

Cressy stared at his handsome face, known intimately to her now, and loved almost from the first few days of meeting. Only – she hadn't known it at all. The smile that touched his mouth was familiar too, but now it invited her to agree how clever he'd been. She turned to look at Marguérite and found her face full of delighted wonder.

"Dearest . . . how *clever* of you . . . no wonder they made you a director!"

"Well, I think it *was* pretty clever, Mama, but I get the impression that our opinion isn't shared. True, Cressida?"

She met his impudent blue glance, trying to convince herself that she was caught up in a nightmare, not a conversation that was actually taking place.

"True, because I can't help thinking what you did was despicable, not clever. Even then, after that, you went on for almost another year, being paid by Credland's and being privy to their affairs. How much more information did you pass on, I wonder?"

"As much as I could," Colin said frankly. "I knew it couldn't last for ever, but the set-up was perfect for as long as Giles didn't realise what was happening." His only regret, it seemed, was that such good fortune had had to come to an end.

"The money Buchard has made has been stolen from Jules Froment and from your brother . . . dishonestly, illegally, *stolen!* Can't you understand that, either of you?" She was finally goaded into shouting the words at them.

"It's *you* who don't understand," Colin said with deadly quietness. "I don't give a damn about Froment, and I care even less what happens to Giles."

"Well, if not Giles, Credland's then. The company your grandfather and father built up; is *that* something to be betrayed?"

"God in heaven, Cressy, listen! Credland's *is* Giles where I'm concerned; the place where I've been humiliated and ridden roughshod over for years. Why should I care what becomes of it? All I've done is level the score at last, not only for myself but for Marguérite as well."

"Of course you have, my dearest," Marguérite agreed warmly, "and I can't thank you enough." Her glance at Cressida was full of reproach. "Now I understand why you've been so unlike yourself all day. Anyone would think it was *our* fault that Colin had to go to so much trouble."

Virtuous indignation trembled in her voice, breeding in Cressy an insane desire to laugh. She felt like Alice, bemused by the

137

upside-down certainties of a Wonderland where black was white and she was the only person standing on her head.

"Poor Colin," she murmured unsteadily.

Marguérite smiled ravishingly, almost sending her headlong into hysteria. "There . . . I knew you'd understand."

"I'm afraid she still doesn't," Colin suggested coldly, "but I'm not going to go on discussing it. I suggest an early film instead; we can eat afterwards."

His glance flicked a question at Cressy, but she did what he expected and shook her head. "No film for me, thanks. Don't let me stop you, though."

She knew beyond doubt that he was infuriated with her because she'd questioned something he chose to do; her duty was to commend, support, and admire, but *never* to find him wanting. A forlorn hope had persisted all day that he would admit to being in the wrong, explain that the corroding hatred of Giles, which she understood and sympathised with, had led him astray. If he would only say that, she wouldn't be suffocated by the terrible fear that they would always be looking at life from different angles. She prayed that what he said next would save them.

"You and me, then?" he asked Marguérite. "We'll leave Cressida here to weep for poor dear Giles."

Five minutes later the door slammed behind them, and she realised there was nothing to save after all. Without conscious thought she trudged the half-mile to the rue Jacob. Even there she packed her clothes without any awareness of pain, governed simply by the need to do one by one the things that had to be done. Reaction had set in, making her slow, until panic sent her stumbling downstairs in a sudden fever of haste in case she was wasting precious time. She asked the concierge to telephone for a taxi, tipped him too lavishly in case he refused, and despised herself for doing so when he looked at her luggage and then at her with an insolent grin.

"You don't like Paris, or you don't like Monsieur?" The jerk of his head indicated the room upstairs that he knew she'd shared with Colin.

The taxi had been rung for and she could say the truth. "Right now, what I like least of all is this hotel."

"There are worse." He said it with a vestige of pride, and she supposed it might be true. But she couldn't wait to get away from it and from this man who stood too close to her, breathing out fumes of garlic and stale Gauloises.

An hour later she was at the airport, and the money Colin had given her just paid for a one-way ticket to London. There was nothing left to do except wait, and spend her remaining francs on a cup of coffee and a brioche. But when it was put in front of her, her stomach heaved at the sight of food, and she sat there waiting for her flight to be called.

Chapter Thirteen

"CRESSIDA'S home," Lady Evelyn said unexpectedly at the Manor dinner table.

"Home for the wedding," Lucy guessed. "Lovely . . . we haven't celebrated something cheerful at St Fritha's for ages."

"Yes, Derrycombe's ageing citizens seem to have been making a Gadarene rush for the churchyard recently!" her father agreed.

Lady Evelyn frowned at this racy way of dealing with a serious subject, then shook her head. "I don't think Cressida has come back to get married. Gwyneth Morgan saw her arrive – alone, and looking very unhappy. A lot of luggage also seemed to suggest that she'd come to stay."

Lucy's face, no longer smiling, was incapable of concealing the shaft of pain that held her transfixed. Andrew saw it and did his best to help by diving into the conversation.

"On the strength of no more evidence than that, Gwyneth will set some wild rumour running round the town, and be made to look a fool as usual when Credland turns up in a day or two."

Lady Evelyn, now also aware of her daughter's blind gaze at the plate in front of her, merely said that they would have to wait and see, and changed the subject.

Lucy set off for the shop next morning trying to decide whether it took more courage to say nothing at all, or to fall on the sword in front of her, Roman fashion. Christopher solved the problem by mentioning immediately that he'd been at Lantern Cottage the previous evening.

"Cressy's home. Things didn't work out in Paris, apparently, but beyond saying that, she left the subject alone."

He made the comment casually, with his head bent over a

publisher's spring list, but Lucy knew about him now the fact that he always sounded casual about important things. She'd learned other things as well about Christopher Goodhew, but still had to guess what he felt about her friend.

"Poor Cress," she said after a moment's silence. "I know she found leaving Derrycombe painful, but she seemed certain that she wanted to spend the rest of her life with Colin. Something must have gone badly wrong." Christopher said nothing at all, and she was obliged to go on. "If she's not going to marry she'll be ready to come back here. I can return to being a lady of leisure."

His eyes were suddenly examining her face instead of the catalogue. "Is that what you *want* to be – a lady of leisure, taking your turn at arranging the church flowers, and putting in an hour or two at Oxfam provided they can be fitted into the social round? Is that what you want, Lucy?"

She was no longer twelve years old, imploring Cressy to teach her the knack of being brave; now she must manage on her own and, first of all, try for a bright smile as she looked at him.

"Perhaps not quite that, but I shall be glad to be able to please myself again. It's been quite fun, but working every day becomes a bore."

"Doesn't it just?" he agreed politely.

She wandered over to the window to escape having to meet his gaze. Did God in heaven forgive a thumping lie if the cause was good? The people outside in Fore Street walked unconcernedly in the cold spring sunlight, busy with their own little lives, not knowing or caring that Lucy Pollack's heart was bleeding to death a dozen yards away from them.

Christopher stared at the back of a girl who up till then hadn't seemed bored at all; in fact he'd managed to convince himself that she was happy there. Training held, it seemed; only the lower orders gave themselves away by allowing the world to know what they were really thinking. He knew that Lady Evelyn had him neatly classified: not quite one of them, but presentable enough to be given a drink when he sometimes delivered Lucy home after a long day. It didn't matter a damn what the rest of the Pollacks thought of him, but it mattered intolerably if he'd been wrong about Lucy.

"I'm sorry if we've been keeping you away from the important things of life," he said coolly. "I've been foolishly tempted to forget that the Pollacks of this world don't have to work for a living."

It made her swing round to face him, and the rare anger in her face confirmed what he already knew – that it had been a cheap and misplaced jibe.

"Whether they have to or not, at least admit that they *do* work, rather harder than most of the people who sneer at them." Reproof stiffened her gentle features, reminding him that she was the daughter of a woman who'd sprung from a long line of belted earls.

"You're right and I stand corrected," he admitted. "Sorry, Lucy. You'll have gathered that I – we – shan't like losing you; in fact you'll be greatly missed."

She thought it sounded like an epitaph, or a testimonial for a housemaid who'd done rather better than expected. It was a relief to pick up a pile of new books and walk out of the room, leaving him to stare at the catalogue again without seeing a word of it.

She made up her mind that she would wait, rather than seek out her friend, and it was Andrew who first caught sight of Cressy, standing on the quay talking to old Nat Selby. It wasn't often Nat managed to forestall Ben Davy and he was making the most of it. There was time for Andrew to watch the girl who stood smiling at him – woman, not girl, he amended silently. She was different in some way he could register but not define. Perhaps it had to do with the way she wore her clothes; the jeans and thick white sweater were standard wear, but she invested them now with an unconscious glamour that Derrycombe girls knew nothing about. No, there were deeper changes: the bones of her face were more evident, and eyes and mouth looked ... used. The word came into his mind, and the scalding bile of hatred came too. If Colin Credland had taken Cressida at all, he should have been able to keep her, so that the rest of them could be left in peace to learn how to manage without her.

As if his surge of emotion had been carried on the breeze between them, she half-turned in his direction and at once said goodbye to Nat. Her mouth smiled, but no warmth lit her eyes to say that she was glad to see him.

"Hi, Andrew. The prodigal is returned, you see!"

"How long for this time? It's hard to keep up with your comings and goings." His voice suggested that it was not only hard but unrewarding, but she persevered.

"Home for good . . . you were right to warn me that I wouldn't transplant abroad very successfully."

"Fortunately there's always good old Derrycombe waiting for whenever you happen to change your mind."

The hostility in his voice could no longer be ignored. "You sound savage about it, Andrew. I'm not sure I understand why."

He recognised the Cressy of childhood, quick to fling back any challenge he'd offered her.

"Because your adventures play havoc with other people's lives. You bring to Derrycombe a family we all hate, then go dancing off to Paris leaving us stuck with the worst member of it. Lucy obligingly steps into the gap when you walk out on Marlow's, works like a galley slave for a couple of months, and now, presumably, gets told she's no longer needed because you think you might like your old job back."

"Are you only angry for Lucy and Derrycombe, or have I wronged you as well?"

"Forget about me, if you were going to offer to make amends. I think I can find a woman who isn't one of Credland's cast-offs."

The words were out of his mouth, and for all that he would have given to unsay them, there they had to stay, written indelibly in his memory. Worst of all was the fact that, although her face went white, she still smiled at him. Time was when she would have picked up the nearest oar and hit him, but now he knew the extent to which life recently had taught her self-control.

"I wasn't aware of making any offers," she said quietly, "but if you see Lucy before I do, please report that I have no intention of going back to Marlow's."

She walked away and, for the first time in her life, passed Ben on her way home without seeing him. He forgave her, though, telling himself that his little maid had looked powerful upset about something.

She tried to conceal dejection at home, but the empty, sleepless

144

nights became something to dread. She was still wide awake at
dawn one morning when the sound of her mother's voice reached
her through the half-open bedroom door.

"Oh, God . . . Cressida, please come . . . come *quickly!*"

She flung herself out of bed and ran along the passage to her
parents' room. Helen knelt beside the bed, and her father lay against
the pillows she'd heaped behind him. His eyes were closed, but
sudden intolerable pain had drawn his face into the rigid mask of
a stranger.

"I'm here . . . what can I do?"

"Call an ambulance . . . but they must come at once . . . oh, God,
we need them *now*."

The ambulance arrived, but the question Cressy had so greatly
feared was already answered. This time Roland Marlow had left
them with the finality of death itself. When they returned they sat
in the kitchen, not to drink the tea Cressy brought to the table,
but simply so as not to have to penetrate any further into a house
that no longer contained him.

"Was it *my* fault . . . for worrying him?" When Cressy's ragged
voice finally broke the silence she had the impression that she might
have shouted the question.

Helen shook her head. "Nothing to do with you, my dearest. It
could have happened at any time . . . in fact we expected it much
sooner than it did. You could say we were very lucky." But she
made the claim despite the tears that streamed down her face.

*   *   *

A week later the whole of Derrycombe, people from all walks of
life, and from other parts of the county, crowded into St Fritha's to
say goodbye to Roland Marlow. Then the time of being suspended
in a kind of mercifully numb limbo was over; the business of living
without him had now to be reckoned with.

The following Saturday Helen was alone in the cottage when
Giles Credland knocked at the door. He came more often than
before, apparently to discuss the progress of the Harbour Master's
house, but she knew that what really brought him was an unspoken

Sally Stewart

intention of keeping an eye on them. He registered the anxiety in her face and, as usual, saw no point in pretending that he hadn't noticed it.

"Something wrong, Helen?"

"Mother-hen complex, I expect!" she said, trying to smile. "I'm worried about Cressida. She's been unnaturally calm . . . frozen with grief inside. But this morning she was suddenly on the verge of breakdown . . . too much has happened to her recently. She's taken refuge in her old sanctuary. I know she's familiar with the moor, but it's no place to wander on when your eyes are looking inward at some private torment. I should have insisted on going with her."

"Then she wouldn't have gone, if she was needing somewhere to lick her wounds," Giles said calmly. "Any idea which direction she would have taken? At the risk of having her push me into the deadliest bit of blanket bog she can find, I could have a look for her."

Helen's strained face relaxed a little. "Would you, Giles? There's a favourite walk she used to take with Roland; they'd leave the car at Buckland and walk to Widecombe from there."

An hour later he was sitting outside Widecombe's pub and thinking that he was probably on a wild-goose chase. Cressida could have done any one of a dozen other things instead of coming here. But even as he thought it, she emerged from the churchyard gate and crossed the green towards him. She walked slowly, weighed down with tiredness or despair, as if this time sorrow had been too great for even the moor to comfort. He waited for the moment when she would look up and see him; half-anticipated that she would turn and run away. But she could only stop and stare, like an animal under threat, frozen into immobility.

"You look in need of a drink and some food." His voice held no trace of the sympathy. It said merely that they'd met by chance and it happened to be lunchtime. "Come and join me . . . outside or in, whichever you prefer."

"Outside, please," she managed, and collapsed onto the bench he'd been sitting on. He nodded and disappeared inside the pub door, giving her time to recover from the shock of finding him

146

there. Only Fate at its most malicious could have brought *him*, she thought, the last man on earth she'd have chosen to find her looking beaten. But perhaps Fate insisted on this one last ordeal before it lost interest in her and tormented some other victim. She managed a smile of sorts when he reappeared with a laden tray.

"I don't think I need quite as much food as that."

"No, but I do. You can nibble as daintily as you please. I require a lot of feeding."

She buried her nose in a tankard of cider, then made a pretence of eating one of the pasties he'd brought. The meeting was desperately ill-timed, but she need only smile and say very little, and it would soon be over. "I'm out of condition," she explained carefully. "Time was when I could walk much further than I did this morning without getting blown."

"Past your prime," he agreed. "At twenty-two, it's downhill all the way from now on."

She was grateful to him for accepting the excuse of physical weariness, and beginning to feel that the meeting wasn't so disastrous after all. Nothing in his manner said that it was anything but accidental, and she should have known by now that he would make a point of avoiding the emotional bog that lay no more than one false step away. He didn't even seem concerned whether they talked or not, and she felt free instead to look at the scene all round her. Widecombe village, constructed out of the moorland materials of stone, slate, and thatch, seemed to have grown as naturally as the gorse or heather that clothed the hillsides. It huddled around the simple granite tower of St Pancras church, confident that it could outlast anybody's present troubles.

"Not a bad place for getting things into perspective again," Giles said suddenly, as if he'd peered into her mind.

"A lovely place at this time of the year. But unfortunately the world comes to Widecombe at the beginning of every summer, and when crowds flock to the fair, I imagine that the villagers must curse the name of Uncle Tom Cobley!"

She'd deliberately edged the conversation away from delicate ground and hoped he would accept her lead. A moment later she realised without any surprise that he never accepted anything he hadn't a mind for.

"I won't talk about your father," he said abruptly. "I imagine it's too painful to be touched on. Tell me instead why Paris didn't work out . . . you seemed settled enough when I saw you there."

His blue gaze fixed on her didn't permit of evasion. "Nothing's ever as settled as it seems," she muttered after a moment. "I suppose the truth is that I don't seem able to manage without Derrycombe."

"I don't suppose it to be the truth at all, but if you don't want to tell me what went wrong we'll simply eat our lunch and admire the view." Her pale face moved him to add more gently, "If it makes the telling any easier, remember that I've been acquainted with the rest of the Credland family far longer than you have."

Cressy stared at him, and the unexpected kindness in his face prompted a question that took them both by surprise. "Will you tell me something instead? Why does Colin hate you so much? I have to judge him by my standards because they're the only ones I know, but to a man who has to contend with so much bitterness inside himself they must seem smugly unfair. The result is that something that might have lasted us a lifetime has been ruined. What I can't accept seems perfectly permissible to him because it's born of loathing for *you*."

She hadn't intended to say so much; it was a mistake to have said anything at all. The tears she'd refused to shed over Colin, and couldn't shed for her father, chose this moment to prick her eyes, spill over, and pour silently down her face. She'd been wrong about Fate – it had had this final humiliation in store, that she should find herself weeping helplessly in front of Giles Credland.

"I won't ask what he did that you found unacceptable . . . I think I know," he said eventually. "If it helps, you can go on thinking that I'm entirely to blame. But it's time you considered another possibility – that my stepmother and her son are made of different material. It's charming and very decorative, but not the stuff for everyday wear-and-tear."

She wiped her tears away – like a child, he thought – smearing her cheeks with the back of her hands. "It certainly comes off worse against the material you appear to be made of, but then almost

148

anything would," she pointed out. "You still haven't answered my question – why did you let Colin grow up hating you?"

A grim smile touched his face, doing nothing to soften its harsh features. "The answer's obvious, surely. I resented Marguérite's marriage to my father, saw my younger brother as a threat because I might have to share Credland's with him, and watched him grow up with the ability to charm everyone he came across, when *my* only talent was to alienate them with equal ease! That's the explanation you prefer to accept, isn't it?"

"I should like the truth, now," she insisted gravely.

"Part of it *is* the truth. I was five when my mother died, six when William remarried. I didn't understand then that he was lonely, working too hard, and still beset by the problems of turning Credland's back to peacetime production after the war. At the time all I was conscious of was the difference between my own mother and the woman who had taken her place. Perhaps that was exactly Marguérite's appeal for my father when he met her during a business trip to the Continent. At the age of six all that registered with me was her unacceptable strangeness, not her undoubted charm. By the time I was sixteen, I'd grown to resent her for William's sake as well as my own. She was a restless woman, mindlessly extravagant, and jealous of every moment of his time that wasn't spent dancing attendance on her. He couldn't, wouldn't, neglect Credland's, but in the end the effort of trying to satisfy them both killed him much too soon; I blamed her."

He said it without emotion, but Cressida knew that it was there, running in a deep-hidden seam through the Cornish granite.

"She was twenty years younger," she pointed out quietly. "Was it reasonable to expect that someone as vividly alive as she must then have been would be content to sit alone in a gloomy house in Plymouth, learning how to cook stary-gazy pie and coping with a hostile child who hated her because she wasn't his mother?"

"Was it unreasonable for William to expect that she'd married him to do the best she could for him and his child?"

A silence fell which Cressy found hard to break, but after a while she tried again. "What happened afterwards?"

"Colin, of course. The age gap between us was awkward, but

apart from that the odds were hopeless – some of them my fault, I now realise. I grew too fast, seemed to get unmanageably large, and went through a phase of being deliberately uncouth just to prove that I didn't want the grace and good looks I obviously hadn't got. My long-suffering father put up with me because he knew he was going to turn me into a good engineer. We shared heroes – inventive geniuses like Trevithick, Humphry Davy, and Goldsworthy Gurney . . . Cornishmen all! It made an unbreakable bond between me and William, but did nothing to commend me to my stepmother."

He stopped talking to take a gulp from his glass of beer, and Cressy had the impression that he'd forgotten he was recalling old hurts out loud. "I'm still here," she reminded him, and saw a smile unexpectedly lighten his face.

"Not bored with this old story? Well, on we go then. My brother was everything I was not – a bright, laughing boy loved by everyone he met, including William, who could never bring himself to admit that Marguérite's unreliability lay below the charming surface. Colin should have done well at school but was sacked for some misdemeanour, should have graduated brilliantly from Cambridge but didn't even last the course. In the end he wasn't properly qualified for anything, and we had to make use of the talents he had – a flair for languages, and the ability to get on terms with anyone he met."

"People can't all be the same," she insisted. "Couldn't you have valued him, at least, for what he *could* do?"

"I valued Credland's more. When William suggested, much against his own better judgement, making us equal co-managing directors, I threatened to leave unless I was given complete control. I had the poor man over a barrel because the company needed an inventive engineer much more than it needed a competent linguist."

"So you did steal Colin's birthright."

"You could say so, and he did; but I kept Credland's safe. It was not, as you no doubt think, to make myself a rich man at his expense, but simply to preserve a company that's become something of a legend in the West Country. Unemployment has been the curse of the region for more than a hundred years, but I try not to turn away anyone who wants to learn and work – especially anyone with guts enough to leave a dole-cushioned life of idleness in Cornwall and cross the Tamar looking for a chance. *That* is what was important, not letting Colin play at being a company director."

Cressy steeled herself to ask the question that had haunted her ever since the night of the Buchards' dinner party. "What about Froment . . . did your association with him fall through after your new machine was copied?"

"Relations are still stiff, but Froment needs me more than I need him. Once I'd salved French pride by accepting that the leak was at our end, he agreed to get on with dealing with the situation."

"How? Surely the damage was done?"

"All we could do was improve on the original design. In the end we left Buchard turning out machines that we could beat."

"Of course. Simple if the inventor happens to have cussed Cornish blood in his veins!"

For the first time since Pierre Lenoir had spoken to her, the sense of being smeared by something fraudulent and unforgivable eased a little. What Colin had done hadn't been the ruin of Credland's or of Jules Froment. It didn't help her unhappiness, but it lessened the guilt of having been, however indirectly, involved. Lost in her own thoughts, she wasn't aware that Giles studied her face, noting its signs of sadness and strain.

"Has my family saga changed anything . . . made it easier to understand Colin . . . changed the standards you can now apply to him?"

After a moment she shook her head. "It doesn't change anything, but I'm grateful to understand better than I did." She cast around for something that would bring them safely back to generalities, and gestured to the view in front of them. A shaft of sunlight slanting unexpectedly through lowering clouds turned the slate roof of the church to silver, and speckled its granite walls with tiny points of light.

"Paris seems a world away already. It's beautiful, but I find that big cities don't agree with me. They weigh too heavily."

Giles nodded. "It's why I like the Admiral's House so much . . .

151

there are times when a sea mist rolls in and I can pretend that I'm the only human being left alive!"

He saw her smile, and thought the effect was much like the shaft of sunlight they were looking at.

"I don't dislike the rest of the human race as much as you seem to, but I agree about the house. I yearned for it even when Admiral Blake was alive, and used to promise myself that I'd live in it one day. Now, I don't mind as long as the person who owns it cherishes it."

"What *are* you going to do now?" he asked suddenly. "I said I wouldn't talk about your father, because I dimly understand what he meant to you, but we can't avoid the subject for ever."

Cressy turned to face him. "I've scarcely allowed myself to realise that we shan't see him again . . . walled myself inside some protective shell that excluded pain because it excluded everything else as well. I know that won't do."

"So what will you do? Go back to the bookshop?"

"No, Lucy Pollack's there now, and I couldn't disturb that arrangement even if I wanted to. But I've discovered what it is that I *do* want to do . . . finish the children's books my father began to write. All the material is there, waiting to be used. I shall spend the summer working on it, and ask Helen to help too, because it will be a comfort to us both. After that, it will be time to think about the future."

She stood up, brushing crumbs from her jeans, and he knew that the conversation and her time of despair were both over.

"Want a lift back to your car?" he asked.

"Please, if you're going via Buckland. I meant to walk back, but suddenly it seems as inaccessible as the moon!" Her thin face was suddenly questioning. "Did you come this way purely by chance? I don't see you as an aimless moor-wanderer."

"I occasionally allow myself a break from the daily grind, if only to convince my doubting colleagues that I'm human after all!"

He hadn't answered her question, she noticed, but it occurred to her with a sense of surprise that he was a good deal more human than anyone except her father had ever had the perception to realise. It made him vulnerable after all, and she was tempted to feel sorry for his solitariness until she remembered that it was self-imposed. It was a mistake she kept on making, the idea that she knew better than the Credlands themselves what they really wanted. Giles didn't want the companionship of other human beings any more than Marguérite had wanted the house she'd tried to foist on her. Even more mistaken had been her conviction that by offering Colin a loving heart she could provide him with peace of mind. She was suddenly swamped by sadness again, and it was a relief when Buckland came into view and she could say a hurried goodbye to Giles.

Chapter Fourteen

MARGUÉRITE was feeling aggrieved. She was in Paris, not Plymouth, and it was spring: she ought to have been happy. But something was wrong, and for the first time Colin was failing her. Even though she knew the subject irritated him, she couldn't help bewailing the loss of Cressy, but when she suggested for the tenth time that he should try to entice her back, he finally lost his shaky hold on self-control and shouted at her.

"I keep *telling* you . . . she *won't* come back. She's a dreary little puritan at heart. Her colour spectrum of morality includes only two extremes – black and white. Not for Cressida the numerous shades of grey that people like you and I deal in."

Marguérite felt miserable enough to argue with him. "You make her sound smug and boring, but she wasn't. I enjoyed everything when she was here, and I miss her."

"So do I." He wanted to scream the words at her, but the aching truth couldn't be admitted to. Marguérite stared at his face and found it chillingly reminiscent of Giles. Just now and then she saw a fleeting resemblance that reminded her they were brothers.

Colin took a deep breath in a last attempt to make her understand. "Cressy was a lot of things we probably shan't find again, but we did without her before and must do so again. If the Buchard business hadn't sent her running home, something else would have done eventually – she sees life differently from us."

He managed to smile at his mother, but knew that if she insisted on harping on the subject he would end by abandoning her. Loss and longing still fought a pitched battle inside him with the self-esteem that Cressy had damaged so badly, and it took all his strength to pretend that he didn't care whether she left him or stayed.

"Never mind, dearest, it's obvious that the Buchards couldn't think more highly of you." Marguérite offered what comfort she could give, but saw the grimace that pulled his beautiful mouth out of shape and was puzzled by it.

"The Buchards . . . yes!" He didn't explain that it was something else to feel ill-used about that success was neither as sweet as everybody supposed, nor nearly as simple. Armand Buchard was no problem; Colin accepted him for what he was – a hard-driving businessman with a subtle, unscrupulous mind. But Jacqueline was another matter. She'd made it patently clear that the position of lover was vacant and that he was expected to apply for the job. Even if he'd wanted a bored, experienced woman looking for fresh excitement, a remnant of caution would have insisted that an affair with her would be much the same as slitting his own throat. Pierre Lenoir or any other of his *chers collègues* would be watching for the smallest clue, and what they couldn't find for certain they would invent. If Cressida had been with him still he could have evaded the summons without giving too much offence to Jacqueline, and even been pleasantly flattered by it. Now, he simply felt sick at heart. It couldn't be admitted to Marguérite, but he knew that the two of them had somehow gone astray. Bearings were lost and so were they.

"We've got in a muddle." He heard his mother's small sad voice put into words the very truth he'd just been shying away from. "Shall we be able to manage, dearest, on our own?" She stopped short of saying that Giles, hated for years, at least had always been there when needed, but her face implored Colin to convince her that they wouldn't come to disaster without him.

"Of course we shall manage, but we must be a little more careful in future . . . less extravagant, for one thing! My job is here, and so is your new home, Maman; it's time to stop flitting about, and settle down."

He only called her Maman when matters were serious. She felt comforted by the unusual sternness, unaware that the more he sounded like Giles, the more certain she could be that he was right to insist that life wouldn't be too much for them.

"Dearest, I *promise* . . . no extravagance and no debts from now

on," she assured him lovingly. "I shall become a model mother –
dull, but good!"

It made him smile at her with his old sweetness, and the
resemblance to Giles disappeared. "I think I prefer you as you
are, *ma mie*. Ruin doesn't stare us in the face; we just have to be
prudent, that's all."

She solemnly agreed, and they celebrated the sensible decision
by going out to dine in the neighbourhood's newest and most
expensive restaurant. Only halfway through the meal did it occur
to her to point out that it wasn't the best way to begin their new,
blamelessly frugal life. It was exquisitely funny, but mopping his
face afterwards Colin realised that they might just as well have
been real tears shed in advance for all the mistakes they would
probably continue to make.

Marguérite moved into her new flat a week later. For the moment
she was too occupied to think of anyone at Derrycombe, and the
subject wasn't mentioned until a letter arrived from Cressida,
forwarded on from the previous apartment, briefly announcing
the death of her father.

*   *   *

Throughout the days following the funeral the memory of her
conversation with Andrew was submerged by what had happened
afterwards. Cressy was aware of it always lodged in the back of
her mind, as something that needed attending to, but it was several
days before she could settle down with Christopher to discuss
the future.

"We want, Helen and I, for things to go on unchanged. It's what
my father would have wanted," she said when they were alone in
his flat above the Derrycombe shop.

"Sure, Cressy? The bookshops are yours now; wouldn't you
rather get away from heart-breaking reminders . . . sell them to
someone else and do something quite different? I refuse to let you
be influenced by the idea that a new owner might not want me."

"Well, we refuse to consider the idea of selling. We couldn't
contemplate abandoning what was my father's life, or his firm

intention of offering you a partnership. That still stands, dear Christopher."

There was a little silence in the room before he said unsteadily, "What about you? Are you coming back to Marlow's, Cressy?"

She gave an odd smile that he couldn't interpret. "No . . . I shall take an interest from afar! My first job is to finish Father's books on Devon; I'm determined that they shall be published as soon as possible."

"Lucy can't wait to get away, either. She was hoping that you'd come back and release her – disappointing, because I'd convinced myself she was happy with – at Marlow's."

He'd taken off the spectacles he wore during the working day, and Cressy thought his grey eyes looked not only tired but sad. A visit to the Manor, she realised, would most certainly have to be her next task.

Her friend, not seen since the funeral, also looked, to Cressy's eyes, somewhat strained although her smile was as loving as usual.

"Cress dear . . . I haven't bothered you and Helen because I knew you'd have a thousand things to do; I also took it for granted that you'd say if there were anything I could do to help."

"There *is* a lot to do, but I'm thankful for it. Time to sit and think would be the hardest thing to cope with."

Lucy nodded, then plunged in bravely. "Andrew delivered your message, and it's very kind of you, Cress, but of course you must come back to Marlow's."

"It doesn't sound as if he delivered it very well! I'm going to spend the summer working on the Devon books and after that it will be time to decide what I do next. But I am *not* going back to Marlow's; it's absolutely fixed with Christopher that everything goes on as before." Her eyes wandered over Lucy's face before she added gently, "As before, that is, unless you're sick of working there . . . he seemed to have the idea that you were."

"Of course I'm not sick of it. I *love* being there." It was a cry from the heart, throwing light on Cressy's darkness.

"Well, why not tell Christopher so? He looked so miserable that I assumed he hadn't sold a book for a week, but he had to admit that sales were very good."

"You mean something else might have been upsetting him?" Lucy enquired shyly.

Cressy wondered how far she could safely go on the evidence she'd had time to acquire. "I had the strong impression that he hated the thought of you leaving."

Lucy examined her fingernails carefully. "I dare say . . . I'm a hard worker." She made the statement with a comical mixture of pride and sadness, then changed the subject abruptly. "Cress . . . I know that what's happened since has driven it into the background, but I'm sorry things didn't work out in Paris. You seemed so certain . . . something must have gone sadly wrong. I can't help feeling it was Colin's fault, but that probably doesn't make you miss him any the less."

"I still ache to have him love me," Cressy admitted with bleak honesty, "even though I know that my idea of him was far from complete. Giles tried to tell me that once, but in my usual pig-headed way I wouldn't listen to him. I thought the gift of myself would be enough to make Colin and Marguérite happy, but I was wrong about that, too."

"Dear Cress, I'm sorry . . ." Lucy hesitated over what to say next, then decided to risk it. "At least you've *tried*; lost, maybe, but lived while you were trying. All I do is settle for losing gracefully! It's inherited from my mother, I think. She'd confront a madman without turning a hair, or embrace a leper, if duty required her to, but full-blooded love . . . sex . . . *that* defeats her. I've never even heard her speak the word. Things might have been different with the pianist, I suppose; but conceiving me and Andrew with poor Bart must have been a fearful struggle for both of them. No wonder I'm so full of hang-ups. I shall run amok and seduce someone one day, just so that experience doesn't completely pass me by!"

"You're not past passion yet," Cressy said firmly. "I promise you that inherited hang-ups will melt like morning mist when the right man makes love to you; wait till then, is my advice."

Lucy looked pensive; at her rate of progress with Christopher, the wait in prospect seemed all too long.

"You're a girl looking for experience, though, so you might try hurrying things along," Cressy pointed out helpfully, "especially if the man in question's inclined to be diffident!" Their eyes met over the shared thought of Christopher Goodhew, and Cressy grinned. "I'm not suggesting that you should walk into Marlow's tomorrow morning with every button of your shirt undone, but why not give honest lust a chance?"

Lucy turned pink, then gave her adviser a warm hug. "Dear Cress, I know it's selfish of me, but I can't help being glad you're back!"

*   *   *

Feeling confident now that Lucy and the bookshops could be left in Christopher's hands, Cressy turned her attention to her own affairs. Helen Marlow wept when she outlined her suggestion that they should spend the summer working together on the children's books.

"Dearest, I'd love to help, but your darling father always insisted, with the utmost gentleness, that my spelling was rudimentary and my sense of grammar non-existent. I can't help feeling that you'd be better off without me."

"No, it's going to be a joint project. We shall both make mistakes, but we shall have to trust him to be looking over our shoulders and giving us a little nudge when we go wrong."

Helen's face was still wet with tears, but she smiled at her daughter. "Of course he will . . . silly of me not to have thought of that."

They began the work straightaway, concentrating first on the draft he had already roughed out of a vividly simple account of the history of Dartmoor. It brought to Cressy's mind the memory of her meeting with Giles at Widecombe. The uncomfortable remembrance of having given too much away left her with the feeling that she preferred not to see him, so it came as no surprise that when she next walked along the quay he was the very man who came towards her. She chose attack as the best method of defence.

"For a man who has great undertakings to run in Plymouth, you seem to spend a great deal of time not there."

"I have great undertakings here as well at the moment." He examined her face with the impersonal interest, she thought, of a vet inspecting a sick horse. "You're looking a bit less haunted than you were. Come and see what you and Ben are partly responsible for."

She was towed willy-nilly in the direction of the Fishmarket, smiled along the way at people she knew, and realised that Colonel Carstairs for one had only raised his tweed hat with reluctance.

"Sorry, I should have asked whether you minded being seen hobnobbing with the enemy," he said when the Colonel was out of earshot.

"Not much, although I don't share your pleasure in being always at odds with people."

"If you mean that I go out of my way to annoy, it isn't true; there are too many other things to do."

"Of course," Cressy agreed cordially, "it's simply everybody else's fault for being unreasonable enough to cross swords with you."

"Exactly so!" He sounded pleased, as if a backward student had found the right answer for a change, and she silently gave him best in that round.

From the quay, the ancient building they'd come to inspect looked unchanged, except that the air of dereliction that had hung about it for years had now disappeared. Next door the Harbour Master's house was equally trim. Not even the Squire at his most lordly could pretend that the restoration had been ill-done; the changes only began inside.

The interior of the Fishmarket had been divided into a series of workshops, which now only awaited the installation of equipment and machinery. An upper floor had been created out of the high-roofed space where, Giles explained, there would be rooms for the boys' recreation and study. Cressy looked about her, thinking that it had all been planned by a man who knew exactly what he wanted, and who spared neither effort nor expense to make it a reality. It was the same next door where the hostel was already taking shape. A dozen small bed-sitting rooms were being contrived and furnished with simple, homely comfort.

"Now you can detect your mother's hand, surely," Giles remarked.

"Because it's colourful, you mean?"

"That, and sensibly planned, but what I've valued above all is her enthusiasm. I like someone who doesn't do things by halves, and I can't abide negative people."

Cressy stared at sunshine yellow walls, and brightly striped curtains and bed-covers. "Negative it is not," she agreed with a smile. "The boys who are lucky enough to come here can't fail to be happy." She thought of the care that had gone into it, and the money that had been generously poured out. Colonel Carstairs and the other people who bowed frigidly in the street should surely be ashamed of themselves. What Giles Credland was doing deserved a better response than that.

"Have you thought of letting Derrycombe see what you're doing . . . a sort of Open Day before it starts operating?"

"By 'Derrycombe' I take it you mean the anti-Credland lobby? If you think it would change their opinion, I don't agree. It's the use I'm going to make of it that they deplore. The boys coming here aren't exactly Borstal material, but they've been used to disadvantages the good Colonel should be thankful he knows nothing about. He's *not* thankful; he prefers to pretend that life is equal for everybody. No amount of public showing-off here is going to change that."

"And in any case you don't feel inclined to truckle to the anti-Credland lobby?"

"There is that too!"

She stared at his impassive face, remembering Colin's first description of him: a thorough-going sod. She was less sure now. He might hope to get skilled workers for Credland's in the long run, but she didn't believe for a moment that he undertook an investment of time and money on this scale for such an uncertain return. The truth was that he was intent on doing good in his own way – a practical way, because he was above all a practical man.

"I hope it succeeds," Cressy said finally. "It deserves to."

"Now we come to the crux of the matter. I know you said you needed the summer to work on Roland's books, but we shan't open here until the autumn: would you consider coming here then – as superintendent, matron, house-mother . . .? I don't care what you call it?"

The thought that he wasn't serious crossed her mind only to die

162

instantly. She couldn't believe that even his most diehard opponent had ever accused him of flippancy.

"Is this another piece of the philanthropy that you're determined to disclaim?" she enquired faintly. "Finding a job for Cressida that will keep her out of trouble in future?"

His mouth twitched in the beginnings of a smile. "If you're hell-bent on getting into trouble, I doubt if I should be able to keep you out of it ... a man knows his limitations. The simple fact is that I have a job to offer. It needs a woman like my mother – strong, resourceful, and kind. You're probably too young, but on the other hand you won't have forgotten what it's like to be an adolescent. If you see it as a sinecure, forget I asked; it will be damned hard work."

"I could feed the boys and generally take care of them," she admitted cautiously. "What else is involved?"

"Creating the feeling for them that they have a home – a luxury most of them have been denied so far. Your roots are here and a lot of people still regard you with affection. If throwing your lot in with me doesn't damage that still more, you might be able to bridge the gap between this place and the rest of the town. I don't want the boys isolated from Derrycombe."

"No sinecure at all. I don't know yet ... may I have time to think about it?"

"I'll give you a week; that's long enough to agonise. The hostel won't be operational for several months and there's still a lot to do, but it would be sensible for whoever's going to take the job to be involved in the next stages. The workshops will be run by a superintendent, incidentally, and his wife will help in here."

"Perhaps she'd prefer the job herself?"

Giles shook his head. "She doesn't want to come at all! Alice Ollerton is a Cornishwoman whose spiritual home is the other side of the Tamar. But Sam was out of work for a long while. He values his job at Credland's, and where Sam feels obliged to go, Alice will follow him."

"Poor Alice. Who says it isn't still a man's world?" Cressy thought she might more truthfully have said that it appeared to be Giles Credland's world. If he was generous in giving, he was equally ruthless in using.

"I don't mind working hard, but suppose I can't bridge the gap you talk about?" she asked at last.

"Then you'd probably feel you'd failed and ask to leave." In other words, Cressy thought grimly, the fault would be hers.

"We needn't anticipate failure," he pointed out kindly. "I have the impression that, unlike Alice Ollerton, you like being in charge!"

"I shall, with an effort, take that as a compliment," she said, hoping to irritate him; but he took the wind out of her sails by smiling instead.

"You overlooked the compliment I *did* pay you. Photographs more reliable than a child's hazy recollection suggest that my mother wasn't particularly beautiful; apart from that, I think you'd have a lot in common."

She was flummoxed this time, the more so because he was perfectly well aware of the fact. "I'll let you know in less than a week," she said with dignity.

A moment later they were outside again, in the softness of a typical April day, overcast and mildly damp. River, roofs, and sky were muted shades of grey against the vivid spring green beginning to paint the surrounding hills. Giles suddenly gestured to the town huddled comfortably round the horseshoe of the estuary.

"Derrycombe maddens me at times, but I can't think of a pleasanter place to create a memorial to my father."

Cressy stared at him, taken by surprise because another unexpected seam of feeling had suddenly been exposed.

"Is that what this scheme is . . . a working memorial?"

"Yes; William wouldn't have wanted any other kind."

Chapter Fifteen

CRESSY changed her mind a dozen times before deciding in the end to accept Giles' job. Her brief letter was answered by one as businesslike from him, stating the terms of her employment. She told her mother that it was just as well she hadn't been expecting any effusions of gratitude.

"What *are* you expecting?" Helen wanted to know. "A challenge, or do you simply want to confound Giles because you think he's expecting you to fail?"

"I dare say that comes into it, but it seems to me that the job itself is worth doing, and I did help to wish the hostel on Derrycombe!" She didn't add another reason scarcely admitted to herself: if she could make the hostel run smoothly, it would go some way towards making up to Giles for his brother's theft of the Credland machine.

To begin with, occasional consultations at the Harbour Master's house were all that were required of her while the conversion was being finished. She was free to spend the rest of the summer working companionably with Helen on her father's great store of Devon material. The Newton Abbot publishers were enthusiastic about the draft of the small book she took to show them, and anxious that it should be only the first in the series her father had visualised. After that the days were spent in the bitter-sweet task of completing what he had begun, and the daily routine of steady hard work became her defence against the loneliness at her heart's core. It was a joyless summer, redeemed to some extent by the sight of Lucy's happiness unfurling like a flower.

Lucy's change of mind about staying at Marlow's was coolly received to begin with. In fact, looking at Christopher's unfriendly face, she almost lost her nerve and insisted that she would leave after all.

"How long might you want to stay this time?" he asked. "It's just that I need to know whether I can count on you or not."

Till death, her heart said. "Until you get tired of me," she promised out loud, with her heart in her eyes.

Christopher stared at her, trying to look severe. "Was it for Cressy's benefit, all that nonsense about being bored?"

She flushed but answered honestly. "Yes; I thought I was making things easy for you both."

Christopher snorted – with disgust, Lucy imagined. "I ought to deliver a lecture on the evils of duplicity but, seeing that I'm rather glad you're staying, I'll let you off with a warning this time."

She thanked him and then smiled blindingly because life looked so beautiful. "My intentions were good, but I know that's what the road to hell is supposed to be paved with!"

She was on her way out of the office when he said suddenly, "Lucy . . . I'm a literal-minded chap, and being always immersed in books probably doesn't help, so I take what people say at face value. When women, especially, mean something quite different, I'm all at sea. Will you promise not to confuse me in future?"

Her promise was given as solemnly as a marriage vow, and thereafter contentment hung about them, scenting the air like perfume. Cressy watched Lucy grow confident, and Christopher faintly proprietorial as they moved towards each other by slow, delighted stages. It wasn't Colin's pace they went at, but she acknowledged painfully that it was probably all the better for that.

* * *

Giles' workshop superintendent, Sam Ollerton, and his wife arrived in Derrycombe to move into their flat on the ground floor of the Harbour Master's house, and Cressy was summoned to meet them there. She took an instant liking to Sam – a small, grizzled, quietly-spoken Cornishman who walked round his empty workshops with the air of a man coming into his kingdom. Alice Ollerton looked merely depressed, and Cressy felt obliged to pity such a reluctant helpmate. While Giles and Sam walked about next door the two women were left to inspect the hostel accommodation and kitchen. The rooms were bright and welcoming enough to merit a word of enthusiasm, but Alice's pale face remained expressionless. Cressy finally decided to grasp the nettle she'd been trying to ignore.

"I'm sorry if you've been brought here against your inclination."

Alice looked disconcerted for a moment, then met bluntness with bluntness.

"Sam's happy, that's all that counts. T'isn't me that matters."

"You matter too," Cressy corrected her gently. "I hope Derrycombe will grow on you in time."

"T'es pretty." Her tone of voice made it clear that she offered the town no compliment. Cressy remembered what Giles had said – Alice hailed from the 'land beyond the land', the wildest stretch of the coast between the Lizard and Land's End. It wasn't hard to imagine that someone reared on the constant background surge of the Atlantic would find a Devon estuary much too tame.

"Pretty, but too peaceful?"

Alice gave a little nod. "The wind was always blowing at home. The men who manned the boat could tell of days and nights when they had to crawl along the cliff-top to the lifeboat station, for fear of getting blown clean over."

"Well, we can't equal that," Cressy admitted, "but Derrycombe isn't always as peaceful as it looks now. You'll feel more at home when we get a Force 10 sou'westerly roaring in." She hesitated about what to say next, uncertain how much Giles had admitted to the Ollertons. "The town isn't altogether happy about this venture, either. It's only fair to warn you that you may find some of the people not very welcoming."

"Happen we'll be too busy to worry about them; any road, I'm not much of a one for talking," Alice said truthfully.

*　　*　　*

The summer was nearly at an end when they put the finishing touches to the inside of the hostel. The beds were made up, the big refrigerators in the kitchen stocked with food enough to sustain a regiment of giants, and the rooms decorated with as many green plants as Cressy could filch from the conservatory at home. Giles surveyed them with a slightly sardonic eye.

"Don't expect the greenery to be appreciated. The boys aren't used to the niceties of life."

"Then it's high time they were," Cressy said stubbornly. "If you're about to tell me they'll fall about laughing at my grace notes, I shan't believe you until it happens."

"Quite right, it's dogged as does it. But I'm afraid it's much more likely that they won't notice them at all!"

By the time the mini-bus bringing the first intake drew up at the door she couldn't have said for sure what she was imagining; a gang of half-grown ruffians hung about with knives and knuckle-dusters had figured in her wilder flights of fancy. But at first glance they looked averagely normal – untidy as to hair, scruffy as to jeans and jerseys, and much given to jostling each other like a bunch of nervous animals not sure of their surroundings. She'd carefully memorised their names, but despaired of being able to tell them apart because they all looked so alike. They weren't even minimally interested when Giles introduced her – again like animals, the strange new place they found themselves in had to be investigated, and their own mark put upon it.

Within half an hour the neatly ordered rooms she and Alice had laboured over had completely disappeared under a sea of bags, books and clothes, and peace was shattered by the first radio tuning in to Radio One. Doors banged as they charged about upstairs looking at each other's rooms, and the air was filled with an argot Cressy could barely understand. When it was time for them to go next door they hurtled down the stairs like a herd of rampaging elephants, the door banged behind them, and silence fell. It was time to realise what she'd undertaken, time to confess to Giles that it couldn't be done.

She didn't tell him then, or in the weeks that followed.

'Ask if you need help,' he'd said merely, and she was damned if she would. From initial indifference, the boys warmed into derision and then downright truculence, because she insisted on the observance of minimal rules, such as the regular changing of clothes, and punctuality at meals. But the truth was that if they mystified her, she was as much of a puzzle to them. They didn't know what to make of someone who remained so quietly, pleasantly obdurate about her own point of view. Immersed in the daily struggle not to let them, or weariness, or despair, get the better of her, she wasn't aware that here and there ground was being given. Even less did she notice that the approval of a woman as stubborn as herself was being won. But Alice smiled at her one morning as she walked into the kitchen, and from then on they were friends.

She needed that encouragement because she was aware of failing so far in the thing that Giles had chiefly required of her. The boys worked hard under Sam's supervision, but out of working hours they still made for Plymouth like homing pigeons. Their only contact with the boys of Derrycombe was an occasional fight, which she and Sam took pains to ensure didn't reach the ears of Giles Credland.

As Christmas approached she took it for granted that the season would make no difference to her working routine. She said this to Giles one day and was taken aback by his reply.

"The boys will go home for the holiday, and so will you."

"Three of them have no home. They can't stay here alone and they're my responsibility."

"Wrong, they're mine! I asked you to take on the running of the hostel as a job, not to devote your entire life to the place, which is what the Ollertons seem to think you do."

"Well, they're fine ones to talk. The Credland crèche fills Sam's every waking thought! However, we've got side-tracked. What happens to the boys who have nowhere to go?"

"They come to the Admiral's House, of course."

He sounded faintly irritated that she needed to ask. Apparently she should have guessed that a man who could spare no warmth or affection for his own family would turn his Christmas upside down to take in three youngsters whom no one else wanted. Cressy had seen him regularly during the past three months, but she was no nearer understanding him. Always just below the surface was the granite on which the rest of the world constantly stubbed its toe, but she couldn't help noticing that the boys were quieter, peaceful

169

almost, when he was anywhere around. Nor was it the quietness of intimidation; they simply reacted to the knowledge that this was the man who had taken their insecure lives in charge.

The workshops closed down the day before Christmas Eve. By the evening the boys had gone, and the Ollertons had left to spend the holiday with Alice's family in Cornwall. For once Cressy had the house to herself. It was blessedly quiet and she could work undisturbed, checking accounts and stores. When there was finally nothing more to do, she walked from room to room, making sure that all was well. She was smiling at a sketch of herself pinned to Kevin Sykes' bedroom door when a sound startled her into spinning round, to see Giles walk into the room.

"I thought there was no one here but me," she said sharply, because her heartbeat had quickened uncomfortably at the unexpected noise.

"Sorry . . . I didn't expect to find *you* here. Why are you? Go home, for God's sake." His glance registered the fact that her face looked thin and tired, and it occurred to him that he asked too much of her.

"I'm on my way, just shutting up."

He came to stand behind her, apparently intent on examining Kevin's masterpiece, and she was visited by a strange idea in the emptiness of the house that it would have been restful to lean against him for a moment.

"It's not bad, but he's made you look too pretty!"

The truth was what you got from Mr Credland, she reflected, but Kevin's approach was preferable. "At least Kevin was being kind," she pointed out.

The ghost of a smile touched the harsh face now staring at her instead of at the sketch. "I was about to add that you can sometimes do better than mere prettiness!"

Before she could think of anything to say he was speaking again, in a different tone of voice. "Regret coming here, Cressida? Do you wish this was one challenge you hadn't accepted?'

"I regretted it bitterly at the beginning, almost caved in, because I seemed to be invisible. Now, I'm occasionally allowed inside the herd and I find it very satisfying." She hesitated and then decided to make the confession that had been worrying her. "There's one thing, though: Derrycombe is still just the place where the boys learn, eat, and sleep. I haven't bridged the gap for them with the town."

"Does the town still cold-shoulder *you*?" he asked abruptly.

She gave a little shrug. "A few people cross the street to avoid speaking to me, but that doesn't matter very much. It's the boys I want Derrycombe to accept, not me."

"I asked more of you than I had a right to . . . I'm sorry. Don't worry about the town, or about the fights which you seem to think I shouldn't know about. A bloody nose or two won't hurt them, and I'd rather they sorted out their differences themselves. Serious trouble will get them sacked and they know it."

"I should miss my little flock now; they can't be driven, but they can be led."

"How? Feminine wiles?"

She thought he sounded disapproving and shook her head. "Music was our battleground. Even if I could have borne the noise of four different pop groups being played at once, I didn't think the rest of the quayside could. Requests for moderation fell on deaf, or deafened, ears, so I explained that too much noise affected my ability to cook. They'd been expecting chocolate pudding, and got a wizened apple each instead! The battle went on for three nights before resistance crumbled. Now the music is on a rota system — one group at a time!"

The rare whole-hearted smile that changed his face warmed it now. "Poor little perishers! I should have warned them about you right at the beginning, and told them to lay down their arms." Then he changed the subject. "Heard anything from Paris?"

"A Christmas card from Marguérite, that sounded rather wistful. Her message said that Colin was working very hard."

"Well, if so, it's for the first time in his life, thanks to Buchard."

He'd known all along, Cressy realised, where Colin had gone.

Froment, of course, was bound to have discovered and told him, or the man who now ran Credland's Paris office. "Is it impossible even now for you to make friends with them?" she asked slowly. "You take endless trouble for the boys here, and seem to understand

171

what makes *them* go off the rails at times . . . can't you spare a little kindness for your father's family?"

She'd overstepped the mark of what he would allow. There was no warmth in his face now, only the sardonic amusement she was familiar with. " 'God bless us all, said Tiny Tim'! I'm afraid you're allowing the thought of Christmas to make you sentimental."

"Well, there's nothing wrong with that."

"There is as far as I'm concerned. I can't stomach Dickensian whimsy, and I don't feel any different about Marguérite and Colin simply because the mawkish claptrap poured over us like treacle by the media insists that it's the season of goodwill. I prefer people as they are – truthfully concerned only for themselves. I suppose you find that unbearably cynical?"

"I find it unbearably sad," she said unexpectedly. "All the same, at the risk of irritating you, I shall insist on wishing you a happy Christmas!"

He was still standing beside her and suddenly she was overwhelmed by the necessity to make some kind of contact with him. Forgetting that warmth and affection had been deliberately excluded from his life, she reached up to kiss his cheek as she went past him to the door. It was as far as she got because his arms closed hard about her and her mouth was held by his in a kiss that held no tenderness, but only the hunger of a man with passion locked up inside him which was never allowed release.

"Another Credland scalp to hang on your belt – is that what you're after?" he asked unevenly when he released her at last, "or is it just that you miss a lover and any man will do?"

Offensive as it was, she felt no desire to retaliate; she'd learned something about him in the course of that hard, hurtful kiss which he would have preferred her not to know. He wasn't any more immune to human needs than she was.

"I miss being loved," she admitted shakily after a moment, "but I wasn't trying to enrol you." From the safety of the doorway she turned to look at him. "Don't let the boys plague you too much over Christmas. If you keep telling yourself that it's only an ad man's fantasy you'll come through it unscathed!"

"Damn you, Cressida . . . go away!"

The expression on his face went with her into the starlit night. She didn't believe in Giles' estimate of Christmas; its sadness lay not in its phoniness, but in its failure to work the miracles she still expected of it.

*   *   *

Her view was shared by Lady Evelyn, who had spent the afternoon at the Manor engrossed in a task that still gave her a secret childish pleasure. A fir-tree glinting in the firelight, golden with baubles and silver with 'frost', had nothing to do with celebrating the birthday of the Prince of Peace, but Christmas without its shimmering presence in a shadowy corner of the hall was unthinkable. She placed each decoration with an artist's eye, walked round the finished tree relishing its beauty, and then sat in the early darkness of the December afternoon. The great room was lit only by fire-glow and tree, but she never felt lonely there, nor oppressed by the vivid sense she had of its past life. The ghosts of unnumbered generations still peopled its high spaces but she found them companionable, not frightening. There'd been times enough when she'd been grateful for their reminder that she was a mere runner in an endless relay race; all she was obliged to do was hand on her baton when the time came.

"Sitting in the dark, Mum?" Andrew's voice broke the quietness of the room, and then he flicked a switch and pools of soft light scattered the darkness. "The tree looks fine – isn't it even taller than usual?"

"Your father's choice; he thinks that any tree is good, but the bigger it is, the better!"

"I left him to do his Father Christmas act alone. He enjoys it more on his own."

"Just as well, dear. It always seems to me that the tenants must feel it's a delegation when you both go."

The opinion, offered in his mother's quiet voice, surprised him, but he didn't comment on it. "Lucy not back? You sound tired, and she ought to be here helping you, instead of toiling in that blasted shop."

"There's nothing left to do, and she's where she wants to be, helping Christopher Goodhew."

"Is she going to marry him, do you suppose?"

"I expect so . . . in fact I hope so. Christopher is the only thing she's ever asked of life. Five years ago I might have hoped she'd make a different marriage, but Lucy knows what she needs for happiness."

Without knowing why, Andrew heard the echo of an old regret in her voice; if he could have seen her more clearly, he thought her face would have looked sad.

"What about you, my dear?" she asked suddenly. "There was a time when you seemed to want to settle down at a very early age; now you don't seem inclined to settle down at all. I'm not sure why – we know a great many nice people in the county—"

"—with a great many equally nice daughters. That's the trouble: they're all nice, all suitable. But I can't bear the idea of settling down with any one of them."

"It's still Cressida, isn't it?" She asked the question with unusual gentleness, and something about that moment, filled with winter dusk and the anticipation of Christmas, suddenly made it possible to talk to her.

"Yes, it's Cressida, and I can't get over the feeling that she properly belongs to me . . . I'm in a perpetual state of rage about it!"

"She's here, unattached again."

"Here, but not detached from the memory of Colin Credland, or his family. I can't think what Helen Marlow was doing to allow her to take that job." He listened to his own words and thought how utterly stupid they sounded. "Not her fault, of course. When did Cressy ever listen to well-meant advice?"

"If you mean *your* advice, I suspect the answer is never," his mother said frankly. "It was my only objection to her years ago that she had too much spirit to be the right friend for Lucy, who didn't have quite enough! But I was wrong about that as well; they've always understood one another."

"Cressida works for Giles Credland, but it's only a job, not a life-long commitment," she said next.

"I said something unforgivable to her when she came back from

Paris. Apart from that, there's a problem of my own." He couldn't, even now, break the reticence of a lifetime to say what it was, but in her present mood his mother seemed capable of flying over every hurdle in front of them.

"You mean you wanted her untouched by anyone else?"

"Something like that," he muttered, astonished but also ashamed.

There was silence in the room, unbroken except for the occasional sigh of a log settling in the grate.

"I don't suppose you're any more ready to accept advice than Cressida is, but perhaps you'll let me say what my own experience has been," Lady Evelyn said diffidently after a while. "I've discovered that nothing about the past can be changed except our own attitude towards it. For years my own attitude was the most stupid one of all: bitter resentment that life hadn't given me what I thought I wanted most. You can't have Cressida as she was before she went to Paris – your choice is Cressida as she is now or not at all."

The thought of Cressy was pushed aside for a moment in considering what she'd said about herself.

"I'm sorry, Mum . . . sorry if you didn't get what *you* wanted," he said gently.

"I got a great deal more than I deserved, but my own stupidity made a duty out of what should have been a joy, and I hurt Lucy, especially, as a result. The fact that she's all right now is largely thanks to Christopher. But you're too like me: inflexible. Promise me you'll try to grow more like your father."

He smiled because she said it so earnestly, then leaned over to drop a kiss on her cheek. "Do my best! Meanwhile I'll have a think about Cressy. It's what she always used to say herself." He'd conjured up in his mind's eye a picture of a long-legged, tousled, laughing girl . . . his girl, as she'd been before life and London and the Credlands between them had set a different imprint on her.

He went out of the room but Lady Evelyn still sat there alone, content for the first time in years to be inactive, no longer forced to be busy, because the resentment she thought she'd been keeping at bay had finally disappeared of its own accord. It was like being relieved of a persistent illness. But she saw in her son the clear reflection of herself and she knew his difficulties. A grudge long held finally became a treasured possession, and resenting the loss of Cressida had almost become a substitute for the happiness he might have had with her.

*   *   *

The Pollack family attended the midnight service on Christmas Eve as usual, but when they arrived at the church Lady Evelyn made straight for the pew where Cressida and her mother were sitting.

"Helen . . . you said you were going to spend Christmas quietly at home. I shall perfectly understand if you still prefer to do that, but could I persuade you and Cressida at least to dine with us tomorrow evening? No strangers – just ourselves and Christopher."

It was the most informal invitation they'd ever received from her and Helen's natural inclination was to meet friendliness with friendliness, although her daughter's face was unhelpfully blank. She accepted for both of them, and told Cressida on the way home that if she was anxious not to go she should have found some tactful way of saying so. "Anyway, if you don't want to go, I can't think why not. It's unneighbourly not to want to share Christmas."

"So it is, but I get the impression that the rehabilitation of Cressida is about to begin," her daughter said ungratefully.

"High time, if you ask me."

"Maybe, but I won't be forgiven by Bart and Lady Evelyn just because it's Christmas and they feel sorry for us. I doubt if there's any danger of Andrew forgiving me."

"Did that sound very cantankerous?" she added suddenly.

"Slightly, let's say!" Helen replied. "I shall put it down to the fact that you're worn out with looking after a dozen troublesome teenagers."

"Good of you, Mrs Marlow," she said, smiling at her mother with affection.

*   *   *

Christmas morning began with an unexpected visit from the three boys staying at the Admiral's House. They were almost hidden behind a glowing poinsettia that more nearly resembled a young tree than a house plant. More of Kevin's artwork had produced a card covered with barely decipherable signatures and a strange assortment of good wishes. Mawkish sentimentality or not, she felt moved to tears by it, and had to leave Helen to invite them in for the mince pies they devoured with the gusto of boys who hadn't seen food for days. Her mind was suddenly invaded by the memory of their host and she knew that she would have liked him to be there, eating her mince pies. Since it was Christmas after all, he might have thrown habitual miserliness to the four winds and spent on her one of his rare, transforming smiles!

She drove Helen to the Manor that evening with an inward reluctance of which she felt ashamed. But the Squire welcomed them with true kindness and Lady Evelyn, for the first time in Cressy's knowledge of her, seemed to have abandoned the reserve which usually suggested hospitality being wrung out of her by a never-sleeping sense of duty. Lucy looked quietly but radiantly sure of herself for the first time in her life. With Christopher beside her, touching her hand when he thought no one else was looking, she seemed to Cressy to be confronting a vision of paradise on earth.

"You're supposed to be exhausted by the Christmas rush, looking haggard, and hating the great buying public! Instead of that, you're as fresh as a daisy and just as beautiful, and I dare say Christopher's told you so already!"

Lucy smiled back at her friend. "He's hinted," she agreed. "Cress, I wish I thought you were as happy as I am."

"I wish I thought so too, but there's no doubt that it's your turn for happiness. You can't share Christopher with the rest of us, so there's no need to feel guilty about it!"

But Cressy was disconcerted a moment later by Andrew's welcoming kiss, which found her mouth instead of her cheek. She thought he'd intended it that way. The effect of the Christmas season perhaps, but why did he stare at her so persistently? She wondered what he expected to see: the traditional scarlet hue of a woman who'd lived in sin, or the dowdy respectability of a hostel manageress? Then he smiled and she was both ashamed of herself and aware of error – even Andrew was in the process of forgiving her!

Chapter Sixteen

LUCY was married to Christopher Goodhew on a typical spring day which began in teeming rain and then, in true West Country fashion, suddenly relented. Feeling only slightly too seasoned for the task, Cressy shepherded a flock of small bridesmaids up the aisle behind the bride, and the whole of Derrycombe crowded the church for a wedding that had taken it a little by surprise: they hadn't somehow expected it of Lucy.

Cressy fulfilled her job as chief bridesmaid efficiently, which she reckoned afterwards was something of a marvel, given the small percentage of her mind devoted to the task. Her thoughts were much more inclined to dwell on the Credlands, sitting somewhere in the congregation behind her. It had been a shock when Lucy had reported some weeks before that she'd invited not only Giles but Marguérite and Colin as well.

"I can't help feeling they still belong to Derrycombe," she'd explained, "and it seems ungrateful to leave them out when Colin was so kind to me." She had no reason to know why they shouldn't have been invited; but an ulterior motive, for once not disclosed, was the hope that Cressy would find she'd recovered from loving Colin and could begin to notice Andrew again. "You don't mind, do you, Cress?" she added anxiously.

Cressy had smiled and shaken her head. The only comfort to be gained was the certainty that Giles wouldn't bother to come, and that Marguérite and Colin were most unlikely to, but in the event they all proved her wrong. Giles was present for reasons of his own, and even if Colin had been reluctant to come, Marguérite had succeeded in persuading him. She wanted to see Cressy, and even Derrycombe, again.

Since her encounter with Giles at the hostel just before Christmas, Cressy had gone out of her way to avoid him, but when she heard that Marguérite had accepted Lady Evelyn's invitation it seemed only prudent to tell him so.

Giles had stared at her for a moment. "What's the kind warning for? So that I don't run amok and interrupt Lucy's vows by having a shouting match with my relatives?"

"I don't suppose you'd do anything so silly," she replied with dignity, "but the truth is that I don't altogether trust you."

"Well, in return for a promise of my best behaviour, I'll ask how *you* feel about seeing Colin again: eager . . . reluctant . . . or, as the pollsters like to say, don't know?"

He waited curiously for her to answer, aware that if she admitted to anything at all it would be the truth.

"All those things," she said finally, and ended the conversation.

She half-expected a telephone call from Marguérite to say they were in London or Plymouth, but by the morning of the wedding no call had come, and she left for the Manor accepting the fact that they still hadn't forgiven her.

The wedding service was over and invited guests were filing into the Great Hall at the Manor when she found herself suddenly face to face with them – Colin outwardly elegant in morning dress, but with an air of anxiety about him, Marguérite dressed exquisitely as usual, in pale-green, with a matching picture-hat that had Paris written in every lovely line. For Cressida the throng of people around them and the buzz of conversation faded to some unnoticed margin of her mind. For a moment of time she was back in a flat in Paris again, listening to the slam of a door closing a brief chapter of her life. It was more than a year since she'd left them without saying goodbye, and for her own heart's happiness it had been a long and lonely year. Marguérite spoke first, and her remark was entirely typical – a generous compliment just slightly tinged with malice.

"Cressida darling, I *love* your dress. Clever of Lucy to choose such a subtle colour; or was she clever enough to leave the choice to you?"

"No credit to either of us. It's Lady Evelyn who has the artist's eye when it comes to colour. You're looking beautiful yourself, and Colin . . ." she made herself smile at him, ". . . is surely every hostess's idea of the spruce wedding guest!"

For a moment he hesitated, then decided on his approach and leaned forward to kiss her cheek.

"You're looking a trifle worn, my dear Cressida – not surprising if what I hear is true. Can you really be running a sort of lodging-house for my dear brother?" There was no amusement in his smile and no trace of warmth either to hint at the memories they shared. The two of them were acquaintances, he seemed to suggest, with a slight passing interest in one another. Cressida thought of the lonely year she'd spent unhappy for this cool, unkind stranger.

"I run a youth hostel, to be exact," she said slowly. "The boys learn engineering in the workshops Giles had built for them. My job is to look after them apart from that."

"It sounds a living death. Surely we offered you a more exciting time than that?"

"Different, certainly," she agreed, and changed the subject. "Things going well at Buchard's?"

"As far as I know. I didn't stay long – bettered myself, as the saying goes."

His glinting smile seemed to suggest that the subject was profoundly uninteresting, and that only someone like herself, boringly obsessed with work, would have bothered to refer to it. Altogether she was finding the conversation hard work, but she persevered with Marguérite.

"Have you moved on as well, or are you still where I imagined you to be, in the new flat you were going into?"

"I'm still there," Marguérite agreed with no great enthusiasm. "It's all right, I suppose, but not what I really wanted."

How could it be, Cressy wondered, when she never knew what she was looking for? Marguérite's face looked pinched for a moment beneath the brim of the beautiful hat, vivacity drained away by some recollection that troubled her. But the Squire arrived to greet a guest so worthy of his full attention and she recovered instantly – a mechanical toy ready to smile and dance because someone had come to wind her up again.

They walked away together and Cressy was left wondering whether the terms she now stood on with Colin permitted them to talk about anything that mattered. Apparently not, because he was determined to make it clear that they stood on no terms at all. With the merest bow he moved away as well, leaving her standing alone. She found it a relief to see him go, and watched him smile at a pretty girl who looked vaguely familiar. Memory, bidden to supply a name, did so: Angela Harcourt-Smith. Memories, unbidden, returned to assail her: lobsters and Lionel, and the evening she'd gone to cook for the Credlands in London – the beginning of all that had happened since. Andrew's voice finally dragged her back from the past.

"A vision in an orange silk dress has no right to be looking pensive."

"Vision I'm happy to accept, but I'll have you know that the dress is a delicate shade of apricot much admired by one and all!"

"I don't doubt it . . . admired by Colin Credland, too, I expect." He smiled at her suddenly, with unexpected and touching diffidence. "In case you didn't recognise it, Cress, that's what's called a leading question!"

"I thought so. Well, the answer is that he didn't seem greatly impressed. I'm looking a trifle worn, apparently, as a result of being the manageress of what he calls a lodging-house!"

"Bloody fool! Do you mind?"

She suspected another leading question and hoped that a truthful answer wouldn't give him the wrong impression.

"I find I don't mind very much. 'A year is a year is a year,' as Dorothy Parker *didn't* say! I suppose the truth is that we've both changed rather a lot in that time."

Andrew's face relaxed. "Clever Lucy! I was irked when she said she wanted to invite them, but she was right after all."

He had got the wrong impression, but there was nothing she could do about it, any more than she'd been able to miss the change in him since Christmas. She felt in need of friends, and Andrew and Lucy had been the earliest of them. If she could have returned to her old footing with him she would have been content, but she was troubled by the different objective she sensed in him. He refused to be irritated when she aired views she knew he disagreed with, and accepted with good grace the times when she refused invitations on the grounds that something at the hostel needed her attention. He was even determined to forgive her for working for a man he disliked, and the fact both touched and terrified her. What if the spirit of forgiveness should finally move him to propose to her again? The thought of inflicting the hurt of another refusal depressed her beyond bearing, and it wasn't only Andrew she would be hurting. Bart and Lady Evelyn went out of their way to make it so clear that she was welcome at the Manor that from time to time she even listlessly faced the prospect of becoming the next Lady Pollack after all, simply because she could see no humane way of avoiding it.

Alone again, Cressy's glance returned to Colin, still deep in conversation with Angela. He was exerting himself to please, and the poor girl could be forgiven for thinking that his only reason for flying over from Paris had been the happiness of talking to her. Cressy knew what it felt like to be at the receiving end of his whole attention – so warmly flattering that caution, even common sense, lay down and died. She felt sickened by her own inside knowledge; it was as inexcusable as peering through someone else's keyhole. She looked away and found herself staring instead at Giles Credland, standing with his back to Colin a yard or two away. For a moment of time she saw them with peculiar clarity – the one so charmingly self-aware, the other totally uninterested in what anyone else thought of him: one brother needing to make his effect on the people around him, the other so confident of himself that he could do without them altogether.

As usual, Giles was listening more than he talked. He'd seen no reason to make himself uncomfortable in conventional morning-dress – a dark lounge suit was his only concession to formality. It was well-cut, but Cressy suspected that his sheer size and indifference to how he looked had long since broken his tailor's heart. Then he looked her way and caught her staring at him. Their eyes met and held in a strangely measuring glance that isolated them for a moment from the rest of the crowd. She acknowledged to herself that it wasn't size alone that set him apart; strength marked him out as well, and the confident acceptance of responsibility for other people's lives as well as his own. She knew it to be true, and in the same moment knew without any feeling of surprise that she would never be able to marry Andrew Pollack.

She saw Giles murmur something to the man he'd been listening to and stroll towards her. "You look overcome . . . not by the sight of my dear brother ogling some other woman, I hope. You ought to be familiar with his party manners by now."

"She's lovely," Cressy felt obliged to point out, then remembered too late that Angela had been a bone of contention long ago.

"Lovely but vapid! Still, her expectations are rosy and, as someone once remarked, 'all heiresses are beautiful'!"

She surveyed him gravely. "Weddings don't agree with you – you're even more sour than usual."

"I don't mind weddings . . . in fact I rather enjoy seeing other people putting their heads in the noose. I was feeling quite benign until I caught sight of Colin doing his party piece."

In spite of herself she was provoked, as usual, by the edge to his voice. "You're as benign as a basking shark, wondering which arm or leg it fancies next for supper."

She expected him to reply in kind, but the blue eyes that always surprised her in the swarthiness of his face didn't gleam with the anticipation of giving battle. If the idea hadn't seemed so strange, she could have believed that her barb had penetrated for once and even wounded him.

"I hadn't thought of myself as a predator . . . self-deception 'o'er-leaping itself', perhaps."

She scarcely heard the murmur as he turned and walked away. There was no time to explain that she'd spoken without thought and, indeed, without justice. So much for Helen's lectures over the years; she still leapt first and looked afterwards. She suddenly felt cross with herself, unhappy, and perversely disinclined to enjoy an occasion which everyone else found pleasurable.

Colin didn't come near her again, and it seemed to Cressy that Marguérite was avoiding her as well, but towards the end of the reception they found themselves side by side, waving the departing couple on their way. Marguérite looked tired now; as usual when her effervescence disappeared forlornness took its place, and Cressy felt sorry for her.

"Weddings are all very fine, but no one could call them restful, or occasions for quiet conversation! If you're not going back to Paris straightaway, or anywhere else, why not come back to Lantern Cottage for a restoring cup of tea?"

Marguérite looked uncertain. "I'm not sure what we're doing. We were supposed to be going back, but now Colin seems to want to stay . . ." She sounded more perplexed than a slight change of plan seemed to warrant, and anxiety robbed her face of youth and gaiety. Cressy remembered that constant loving kindness was the only element in which she could live; it made her very vulnerable, and put on Colin's shoulders the whole burden of her peace of mind.

"He's found an old friend. Perhaps he's even discovering that Angela's more interesting than he used to think her!" It was the wrong thing to have said. She could see Marguérite recalling the first time they'd met, and suddenly the past was in their laps like an unwanted child that couldn't be ignored.

"You didn't reply to my letter," Cressy said bluntly. "Colin didn't either, so I suppose neither of you could understand why I had to leave Paris."

"We still don't understand. You knew how badly Giles treated us. When Colin managed to get the better of him for once, you should have been *glad*."

It was a subject on which they would never be able to agree. Cressy abandoned it and tried another tack.

"Why did he leave Buchard's? I thought he was happy there."

She couldn't read the expression that touched Marguérite's face for a moment. "I don't know . . . something to do with money, I expect – it usually is. Colin said he could earn more doing whatever it is he does now."

She sounded genuinely vague and there was no point in pressing her. Cressy returned to her original question. "Won't you come back with us if you're at a loose end?"

Marguérite shook her head with unexpected firmness. "I can't do that, because you've gone over to Giles' side. Colin says you're even working for him now. That is *really* treacherous, Cressida. I wouldn't have believed it of you."

Cressy tried to answer calmly. "I make sure that a dozen teenagers who haven't had much of a chance in life so far are properly looked after and fed. Is there anything so very treacherous about that?"

"They shouldn't be here at all. Giles is salving his conscience by squandering Credland money on a lot of back-street brats – he'd rather let anyone have it than the one person who has a right to it."

She was only repeating Colin's view but Cressy was angered by it all the same. "If you remember, I was present when your stepson explained how Colin's claim on the company was to be settled. It seemed generous. Giles is now free to do what he likes with the Credland money; it's his. In the matter of the hostel, he chooses to do something good."

"There you are . . . you *are* on his side." Marguérite's eyes were huge with reproach. "We were quite wrong about you." Moved by a maternal longing to hurt the girl who had hurt her son, she added something else. "Giles wasn't wrong about you, although I refused to believe him at the time. He said from the beginning that you were chasing Colin because he couldn't help looking wealthy! You may think that my stepson's a better bargain, but I can tell you that you won't get him; no one will, but especially not you."

Cressy was feeling sick again, which seemed bitterly unfair on the strength of one glass of champagne and two smoked salmon sandwiches. Something more should have been left of friendship than this parting piece of venom. "I'm not aware of having chased Colin," she said quietly. "I thought we loved each other. As far as Giles is concerned, he pays me to do a job. We argue from time to time, and otherwise ignore each other. The arrangement suits us both." It was as nearly the truth as made no matter. "Now, if you'll excuse me, I can see my godfather signalling to me."

James Jessop was in fact enjoying a quiet conversation with a friend but he smiled at Cressida when she appeared.

"Hello, my dear. You're looking wan. Is it the heat, or that colour you're wearing . . . it's a bit sapping, if you ask me."

"Don't blame the dress, blame wedding indigestion! Everyone

186

else seems to have enjoyed themselves, so it's probably the fate of spinsters to be cast down by these occasions. Never mind, if I'm looking glum Gwyneth can choose her next rumour – either poor Cressida was snubbed by Colin Credland, or she's moping because Lucy snaffled the other man she was hoping to marry!"

"Were you hoping to marry Christopher?" he enquired mildly.

"No; but don't let's spoil her fun."

James smiled, but his eyes lingered on his god-daughter's pale face. "Something's spoiled your fun . . . seeing Colin again?"

"Not in the way you're thinking, but I'm rather floored by my own fickleness. Colin probably hasn't changed at all, so the changes must be in me it's going to be disconcerting if all my eternal verities turn out not to be eternal at all!"

She grinned as she said it but James had the feeling that she was both serious and sad.

"I scarcely knew Colin when he was here, so I can't venture an opinion about him. But I can see when another of your beaux doesn't change. I doubt if Andrew's even noticed another girl all day."

He'd intended to give comfort, but a glance at her face told him he'd failed. She nodded and walked away to comfort a small bridesmaid whose posy was disintegrating under the strain of being too tightly held and too much loved. James watched her go, aware of a sense of discouragement in her he didn't associate with Roland's daughter. She'd always been a fighter, but the events of the past year had temporarily vanquished her. He wished she knew the effect she had on people: while she sat talking Amabel Pollack into smiles again, other women watched almost without envy and men, depending on their age, admired or looked regretful. She didn't even notice them, James thought; the loss of her father had been survived at the cost of shutting her heart away from the risk of being hurt again in future. It excluded pain, but he feared that it excluded the possibility of happiness as well.

Chapter Seventeen

IT WAS Andrew's boat, *Seamew II*, that now rode the current at her mooring in the estuary – a lovely thing to look at. Lovely to sail as well, Cressy thought, but as the season moved into summer she resolutely refused all his invitations. Her excuse was almost true, though too heavily relied upon – the hostel left her little free time, and what there was of it must go to finishing the second of the Devon books: the story of Exeter's royal and tumultuous past. She expected, hoped, that Andrew would stalk away from her in disgust; instead, he was more patient than she had ever known him. For once even the Derrycombe bush-telegraph system was letting her down as well. The town gossips must surely be aware that Giles Credland was a frequent visitor to Lantern Cottage, and so, therefore, were the inmates of the Manor. The Marlows were not only working for the enemy but hobnobbing with him as well – it should have been enough to put Andrew off for ever.

Cressy expected Giles to visit the Fishmarket regularly to check up on the boys' progress; it was less expected, and very unwelcome, to find him often calling on her mother en route to spend the night at the Admiral's House. She preferred him safely in Plymouth – he was a man to be kept at arm's length. But, far from understanding this, her mother seemed more and more to depend on his advice. It led finally almost to a quarrel between them.

She came home late one evening to find Giles there, listening to Helen's racy account of a meeting of the Drama Society. Feeling tired, depressed and unaccountably in the way, she said a curt goodnight and stalked off to bed. The next morning at breakfast, when she was no more talkative, Helen took the bull by the horns.

"As well as very tired, you looked cross last night . . . as if you didn't like finding Giles here."

"He's my employer – I see all I want of him at the hostel," Cressy snapped.

"He's also our friend, for your father's sake. He comes out of kindness, to keep an eye on us, and perhaps also a little out of his own loneliness. I see nothing wrong in that."

"You're wrong about him, that's all," Cressy insisted. "He chooses solitude. The Admiral's House all to himself is the way our self-sufficient Mr Credland likes it."

With the words barely out of her mouth, colour surged into her pale face at the memory of a moment when self-sufficiency *hadn't* seemed enough for him. She might have forgotten it more easily but for the fear of having given herself away at the same time. He'd never touched her again, and she was aware nowadays of the care he took not to come near her. Remembering his stepmother's jibe at Lucy's wedding, she was just as anxious to avoid him.

Helen registered the change in her daughter's face but spoke so firmly that it amounted to a rare rebuke. "He is a good, kind man, Cressida. You must think of him how you please, but I hope you won't always let Colin's view of him colour your judgement. That would have disappointed your father."

Suddenly close to tears, Cressy thought she was a disappointment to herself as well. Lucy's wedded bliss was wonderful to watch but also heart-wrenching; Andrew's patient pursuit was becoming more and more of a worry; and the emptiness at her own heart's core seemed as if it might never be filled. She got up to kiss her mother in atonement for the previous evening's rudeness, and tried to smile.

"Take no notice of me . . . I dare say I'm growing into a spiteful old maid – another Gwyneth Morgan!"

"I see no resemblance at all, my dearest," Helen said gently, "but I think you need a holiday – you work too hard."

"I'll take one soon. The boys are being given a trip to France. Alice fears the worst in the matter of contagious French habits, but at least we can close the hostel for three weeks."

It ended the conversation with the inference that only tiredness

190

ailed her; it wasn't the truth, but it would have to suffice, and the subject of Giles wasn't mentioned again between them.

* * *

A wet and dismal summer finally redeemed itself in time for the most important event in Derrycombe's annual calendar: the Town Regatta. Hoping to revive memories of times past when he had rowed in it cheered on by Cressy, Andrew called early in the day at Lantern Cottage. Not early enough, Helen had to say. Cressy was already down on the quay with her hostel team; the boys were involved with the town at last, even though the day might end with them getting into a free fight.

Andrew's set face refused to smile, and she was tempted to say that neither glumness nor continuing rancour against the Credlands would win him back her daughter. But this stiff, resentful stranger wasn't the boy she'd watched grow up, and she let him leave without the counsel he would almost certainly have rejected.

He found Cressy ten minutes later, perched on the sea wall above the finishing-line. She was hemmed in by a crowd enjoying the morning sunshine, the town's gala air, and the excitement of some spirited racing. Her duties seemed to be mixed – keeping the score, dishing out tactical advice to her team and, more impartially, cold lemonade to any thirsty combatant who needed it. When Andrew hoisted himself on the wall beside her the awkwardness she felt with him nowadays seemed absurd.

"I shall expect you to cheer my lot," she said with her old friendly smile.

"I'm not well enough disposed towards them for that," he said bluntly. "You think about nothing but Credland's bloody hostel, and I never get a chance to see you – alone, I mean, not shared with a dozen teenagers and half of Derrycombe looking on."

She was silenced for a moment by the grimness in his voice, and the knowledge that his patience had finally been exhausted, and he went on quickly, "Lucy seems to think that Giles Credland spends a lot of time at Lantern Cottage. I find that hard to believe – you must have learnt all you want to know of that damned family."

191

She thought it was entirely typical of Andrew that, having finally made up his mind to corner her, he should do it in the middle of the regatta. It would have been a relief to be angry with him, but there was too much misery in his face. Ill-timed though it was, some long-awaited moment of truth had been reached between them.

She abstractedly chalked up another result, waved to Trevor and Billy who sat, chests heaving, in the losing boat, and then spoke to the man by her side.

"Giles does come – to be helpful to my mother. What I've learned about him is that he does the work of two ordinary men, provides good employment for hundreds of people, and uses his own wealth to give boys like these a decent start in life. Does any of that entitle you to despise him?"

Andrew's brown face paled a little under the directness of the attack, but he only half-believed that she meant what she said.

"He's still an ill-mannered, arrogant pig who seems to have treated his own family badly. That was *your* opinion not so long ago."

"Yes, before I knew what I know now." She broke off to pour lemonade for a scarlet-faced Billy who'd come to plump himself down beside her. "Hard luck, Billy, another five yards and you'd have done it."

"Sorry, Cress, but we'll catch that soddin' boat next time – see if we don't." He smiled his gap-toothed smile, and she tried to remember a time when she'd found his sharp-featured mug unappealing. Billy stared at the stiff-faced man next to her, and Andrew found himself obliged to say something.

"If you win the toss next time, choose to row on the other side. You'll get an advantage in mid-stream now that the tide is on the turn."

"Is that so? I'll tell Trev." He wandered off, with lemonade for his friend, pondering the fact that there was still a lot to learn in life. He just hoped he was going to find time for it all.

Cressy watched him go with regret, hoping not to have to resume the conversation he'd interrupted. "At least they're competing at last. I live in hope that they'll finally make friends with Derrycombe."

Andrew stared at her, wanting to shout that she must think about *him* for a change. With dark hair blowing about a sun-tanned face, she was the girl he'd known since childhood, but not that girl at all.

He was aware of having chosen his moment badly, but choice really hadn't come into it, only sheer, aching necessity. If he didn't say now what was in his over-burdened heart the chance might never come again – he knew that with some strange certainty that made him feel cold despite the warmth of the sun on his face and hands.

"I can't pretend not to hate the Credland family," he said slowly, "but they aren't who I need to talk about now."

Her low answer barely reached him amid the buzz of conversation around them. "Don't, Andrew dear, please don't, not now – in fact, not ever if you mean to talk about us."

His hand gripped hers, hurting her. "Cress, listen, please. Will you forgive what I said when you came back from Paris? It's no excuse, but I was eaten up with jealousy. I'd spend my life trying to take care of you if you'd let me, and Bart and my mother would give anything to have you at the Manor as well."

She couldn't doubt him, couldn't even say this time that it wasn't true of Lady Evelyn. However surprisingly, Cressida Marlow had become for all of them the girl they wanted to see take her place in the long, long Pollack procession. Somehow she must find the strength to disappoint them.

"Nothing's changed," she said gently. "I'm still the opinionated, unbiddable piece who ran off to Paris to follow a will-o'-the-wisp and got badly damaged in the process. I still believe in what Giles Credland is doing here, and I should vote for him again instead of anyone who tried to stop him."

At last Andrew spoke again. "I want to marry you, Cressy, but I'm asking you for the last time."

She met his anguished glance and he read the answer in her sad, dark eyes. Ben shouted that it was time to set her stop-watch for the next race. The world around them insisted on still turning; the regatta was still on. Derrycombe didn't know or care that, beside her, Andrew was muttering, "I hate *all* the Credlands. I shall die hating them." Then he dropped off the wall and walked away.

After a moment Cressy stared down at the stop-watch in her hand, trying to remember what she was supposed to do with it.

*   *   *

The clear skies that had smiled on them didn't outlast the night. With a sudden change in the wind, great rain-laden clouds sailed in from the sea in a race towards the moor, and spent themselves in a downpour that, once started, seemed to see no reason not to go on for ever. It was scarcely a day for walking, but the alternative of sitting indoors reliving her conversation with Andrew seemed worse than a Dartmoor soaking. Cressy was about to tell Helen so when a knock sounded at the front door. Giles Credland stood there, apparently indifferent to the rain streaming down his face.

"I thought we might have a picnic," he said by way of greeting.

After an astonished moment Cressy decided to call his bluff. "Why not? Just the day for one."

But she could see him beginning to smile before he answered. "Good! Don't worry about food – it's in the car."

"I'm not dressed for lunch al fresco – you'll have to give me time to change," she said bravely, leaving him to explain to Helen what was in store.

They made a dash for the car a few minutes later, but her aloof expression said how much she regretted accepting a ridiculous invitation.

"Your mother says I overwork you," he commented before starting the engine. "If that's true, I must do something about it. Right now you look as if you'd rather change your mind and go indoors again."

Offered the let-out, she perversely decided not to take it. "Chickening out, Mr Credland? This picnic was your idea."

He simply answered with a nod and settled down to drive them westwards as swiftly as the rain-drenched roads would allow. It seemed long to Cressy before he finally stopped the car on a starkly exposed cliff-top. Hard as it was to believe, they seemed to have arrived. Its disadvantages as a picnic spot on such a day were obvious, but she was merely told to follow him carefully because the path was treacherous. Since it was a steep, downward track now running with water and loose shingle, this at least was undeniable.

She did as she was told, and finally stepped safely onto a curving wedge of beach that lay at the foot of the cliffs. At each end it was protected by a line of rocks stretching out like arms to break the thrust of turbulent grey-green sea. A disused day-mark raised its pencil of stone on the farthest rock, dematerialised into a different element each time it was veiled in foam, and then reappeared again, fragile but apparently indestructible.

Lost to everything but the sight in front of her, Cressy waited for each incoming wall of water to hurl itself over the rocks and die in a fountain of white spray. But at last she heard Giles say something.

"I wanted to show you this. Today seemed the perfect moment."

He pointed inland. Tucked between the beach and the cliffs a tattered sign-post still faintly bore a name: Poldinnick. Of the place itself all that remained were the inner walls of cottages that must once have seemed to grow out of the cliff-face itself. The cycle was now almost complete – the stone fragments were being absorbed back into the cliffs again. The air was tinged with the melancholy of a place only inhabited by ghosts, and a boat quietly disintegrating on the beach added to the sense of heart-breaking decay.

"Colin took me to Versailles once," Cressy said after a while. "He didn't understand when I said it was haunted. Poldinnick is, too. What happened here?"

"Very little for a long time. Its existence must always have been precarious, but if life was harsh by today's standards at least it was real. My grandmother was born here, and when I was small she used to tell me about it. They're the first stories I can remember, handed down as all good legends should be, by word of mouth. Apart from the cottages of the fishermen themselves there was nothing here except the post office, a single shop and the ever-necessary pub. The only way in or out was by the track we used; supplies came down on the backs of pack-horses."

Giles stared at a row of shags hunched miserably on the wreck on the beach, but she had the impression that he saw instead the living Poldinnick that his grandmother had described.

"I suppose the mackerel shoals failed eventually," she prompted him.

"Yes, poverty became destitution, and those who could find work elsewhere drifted away. A stubborn few clung on to the only life they could imagine, aware that when they died, Poldinnick would die too. In fact it died even sooner then they expected. A freak combination of wind and tides brought in seas that took only a couple of days to rip the place to pieces. No one's had the heart to try here again, and who can blame them?"

Cressy stared at his rain-wet face. "I have the feeling that *you'd* like to," she said gently. He didn't reply, and she thought that what she'd told Helen was true. By inclination as well as habit, he was a solitary man, unaccustomed to sharing mind or heart. She gestured to the desolation around them. "At least it was natural destruction, not the fate that's overtaken places like Polperro and St Ives. I wish Derrycombe could understand why you want to keep it alive by other methods."

"Derrycombe understands well enough; it just has a preference for soft options!" She nodded, still thinking of a night when wind and waves had met in the disastrous combination feared by all people who live on the edge of the sea. Then a wave driven higher up the beach by the force of the wind spent itself over them in a veil of silver spray. She laughed out loud, for the sudden happiness of feeling cleansed of guilt and grief and regret; she was glad to be there with him, knew herself privileged to have been allowed to share what was for him a hallowed place.

He stared at her for a long moment, seemed about to say something, and then changed his mind. Instead, with her hand gripped in his, they struggled up the path again. Under a convenient overhang of rock they devoured pasties and fruit, and drank coffee from the thermos. Rain showers still swished curtains of silver around them, but out at sea the sky was slowly lightening, promising an evening that might be fine after all.

"Thank you for showing me Poldinnick," Cressy said suddenly. "Brought up on its folklore, and with your mother's Cornish blood in your veins, you had to be entirely different from Colin. But having chosen Jane as his first wife, I still wonder why your father then chose Marguérite."

"He was forty when he met her – too young to accept that life

196

and loving were over. Marguérite was everything my mother had not been: demonstrative, vivacious, and full of feminine appeal. My mother would have despised such weakness, but by then William was probably flattered by it."

The appeal hadn't worked for her stepson, Cressy reflected. She still pitied Marguérite, but saw in her mind's eye a small, bewildered boy, stubbornly determined to reject what he couldn't understand. There had been no hope of happiness in the new Credland family.

With her face turned towards the view in front of them, Giles could inspect only its delicately-carved profile. Helen was right – her daughter looked noticeably more fine-drawn now than before, and sad when some absurdity or other didn't move her to sudden laughter. She had loved his half-brother – he had no doubt of that; and Colin, careless of the treasure he'd been given, had been fool enough to let her go.

"We Credlands haven't done you much good," he said abruptly. "I'm sorry about that, Cressida."

She turned towards him, touched by the sincerity in his deep voice. Her smile admitted what was true, but seemed to absolve him at the same time. Then she pointed out to sea – the sun had finally won its battle with the clouds and the colours of an almost perfect rainbow deepened over the horizon as they watched.

"I've been in some muddles lately," she confessed, "but I think I shall be all right now."

He pulled her upright, but instead of releasing her at once, leaned down to kiss her lightly on the mouth. "I think it's time I took you home," he said, stamping firmly on an inclination to do something that wasn't that at all. They had made progress today, but they still had far to go, and life had taught him to be patient. Cressy followed him back to the car, aware that what she was feeling now was nothing but disappointment. Then he opened the door and smiled at her and she realised her mistake. There was no need for disappointment because life seemed suddenly full of the most lovely promise.

Chapter Eighteen

MARGUÉRITE tried not to give in to despair these days. It was the only thing she could do for Colin; but when he went back to her flat late one evening his face told her that things were worse than usual. Her mind was often muddled now, because she ate too little and took too many of the tranquillising pills that made the long nights bearable. But a picture of Derrycombe often floated to the surface of her thoughts – a mirage of a place where life had been untroubled and secure. The Admiral's House had been beautiful . . . why had she wanted to get away? She couldn't remember now. But it belonged to Giles, that she could remember. Everything belonged to him, and the more he gained, the more she and Colin seemed to lose. She didn't ask questions about the import–export agency that was supposed to occupy him, but she knew it wasn't going well. He no longer lived in the rue Jacob; if a girl didn't offer him somewhere else to sleep, he came back to her own small spare room. He came more and more often now, and she wasn't surprised. She could sense the anger and resentment that raged inside him, burning up the surface gaiety that people had once found so irresistible.

"Have you eaten, dearest?" Her tremulous enquiry now seemed scarcely to penetrate whatever bitter train of thought obsessed his mind. But he answered her at last.

"It's money I need, not food." The stark sentence broke down the door she'd been keeping barred in her mind against some threatening calamity. She suddenly looked old and defeated, and for Colin it was the last, most dreadful thing to bear.

"We – we haven't any money," she whispered. "I promise you I've bought *nothing*, but this quarter's allowance has gone . . . I don't know where."

He tried to smile at her. "It wouldn't make much difference anyway, *ma mie*. I need a lot of money, not a few thousand francs."

"Why?"

He shrugged the cry aside, poured himself a whisky, but stood staring out of the window instead of drinking it. "It doesn't matter why, but I'm sunk without it."

It was delivered with the flat simplicity of despair. Coming from a man who normally dealt in exaggerations, she knew it for the truth she'd long been afraid to hear.

"What – what shall we do next? Ask the Trustees? Sell this flat if they won't give us any more money?"

"And live in the street?" he shouted. "Does *that* seem the next thing to do? Oh God, what an unutterable mess."

His voice broke on the words, and she thought her heart was breaking too. "We could ask Giles," she ventured finally.

"I'd rather starve – die – than give him the one final pleasure of turning us down. He's got everything else, even Cressida working for him like some domestic slave."

Marguérite was distracted for a moment from despair. "She looked beautiful at the Pollack wedding – not like a slave at all."

But it made Colin more angry still. "*I* should have her, and Credland's too; instead of that I'm here, scratching about for a living among a lot of hard-nosed Frenchmen."

Her heart ached with pity for him, and for herself; but for the first time in her life fantasy had been stripped away and she saw them both for the broken things they were. Life should have been more kind to them, because – as she'd feared all along – they couldn't manage on their own.

"Credland's belongs to Giles because he paid you off," she said with quiet desperation. "Perhaps Cressy rightly belongs with him too. You always said they saw things the same way."

"For once there's no pleasure in being right!" His mother's unexpected calmness shamed him into making an effort to match her own. He drank the whisky in his glass and gave her the travesty of a smile. "Don't worry if I'm back late, I have to hunt up one or two people. They're hard to find if they think you're about to ask a favour!"

The slam of the front door echoed in her mind long after he'd

200

gone. An empty flat, another sleepless night to get through with only her own thoughts for company. Useless to ask where they'd gone wrong. The truth was that without Giles they were like a boat without a sail, drifting along on any current that took hold of them. It didn't occur to her to blame Colin; things were as the stars ordained, unless you were like Giles, able to wrestle them into submission. She thought prayer might have helped, but she was out of practice, and a remnant of pride forbade her to beg for the help of a God she'd turned her back on in happier times. There remained only the tranquillisers to get her through the night; if she could sleep, things might look less hopeless in the morning.

*　　*　　*

The telephone call from Paris reached Lantern Cottage at breakfast-time, and Helen Marlow called Cressy to the phone.

"It's a bad line, but it sounds like Colin Credland asking for you."

She went to the telephone, seized by the sudden dread that Giles, on his way to a business meeting in America, had met with an accident about which Colin, as his next of kin, had been informed.

"Cressida, can you come? I found Marguérite unconscious early this morning. She's in hospital and badly needs a friend."

Above the thumping of her own heartbeats she heard the desperation in Colin's voice. He was only just holding on to self-control and she had the feeling that it could shatter into pieces at any moment. "Cressy . . . please come . . . I could do with a friend myself . . ."

"If Giles were here, I'd ask him, but he's on his way to America," she said at last. "If you really think there's something I can do to help, then of course I'll come."

"We don't want Giles, just *you*."

"All right. I'll do the best I can. With luck I should be there this evening." She put the telephone down, thinking that there were questions she should have asked about Marguérite. But better, perhaps, to find out what was wrong when she got there. She stared, pale-faced, at her mother. "It seems I have to go to Paris. Marguérite's in hospital, having been found unconscious this morning, and Colin sounds at the end of his tether. It's a mercy the hostel has just closed for several weeks. I don't know what I should have done otherwise."

"Something's worrying you apart from Marguérite," Helen said.

"I suppose Giles is worrying me!" The admission took her mother by surprise and she felt obliged to explain it. "I expect you've noticed that we've been getting on rather well lately, but we haven't yet agreed to differ amicably about his family. I know what he would say – they must manage on their own."

"But you must do what *you* think is right," Helen insisted quietly. "Go and pack while I look up a train."

The conviction in her voice steadied Cressy, and her strained face broke into a smile. "I don't suppose I've ever mentioned it, but I did *very* well when parents were handed out!"

Half an hour later Helen drove her to Totnes. "What shall I say if Giles gets back before you do?" she thought to ask almost as the train was pulling out of the station.

"He won't. I'll only be away a day or two at the most."

She smiled as she said it and waved goodbye, but driving back to Derrycombe Helen wondered again about her daughter's changing relationship with Giles Credland. Occasionally she felt optimistic about it; told Roland in her night-time conversations with him that perhaps Cressy was going to be happy at last. But this was not the moment – she felt that stongly – for Colin to interfere again.

When the telephone rang that evening she expected to hear Cressy's voice at the other end. The deep notes were those of Giles instead, sounding as clear as if he were talking to her in the same room.

"Cressida's not here; she's had to go to Paris for a few days." Flustered, she blurted out the information and wished she'd found some other way of delivering it.

"Sudden . . . she didn't mention it," Giles said briefly. "I thought she'd had her fill of Paris. Is it a holiday visit?" His voice, even across transatlantic cables, sounded unmistakably cool, and Helen remembered wretchedly that Cressy had expected him to disapprove of her going.

"It was an SOS from Colin," she said, hoping to improve

matters. "Marguérite's been taken ill, and Cressy felt obliged to rush over there."

"She would, of course," he agreed. Mercifully he didn't wait for Helen to say something else that would turn out to be the wrong thing, merely enquired politely after herself, confessed that New York was unbearably hot, and then rang off.

"I made a thorough mess of it," she told James Jessop when he called in. "Giles is miffed, and I was too flustered to make him understand that it was a real crisis of some kind . . . now he thinks that Colin only has to snap his fingers and Cressy goes running back."

"My dear, does it matter what he thinks?" James asked in some surprise. "Credland isn't fool enough to boot Cressy out of a job she does extremely well just because she helps his stepmother over a crisis."

Helen still looked anxious. "I know that sounds reasonable, but I wasn't thinking of the hostel. Cressy doesn't quite know it yet, and I'm not sure Giles does either, but there's more than a job at stake. The trust between them is fragile, though, easily destroyed."

To her surprise James didn't accuse her, as Roland might once have done, of over-dramatising things; in fact his pleasant face looked sombre. "Pity," was all he said, being a man of few words, and she was left with the feeling that he wasn't optimistic about the happiness of a god-daughter he adored if it depended on Giles Credland.

*   *   *

Her last sight of Colin had been back in the spring at Lucy's wedding. Even then she'd been aware of something slightly raffish beneath the surface gloss, but nothing had prepared her for the deterioration she found in him now. His arms were held out and she walked into them, impelled only by the need to give comfort. But the time when his eyes and hands and mouth had been able to evoke a shattering response was gone. She released herself after a moment or two and he stood staring at her, as if trying to convince himself that she was there at all.

"Tell me about Marguérite first," she suggested.

"She's a little better, conscious again, and longing to see you. I said you were on your way."

"What happened? Did she suddenly fall ill?"

"I told you . . . at least I think I told you, but I was half out of my mind when I telephoned. I had to go out last night; when I got back she was unconscious. She's been depending too much on tranquillisers recently." He forced himself to answer the question in Cressida's eyes. "I think she forgot she'd already taken her pills and swallowed some more . . . it wasn't deliberate. I'm *almost* sure it wasn't deliberate," he added sombrely.

"Was she so miserable that there could be any doubt about it?"

"Yes. Things haven't gone very well for us lately." A travesty of the smile she remembered twisted his mouth while he considered what he'd just said. "Understatement worthy of a full-blooded Englishman, Cressy! Things have been just about as bloody awful as they could be."

He was desperate to talk, she realised, to explain yet again the ways in which Fate had been unfair to them. Perhaps it was even what she'd really been fetched for, to listen, and be made to feel that she was partly to blame for walking out on them.

"Let's talk about Marguérite first," she insisted. "Is she really getting better? Would it help if I went to see her this evening?"

"I saw her this afternoon, and she'll be resting now. She's out of danger but still very weak. I promised that you'd be here to visit her tomorrow."

"In that case, I'd like to make myself a sandwich and a cup of coffee. I seem to have been travelling all day."

He was resentful of a mundane request for food when she was supposed to be listening to him, but there was nothing to be done except follow her when she walked into the kitchen. Cressy felt desperately sorry for him, but anxious to prevent the threatened launch on a sea of self-pity. To the puritan he'd frequently told her she was, there was also the fact that adversity was something to be grappled with; she had the feeling that he hadn't done much grappling so far.

The refrigerator offered very little and her stomach, though empty, rebelled at the sight of what there was. She brewed coffee for them both instead, and Colin gulped it down eagerly.

"Just having you here makes me feel better," he explained unsteadily. "Nothing's gone right since you went back to England."

"Tell me why you left Buchard's . . . I've lost track of things after that."

"Buchard treated me like an office boy. Even after I helped him make a fortune out of Giles's new machine, I never got the recognition I deserved."

She wondered whether anyone but Colin would have been surprised to find that Buchard hadn't felt able to trust him. Before she could make up her mind to say so he was off again, the words tumbling out in his feverish need to talk.

"The real trouble, though, was Jacqueline. You were right about her, Cressy; trust a woman to see through another woman. She turned out to be a bored, demanding bitch who became dangerous when she didn't get what she wanted."

"You mean she wanted you?"

He nodded and even looked faintly solaced for a moment. It was a comfort to make Cressy realise that he'd been sought as a lover by a rich and experienced woman. "Anyway, in the end it was a relief to leave Buchard's. I disliked the people there and they were jealous of me, especially ambitious sods like Pierre Lenoir, always scheming for a foothold on the next rung of the ladder."

"What happened next?"

Colin frowned, as if he could scarcely remember. "I helped one or two people," he mumbled, "invested in things that ought to have worked for them and didn't; then I took some gambles of my own that *should* have worked for us but didn't. It's always the same: by the time you desperately need success it's constantly dancing away from you and pouring money into someone else's lap."

"But what do you actually do?" she persevered.

"Now? Oh, imports and exports," he said vaguely. "We ship electronic stuff out to North Africa, and bring in Algerian wine, Moroccan jewellery . . . that sort of thing."

"Do you want to spend the rest of your life doing 'that sort of thing'?"

"Of course I don't," he shouted suddenly. "Cressy, I hate, loathe it! The people I have to deal with – Arabs at one end and French at the other – are all as slippery as hell and up to every illegal dodge you can think of. They seem to get rich, but I'm the fool in the middle, taking all the risks and getting nothing out of it."

"Why stay, then?" she asked reasonably. "Do something else."

"I *can't* – not until I find some way of paying off the money I owe them."

It occurred to her that since there was nothing particularly illegal about trading in the things he'd mentioned, and no risk attached to it, there must be other merchandise that he hadn't referred to. His white face and trembling hands might be the result simply of stress, and of his worry about Marguérite, but it seemed more likely that among the items he'd helped bring into France drugs had been included, which his associates had encouraged him to sample. If Marguérite had known what he was doing, perhaps her own overdose hadn't been accidental after all. Cressy thought of Giles' determination to let them fend for themselves, and the anger that suddenly burned in her was against him. He should have known better, and cared a little more, than to turn his back on two people whose lives seemed fated to fall apart.

Colin's ragged voice dragged her away from her own thoughts again. "That's what I was doing last night, trying to raise money. But even people you've helped are always well out of sight when you need them."

"How much do you need?"

Colin gave a little shrug. "Five thousand pounds or so, but the figure scarcely matters; I can't find a fraction of that amount."

"Nor can I," she said bluntly, "so there's no alternative but to ask Giles. If you don't like the idea of doing it, I shall have to ask him myself." She was on the verge of adding that Giles would think better of him if he did the asking, but reflected that she was there to help, not to make suggestions that he would find impossible.

"He'd turn me down, and be glad to."

"Perhaps," she had to agree. "He might not turn *me* down."

"Why? Is he so grateful to you for running his wretched hostel for him?"

"Yes, I think he's grateful, but I look on him now as a friend." It wasn't an extravagant claim, but she prayed that it might still be true when she needed him.

Colin inspected her face, saw in it more than she wished to reveal, and reached his own conclusions. The outburst she anticipated didn't come, but it would have been preferable to the smile that touched his mouth. "Clever Cressy, but unexpected, too! I should never have guessed that my little puritan would go in search of wealth instead of love."

She was stayed on the very brink of storming at him by a sudden stab of knowledge. It was the wrong moment for a discovery that took her breath away, but she knew now beyond the slightest doubt where her only chance of happiness lay.

Malice brought Colin's eyes to life again as he looked at her. "Don't expect tenderness or pleasure from Giles, my dear; he's a bloodless machine!"

She could have insisted that he was wrong about his brother's bloodlessness, but no one knew better than herself how little Giles had to do with tenderness – like Christmas, it was probably something else that came into the category of Dickensian whimsy.

"We're discussing your affairs, not mine," she managed to say after a moment or two. "These people you talk about . . . can you hold them off for a week or two? If not, I must try to contact Giles in America."

"I can hold them off for as long as I have to, but if I renege on the promise I shall be found in a gutter eventually with my throat cut." He tried to smile at her. "That might be the best solution, anyway!"

The mock pathos would have been irritating except for the desolate reality she glimpsed underneath. He was afraid, staring at a vision of himself spiralling downward into ruin, but also mortified with self-disgust that she should have to see the mess he was in.

"You know you're talking nonsense." She tried to sound sympathetic but firm. "Everybody hits a bad patch from time to time, and you're in the middle of one now. As soon as Marguérite is well

207

again and these loathsome people have been got off your back, life will begin to seem possible again. But right now it's late, and the day seems to have been very long. May I use Marguérite's bed?"

It hadn't occurred to him to make it up freshly for her and she had to unearth sheets herself. She finally crawled between them too exhausted to do anything but sink into a restless sleep.

*　　*　　*

At the hospital the following morning Marguérite wept at the sight of her.

"Cressy, we've missed you. Nothing's gone right, Colin's got into some dreadful muddle over money, and I took too many pills. Now, I don't know what we're going to do . . ." The words tumbled out in a febrile whisper that could hardly be heard, but her white, haunted face spoke of the lonely region of despair in which her mind wandered.

"You should have let me know sooner," Cressy said, trying not to weep herself. "I'd be cross with you if you didn't look so much in need of cosseting."

Marguérite's face was riven with the pain of past memories. "Funny English word . . . but it's what William used to do, I suppose . . . cosset me." Her eyes filled with tears again for a life that no one could give back to her. "Are you going to stay with us now?"

"Only till you're a bit stronger; then I must go home because Colin needs some help and I have to talk to Giles."

"My stepson will refuse to have anything to do with us. He'll say we have to manage on our own." Her shadowed eyes looked enormous in her sunken face. "We can't seem to, Cressy; I don't know why." It was the simple truth, delivered with a sad finality that was almost beyond arguing with.

"If you'll promise not to give up hope, I promise I'll make him understand. So do what Ben Davy would recommend and 'hearten up, my dearie'!" She saw Marguérite try to smile, and bent down to kiss her cheek. "Rest now . . . I'll come back this evening."

Chapter Nineteen

BY THE time she flew back to London Marguérite had been brought home to a flat that Cressy had cleaned and made welcoming with flowers; there was food in the larder, and an apathetic but definite promise had been given that she would eat more food, swallow fewer pills, and not allow herself to give way to despair. In front of his mother Colin made an effort to control his own worries, and Cressy left them thinking that it was still the nicest thing she knew about him – the unselfish affection that he seemed to reserve for his mother alone.

She got back to Lantern Cottage looking so tired that Helen offered a carefully edited account of her telephone conversation with Giles; but it wasn't hard to read between the lines.

"He was angry because I went to Paris?"

"Not enjoying America, perhaps," Helen suggested hopefully. "Either that, or the long-distance call gave the impression that he was feeling a little irritable!"

Cressy shook her head. "You're doing your best to be tactful, but Giles doesn't go in for 'impressions' as a rule. If he's irritated, you're not left in any doubt! I need to see him very urgently though – it's too important to wait."

"He'll be home later today – I checked with his office," Helen admitted.

Cressy tried to look more confident than she felt. "That's where I'll beard the lion in his den then."

But walking to the Admiral's House later on, she acknowledged to herself that she'd made no dent at all in the armour Giles buckled on whenever he was asked even to think about his relatives. His attitude was unchanged, and the subject she must discuss with him was the one he would most dislike.

She arrived at the house before him, and was wandering about the garden when his taxi drew up at the gate. The contrast between him and the hopeless man she'd left behind in Paris was enough to make her angry all over again. She wanted to be angry, the better to do battle with him, but she was hampered by the discovery also of how very happy she was just to see him again.

He stopped in his tracks when he saw her waiting for him.

"It's very nice to have you back," she said gravely, but her impression was that he had no pleasure in seeing her.

"I'm surprised you're here. You didn't say you were going to be rushing over to Paris as soon as my back was turned."

"I didn't know. I went at a request that sounded too urgent to be ignored. If you were about to ask, by the way, Marguérite is better, though very weak and languid still."

"And my dear brother? How is he?"

"In trouble," Cressida said bluntly. "I'm sorry to confront you with it the moment you get home, but it's too pressing to be allowed to wait."

"I realise that Colin's problems are all-important, but they'll have to wait while I get out of this damned uncomfortable suit and pour myself a glass of cold beer. After that I'll listen if I have to."

She followed him inside, aware that she hadn't made a very promising start. Her favourite retreat, the Admiral's tower, was full of September sunshine, mellow and golden. From the windows she could see a little armada of sailing boats scudding along the estuary towards the bay. Time was – a lifetime ago, it seemed now – when she had been among them, with not a thing in the world to worry about except carrying out the instructions Andrew shouted at her. Now, everything was a worry. She'd promised Colin help, and assured Marguérite that she wouldn't let Giles ignore them. But if she couldn't persuade him to listen, no amount of cajolery or pressure would make him change his mind.

She was still deep in thought when he came back into the room carrying a tankard of beer for himself and for her the cider which she always preferred. Wearing slacks and an open-necked shirt, he looked less stern and formal, but there was still a hostile air about him that discouraged her.

"Travel doesn't agree with me as much as it seems to suit you. You're looking very fetching!"

She'd dressed with care but even that, it seemed, had been a mistake. "Are you ready to listen now?" she asked coolly, and got a nod by way of encouragement to begin. "Colin rang soon after you left. Marguérite was in hospital, unconscious after an overdose of sleeping pills. He sounded distraught and, with the hostel closed, there seemed no good reason not to go and help them if I could. By the time I got to Paris she was recovering physically, but mentally sunk in despair. Colin was anxious about her, but with appalling problems of his own. The money you paid him off with has gone – helping friends who'd fallen on hard times, and financing high-risk ventures of his own that subsequently failed. He got a job again, working for a group of people he is now afraid of. Actually *afraid* of, Giles. They're French and Arabs who use legitimate trade with North Africa to cover activities which he knows are anything but legal. But he's tied to them because he owes them money. If he can't pay it back, he expects to finish up in a gutter with his throat cut."

"Colin's histrionics as usual."

"I don't think so," she said steadily. "You must take my word for it that he's genuinely in fear of them, and desperately in need of help – five thousand pounds' worth of help, to be precise."

"And it's going to be my privilege to bail him out?"

"There's no one else to ask. I wouldn't have asked if I could have thought of a way of coping with it myself."

"Doesn't it occur to you that at the age of twenty-nine he might be expected to cope with it himself? God damn it, Cressida, he's supposed to be a *man*!"

"Don't shout at me," she shouted back. "I know what he's supposed to be – a man like *you*, devoid of human weaknesses and devoid of human warmth! Why can't you, *won't* you, understand that he's Marguérite's son as well as William's . . . not descended from a long line of Cornish wreckers, tinners, intrepid fishermen, and heroic engineers? They must both have help, and even giving

Colin the money he needs is only part of the story. Without you and Credland's behind them they're like a wheel minus its axle, spokes flying loose in all directions. Giles, you *can't* disown them."

She was beautiful in her anger and distress – and she was still completely absorbed in the thought of his brother.

"Where are they now?"

"At Marguérite's flat. Colin is living there as well at the moment."

He nodded and emptied his glass. "All right. Don't let me keep you, Cressida. I shall work off jetlag and general spleen in the garden, and then catch up on the sleep I'm short of. I'll be in touch when I've decided what to do."

It was dismissal of the most brutal kind, and she wanted to shout that she wasn't a junior member of his staff to be sent packing, but something in his face stopped her. Not only was there evident fatigue, but some deep sadness, that wiped away her anger.

"I'm sorry it's such a mess," she said quietly.

"So am I. Just for a little while I thought everything was going nicely."

She had meant Marguérite's and Colin's affairs, but knew that he was talking about something else. It was the chance of happiness that they had briefly seemed to have together.

A note was dropped through the cottage letterbox next morning, with a message that ought to have been comforting. He was on his way to Paris and would see her when he got back. It was what she'd wanted him to do, so why should the bald message not seem enough?

She was hacking down undergrowth in the herbaceous border later in the morning when Lucy called, radiating the contentment of a woman who was pregnant and happy to be so.

"Thank Heaven for you," Cressy observed. "No need to ask how you are, I only have to look at you. Will perfect bliss get boring, do you suppose?"

Lucy shook her head. "I doubt it. It's too much of a responsibility. I feel like one of those Greek vestal ladies, devoted to tending the sacred flame!"

Cressy tried to take this statement seriously. "Just as well you

212

aren't, you'd have been buried alive by now for so obviously deserting your duties!"

"Not looking entirely virginal, you mean?"

The pleasure with which Lucy asked the simple question was too much for Cressida. She began to grin, infected her friend, and a moment later they were both helpless with laughter.

"Just what I needed," Cressy said when she finally mopped streaming eyes. "I haven't laughed like that for ages, but it's exactly how we began, if you remember, laughing ourselves sick – only then it was at poor Andrew, dripping with milk!"

Lucy had turned thoughtful. "I don't think he's changed much since then, but *we* have – I have, especially, because I had such a lot of catching up to do."

"Well, you've managed it very nicely – made a better job of growing up, in fact, than either Andrew or me."

Lucy shook her head. "No, but it no longer matters, because I wouldn't change places with any other woman on earth. The fact remains, though, that nobody looks at me, Cress, if you're in the room – star quality, don't they call it in the theatre? Something's wrong, all the same. Are you still worrying about things in Paris?"

"No, because Giles has done what I wanted him to do – taken matters into his own hands. He's in Paris now. I should have liked him to go more willingly, but at least he's there, dealing with the problems."

Lucy stared at her sombre face. Beside her own swelling body, Cressy looked as slender as a wand, and her face was thin almost to the point of gauntness, revealing clearly the delicate moulding of temple and cheek-bones. She looked older than twenty-three, and schooled by experiences that had been painful. Lucy found herself regretting the change; Cressida learning at last to look before she leapt would mean that they were all growing old.

"Giles got back safely from America, then?" she asked after a little silence. "I should think he'd go down well there – aren't they supposed to like a man who knows his own mind and doesn't give a damn for anyone else's?" Then she shook her head. "Unfair. We're still tying on him the label that Colin always insisted he wore."

213

"By and large it's not unfair," Cressy said bleakly. Then she tried to smile again. "All well at the Manor?"

"Yes. Parents delighted that we're going to move into the empty wing. We've been happy in the flat, but Christopher agrees that a baby exercising its lungs above the shop isn't conducive to trade! Bart is tickled pink at the thought of becoming a grandfather, and even Mama's looking forward to The Event. Funny how things have changed at home, but very nice."

"And Andrew?"

"Working like a madman, and doing his best to bite everybody's head off. Poor Angela Harcourt-Smith is occasionally visible in the line of fire. Even Bart thinks she's a bit of a bore, but I can't help feeling sorry for her, because Andrew treats her like a doormat."

"Odd how life insists on completing patterns," Cressy said thoughtfully. "She and her parents were at a dinner party Marguérite gave in London, and I cooked for them. It was the first time we met, and I didn't realise then that both Colin and Giles had known her down here. As a result of the menu Marguérite chose, lobster and the name of Harcourt-Smith are inextricably linked in my mind."

"Like babies and Dot Endacott! I wonder if I shall be as fertile?"

"Do you hope to be?"

Lucy smiled with great contentment. "Of course. Happiness should be shared among as many children as possible."

"Then I foresee godchildren arriving like summer rain!" At least it sounded like a good exit line, enabling Cressy to kiss her friend a cheerful good bye.

*   *   *

Giles returned from Paris three days later, bringing Marguérite with him. He rang Lantern Cottage to say briefly that for the time being, at least, she would be staying with him at the Admiral's House. The terse comment seemed to be the extent of his report and Cressy was forced to ask for more information.

"What about Colin?"

"His affairs have been settled. The details don't matter, but if you're sufficiently interested, you can ask him. I left him to dispose of his mother's flat, and ship whatever she wants to England." His cold voice warned her not to pursue the conversation; what had had to be done was done, and that was the end of it.

When she went to the house the following day Marguérite was lying in a hammock in the garden, listlessly content. The old restless search for excitement seemed to be over; all she craved now was the reassurance that Giles wouldn't cast her adrift again in a frightening world she couldn't cope with on her own.

"Your stepson being kind to you?" Cressy asked smilingly. "You look as if he is."

Marguérite roused herself to answer a question she hadn't considered in those terms. "I suppose he's being very kind. He even takes the trouble to come back from Plymouth each evening, although I didn't say how much I still dread being alone at night."

"He wasn't very forthcoming on the telephone about Colin. Tell me what happened."

"I know the debt was settled. Giles went to see some dreadful creatures in a sort of thieves' den and made it clear that Colin's involvement with them was being ended."

Cressy was distracted for a moment by the scene that imagination painted in her mind. In circumstances that had been unpleasant, and perhaps perilous, there was a lot to be said for being very large. Giles had the advantage of not looking like a man who could be easily intimidated, and added to it an air of ruthlessness just as hard to miss. His brother's shady confederates would have had no difficulty in recognising that.

"Colin's going back to Credland's," Marguérite's voice broke into her thoughts. "Not at Plymouth; Giles is sending him to an associate company in New York. He says Colin will be kept too busy to get into difficulties – it's what my darling son needs."

It was a more realistic attitude than she'd taken in the past, but Cressy was saddened by the extent of the change in her. Warmth and vivacity, and even fecklessness, had been the greater part of her charm; the old Marguérite had little to do with this quiet, detached woman surveying life from the safety of the sidelines.

"What about you, if Colin goes to America?"

Marguérite gave a little shrug. "I shan't go with him. I've been a burden to him for too long; now he must make a fresh start on his own. If Giles doesn't want me to stay here I suppose I shall find somewhere to live nearby." She tried to sound calm but fear shadowed her eyes again, and Cressy contemplated almost with despair the likely outcome of trying to tell Giles Credland that he couldn't rescue his stepmother only to abandon her. He'd gone to Paris irritated enough by her insistence that he must do something to help his family; but he'd returned a coolly indifferent stranger. She preferred him in full cry, angry with her for some reason she didn't have to guess at. With this withdrawn and inimical man she could never have shared moments that her memory treasured.

When Colin arrived from Paris, Helen dismayed Cressy by announcing that she'd invited all three Credlands to dinner.

"If you'd told me what you were going to do, I'd have begged you to change your mind," Cressy felt obliged to point out. "There are some risks that we don't actually have to take."

"Darling, you're letting imagination get the better of you. Giles and Colin aren't going to have a free fight at my dinner-table; in any case, you've insisted all along that they're a family and should be made to behave like one."

Cressy forebore to say that this was a far from typical family, doomed by Fate and circumstance to be always at odds with one another. But in the way of things greatly dreaded beforehand, the evening went with unexpected smoothness. Marguérite recovered some of her old animation, James Jessop, invited by Helen to complete the party, was a serene and easy guest, and Giles looked much too tired to be troublesome.

As far as Cressy was concerned, Colin represented the only problem. He kissed her by way of greeting, which only seemed an embarrassment when he released her and she found Giles staring at them, but from then on he seemed determined to throw off the memory of near disaster in Paris. With a fresh start ahead, dejection was sloughed off like an unwanted skin. Only Giles was resolutely unaffected by his gaiety, and Cressy found herself angered by an attitude that seemed as unkind as it was stupid. 'In the Fire of Spring the Winter garment of Repentance fling'! The season wasn't spring, but the sentiment exactly fitted a man whose nature simply refused the sackcloth and ashes his brother expected him to wear. Cressy's sympathies were with Colin, and the only thing she regretted was his insistence, as the evening progressed, on reminding her and everyone else that they had once been intimate. She didn't suspect him of wanting to embarrass her only of hoping to annoy his brother.

It was a relief when the conversation turned to Helen's new Christmas pantomime, and she could wander over to the window to join Giles, apparently admiring the last blaze of colour in the garden.

"Thank you for what you've done for Colin," she murmured. "He's unrecognisable for the wreck he was a week or two ago."

"Don't mention it. In any case most of the credit is yours!"

He sounded dauntingly civil, but she persevered. "Will the American scheme work out, do you think? Will he be sufficiently . . . controlled?"

"He'll be tied hand and foot," Giles said with sudden grimness. "Hank Wallace over there will watch him like a Victorian father, and he'll be made to damn well work his passage. Does that set your mind at rest, or do you fear that we're being too unkind? I realise how important it is to you."

She searched his face in vain for some clue to what he was really thinking. Their friendship hadn't so far given her the right to know what was in his heart, but she was excluded from his mind as well; the solitary man was back in the safety of his shell again.

"How can his future not be important?" she asked uncertainly. "You're involved in it."

Giles's blue glance swept her face for a moment, then resumed its study of the garden. "If you're about to offer me the hoary quotation from John Donne, don't bother. There's a lot of mankind I'd rather *not* be involved with, and it includes my brother."

He spoke with a weary disgust that silenced argument because, although she didn't know why, it now seemed to cover her as well. Her eyes, huge and shadowed in the thinness of her face, questioned a bitterness that was more than she could understand, but before she could find the words to say so Giles gave a little nod and walked away, leaving her standing there with the knowledge that friendship and trust had shrivelled as surely as tender plants under the blighting touch of frost.

Chapter Twenty

A WEEK later the silence of the Harbour Master's house was shattered by the boys' return from France. They were noisily excited to be home, and when Billy Street unthinkingly used the word he was disconcerted to see his lady burst into tears.

"Somethin' wrong, Cress?" he asked anxiously.

"Not wrong . . . right!" It added to his puzzlement, but she was smiling again, and he quickly handed over the present he'd brought back for her – a T-shirt decorated with the Eiffel Tower picked out in gold sequins, which she swore she would never cease to wear.

She was writing lists at the kitchen table when the door opened and Giles walked in. His expression didn't encourage chattiness but she did her best.

"The French expedition was a great success – the boys are full of it. Billy informs me that he's even got used to garlic now, being full of that as well."

Giles continued to frown, but for once she had the strange impression that he hesitated over what he'd come to say. At last he managed it, and took her breath away.

"I shan't hold you to any contract – but I should be grateful to know in good time when you think of leaving."

It couldn't be a joke – his face was too coldly controlled for that. She steadied herself by gripping the table and tried to answer him calmly. "Thank you, but I have no thought of leaving at the moment."

"Now you're being ridiculous. Why not admit that the novelty of running a boys' hostel has worn off?" Her blank expression only seemed to release the anger she felt him to have battened down inside. "I won't allow you to leave the boys in the lurch by walking out just when it suits *you*."

"Well, I won't be bullied into leaving just because it happens to suit *you*. There are laws . . . tribunals and things . . . and Billy and Trevor and the others won't *let* you send me packing . . ." She blinked away the tears that pricked her eyes and tried to stop shouting at him. "My plans needn't concern you, but they don't include letting down the boys."

"Then do what you damn well like; I don't care."

The door slammed behind him and she was left alone with her half-completed menus, 'chicken Maryland and apple pancakes', specially requested by Trevor to mark Andy Street's birthday. She swallowed the nausea in her throat and went back to writing her list.

*　　*　　*

Colin spent a month at the factory in Plymouth. During that time no one cold-shouldered him or threatened to black his eye, and he was forced to admit to himself that Giles hadn't seen fit to inform his colleagues about the Buchard episode. Giles didn't see fit, either, to spend any more time than he had to in his brother's company, and usually managed to be away from the Admiral's House whenever Colin went to visit his mother. Cressy seemed to be avoiding him too, but one morning their visits to Marguérite coincided, and he insisted on walking back to Lantern Cottage with her afterwards.

After glancing at her pale face he said quietly, "If the way you look has anything to do with the amount of work Giles expects you to do, I shall be happy to inform him that he's an inhuman swine."

There was something in his voice that sounded like genuine concern and she was touched in spite of the wry smile she gave him. "Do I look as bad as all that? It's nothing to do with Giles. The reopening of the hostel after a holiday is always a strain. I love the boys dearly, but the amount of noise they make has to be got accustomed to again!"

"Cressy . . . I know everything seemed to go wrong, but it wasn't always so, was it? Couldn't we both leave mistakes behind and start again in America? I wish more than anything that you'd come with me." He read in her face the refusal she was hesitating over how to phrase, and tried again. "Is it because you despise me for making such a mess of things?"

"I don't despise you . . . haven't the right to when I make so many mistakes of my own! But we can't start again, Colin; even to try would be the worst mistake of all. Our time in Paris shouldn't be – exhumed, I think, is the word a pathologist would use!" She smiled at him with the candour he recognised as her special quality, the thing that he would remember about her however many women he met who were more beautiful than she. For the first time in his life he found himself regretting a time too carelessly mislaid; if he could have gone back and done things differently, he would have wanted to do them with her.

"Friends still?" he asked.

"Always, I hope." She kissed his cheek by way of goodbye, and he didn't see her again before he left for New York.

* * *

His departure was the signal for a golden Indian summer to dwindle almost immediately into a rainy autumn. Giles struggled in the soaking garden with bonfires that smouldered sullenly or went out altogether, and thought them remarkably like life: full of effort and no reward. His only consolation was his stepmother's continuing docility. She seemed content to stay where she was, and gradually a relationship grew up that surprised them both by its pleasantness.

One evening he came back to find her not in her usual place in the tower room. She was in the kitchen instead, poring over the sheets of drawing-paper that covered the large deal table. Her face went white at the sight of him. "Giles, I'm sorry! I was supposed to get supper . . . it's Mrs Baker's evening off . . ." She began piling the sheets together feverishly while she murmured apologies, until he bent down and took hold of her trembling hands.

"Calm down, Marguérite. There's no great harm done if you *have* forgotten the supper, and you're ruining whatever it is you've been doing."

He was tired and hungry, and no more than mildly interested that she'd found something to occupy her, but the change in her

221

face a moment ago had shocked him into realising that she was still afraid of him. Contentment had suddenly been wiped away by the fear of displeasing him.

"Show me what you were working on," he suggested gently.

"They're costume sketches for Helen's pantomime – *Cinderella*. Her previous designer moved too far away to go on doing it . . . I said I'd like to try," Marguérite explained nervously.

She watched him leaf through the sheets in his hand, that depicted in simple, clever outlines Cinderella's progress from tattered waif to ball-gowned beauty.

"They're good . . . in fact, rather brilliant, I should have thought," he said with an air of faint surprise. "I didn't know you could do this sort of thing."

"Nor did I," she admitted, smiling now, "but when I couldn't find a dress I wanted I used to make a rough sketch and show it to the dressmaker. Cressy suggested once that I ought to set myself up as an interior decorator. I knew that wouldn't work, but perhaps I could become Derrycombe's first couturière!"

He changed the subject abruptly by suggesting that they should go out to dine. She thought that her thoughtless reference to Cressida had been the cause of his change of mood, and regretted it because she no longer wanted to hurt him. He suggested a restaurant in Dartmouth and she went to get ready, pleasantly excited by the prospect of an outing that wouldn't have seemed possible a short while ago. The food and the change of scene were enjoyable, but her real pleasure lay in the knowledge that they were steadily moving towards something that could be called friendship. When he laughed at something she said, she was suddenly reminded of William, and all the years of hating him for Colin's sake and feeling intimidated herself, suddenly seemed to have been a heart-breaking mistake.

After that evening Giles watched her slowly gaining confidence in the idea that they were no longer enemies. In return, he found pleasure in offering her a kind of teasing affection that he now realised could have been offered years ago without the slightest disloyalty to his own mother. He regretted the waste of time for Marguérite's sake, and even more for William's.

Apart from the new-found pleasantness of life at home, work

was the only panacea for the emptiness within himself that honesty forced him to recognise. Time was when Credland's had been enough to fill his life. The affections he'd despised other men for needing had begun to take insidious root. The self-sufficiency that he'd relied upon for years was wearing thin. He drove his staff hard, and himself harder; they walked around him as carefully as Agag, ran when mere walking seemed to try his patience too far, and longed for the day when exhaustion should overtake him as it did ordinary men. If they supposed that he slept on Sundays, they were wrong: he toiled in the garden of the Admiral's House, laying out the schemes that Roland Marlow had devised for him, determined that sheer effort, if nothing else, must create what his friend had visualised.

Cressy found her own solace in working at the hostel, provided she could be sure of avoiding Giles. There was no question about it; she was finally inside the boys' magic circle, and they offered her the same rough care they took of each other. The first Derrycombe boys, Danny Endacott among them, had now joined the original intake, and were taught the only house rule that mattered. "Give Cress any trouble and I'll thump you," said Billy briefly.

She didn't hear the conversation but had no trouble with her new recruits, and knew that her friends were always looking out for her. Affection for them kept her there even though she found her relationship with Giles bizarrely unreal. They talked to each other, if they had to talk at all, like courteous strangers, and all the time she had the heart-breaking conviction that he waited for the day when she would go away. One morning desperation impelled her to raise a subject more personal than new bedlinen or the football team which Trev wished to challenge the might of Derrycombe.

"Are you getting good reports from Hank Wallace?" she asked suddenly. "Colin's letters brim over with cheerfulness, but it would be nice if you were to confirm that he's doing well."

Giles stared at her strained face, wondering yet again what kept her there.

"If my opinion matters to you at all, yes, I think he's doing very well. You shouldn't keep him waiting too long, though, before you decide that he's making a go of it. Not a patient man, my brother Colin!"

The ironic note that always edged his voice moved her to unexpected rage. Instead of mutely accepting it any longer she would shout at him, kick down the barrier that grew daily higher, separating them from one another – and she would begin by informing him that she'd never had the slightest intention of going to America.

"Cress—" Andy barely remembered to knock, then came hurtling through the door, "—Mr Ollerton says to come, please. Danny's cut hisself, and he's bleedin' like a pig all over the workshop floor we washed this mornin . . ."

It was a morning like any other after all, made up of meals and minor accidents; what did it matter that Giles Credland seemed to think she waited in Derrycombe only for some selfish whim of her own?

Christmas came slowly, and this time the Ollertons chose to spend the holiday in Derrycombe. Alice even smiled when she confessed that they'd be glad to. Sam had missed something, having no children of his own. Giving the boys Christmas would be something he'd enjoy. When Christmas Eve came Cressy staggered home under the weight of a strange variety of objects made for her in the workshops. She was now equipped to weigh precisely minute quantities of herbs, produce a screwdriver for any domestic difficulty, and offer Helen picnic plates guaranteed not to break even if dropped from the top of Rippon Tor. Her pleasure in the gifts was the most she could expect this season of good cheer to offer.

Much to Marguérite's disappointment, Colin had written to say that he wouldn't be home for Christmas; there was talk instead of a holiday at the Wallaces' skiing lodge in Vermont. His telephone call on Christmas morning sounded even more ebullient than she had expected.

"Dearest, news for you, and you must promise to be pleased about it. Kim is here with me, waiting to talk to you. I've done my best to convince her that she's mad to agree to marry me, but she refuses to be put off." The news wasn't entirely a surprise, even though it came sooner than Marguérite had anticipated. His letters and telephone calls had contained more and more references to Hank Wallace's daughter. A moment later her voice, a flat, confident drawl, was wafted along the line.

"Marguérite . . . may I call you that? . . . Colin says you haven't been well . . . but you'll be sure to come to our wedding, won't you? We shall come right over and fetch you if you don't like the idea of travelling alone . . ."

Marguérite heard herself agree that she would be sure to attend, she also promised to have a *good* Christmas day, and even undertook not to think for a *moment* that she was losing her only son to America. Colin resumed the conversation, remembered to ask in the middle of his own euphoria how she was, and sent breezy good wishes to the rest of Derrycombe. When she replaced the receiver, Giles was staring at her fixedly.

"What was all that about, apart from the usual Christmas outbreak of family affection?"

"Colin's just got engaged to Kim Wallace. She sounded confident, he sounded bemused, and I was required to sound delighted!"

At any other time he would have been amused by the unaccustomed dryness in her voice, but overriding everything else for the moment was the uselessness of his warning to Cressida: she'd waited in Derrycombe too long. For some reason he couldn't explain he was enraged by her stupidity as much as by Colin's inability to wait.

"What the hell does he mean by playing about with Hank's daughter? I thought he was going to marry Cressida at last."

Marguérite stared at his expression, then picked her words carefully. "I think he might have done, but dear Cressy had . . . outgrown him. She only came to help us because Colin begged her to and her heart is very kind."

Giles smiled, but Marguérite thought it more terrible than if he'd offered her violence of some kind.

"It wasn't quite the impression he gave me in Paris. I was meant to understand that they were lovers again from the moment she arrived – it *pleased* him to be able to tell me that."

"It would have done, but it wasn't true," Marguérite said slowly. "About that you must believe me, I know my son better than you do. He said what he hoped would hurt you. The truth is that she

225

never loved him, only some idealised conception she had of the man she might have made him into."

"Did she know that he'd sold the Credland machine to Buchard?" Giles asked after a long pause.

"Only after your visit. Pierre Lenoir told her at dinner one night, and that was the end of dreams. Colin might have retrieved himself with her if he'd been repentant, but he wasn't – and nor, then, was I. It's time to tell you that now and something else besides. Even I wanted to hurt her once, although I can't remember why. When I knew that she was working for you at the hostel I told her she was only after the Credland money; I said it was a waste of time because you'd disliked her from the beginning. I'm sorry, Giles."

He sat staring into the fire, not saying anything for a long time while his thoughts ranged further back over the past.

"Shall I make a confession now?" he suggested finally. "I used to blame my father's death on you, but now I realise it was something in which we all shared. I was so busy resenting you for years that it didn't occur to me that William was between the devil and the deep blue sea, trying to keep Credland's going, you happy, and me within reasonable bounds – more than one man's work when you think of it."

"Giles, will you try not to hate Colin, please? He may not even have wanted to hurt you and Cressy, but when you saw him at his lowest ebb he had to pretend that *something* had gone right for him."

"It scarcely matters; I've done more than enough damage on my own account to make her think that the only sane course is to avoid the Credlands in future."

"I see," Marguérite agreed doubtfully, not sure that she saw at all.

"She told me once that I couldn't disown you and Colin. She was right about that, and about other things she's hurled at my head in the course of our acquaintance. With her help we seem as a family to have got ourselves sorted out at last, but in doing it we've ground her between our mill wheels."

"Yes ... despite the fact that we've all loved her in our different ways."

Giles made no answer to that, but then she hadn't expected him to.

Chapter Twenty-One

FOR ONCE Christmas provided them with weather to match the season. Snow began to fall on Dartmoor, first 'deep and crisp and even', and then not even at all, because a wind rose steadily that scoured the moor bare in exposed places and piled up huge drifts elsewhere that were carved into shapes as weird as the rocks on Combestone Tor. There was even heavy snow in Derrycombe itself, almost unheard of except by old men like Nat Selby, whose memories reached far back into the past. The hill-farmers grumbled that the sheep and ponies would need a lot of feeding, and people living in the moor villages found themselves isolated from the rest of the world. Suddenly bread was something to be made again, not bought from the travelling van; and when the electricity failed, oil-lamps and candles shed light enough to talk by. Conversation, like self-reliance, was rediscovered and found to be rather enjoyable.

The strange new pattern of life didn't last very long. The arctic weather departed almost as suddenly as it had arrived, and with the usual coverlet of cloud unfolding rain instead of snow, people told each other that things would soon be back to normal again. Only Ben, met in the town one morning, didn't seem happy about the swift return to mildness.

"Too sudden, Cressy love, the thaw should have come more gentle-like. There's a powerful lot of snow up on Moor that should 'ave melted nice and slow. You mind what happened when the Lyn all but washed Lynmouth into Bristol Channel."

She minded it very well; it had been a tragedy no one belonging to Devon was likely to forget.

Ben pointed to the boats moored in the river, already being tossed about by water that was higher and more turbulent than usual.

227

"Level's risin' too fast for my likin'," but he forbore to mention what worried him most of all. His barometer was falling as steadily as the river was rising, and the wind was shifting to the quarter from which their worst gales came. A word at the Town Hall about the sense of sand-bagging the harbour walls would ease his conscience, but not do a particle of good otherwise, because Mr Credland was right, and the town was in the hands of a lot of old women from Midland places who'd forgotten, if they ever knew, what a wicked combination of wind and water could do.

Cressy agreed with him about the river level, ashamed to realise that she'd been concentrating too hard on her own affairs to notice it properly. She was glad to be done with the year that had just ended; with a fresh start she could take control of her life again, not drift about like a kite in a fitful wind.

Her god-daughter, Victoria, was born on a January day which happened to be her own twenty-fourth birthday, although Lucy claimed that she'd planned things that way.

"Present for you, Cress, a good omen for the new year." Then she added in a different tone of voice, "Did I say something wrong?"

Cressy shook her head, trying to ignore the shaft of pain that seemed to be burrowing to her heart's core. "Nothing wrong at all, but I once watched a rainbow born of a storm and thought that was an omen too, but it turned out to be no such thing; I distrust omens!"

Lucy didn't ask who she'd watched the rainbow with. Happiness fell 'like the gentle rain from heaven upon the place beneath', but the places of its choosing constantly defied expectation. Her own vast contentment had grown out of unlikely beginnings: Roland Marlow's heart attack and Cressy's unsuccessful search for happiness with Colin Credland. It seemed very unfair, when she'd done so little seeking of her own salvation.

"Shall you stay on at the hostel?" she asked diffidently after a glance at her friend's withdrawn face.

"I'm not sure what I'll do yet, although the idea's growing on me that I might open up an agency like Aunt Ag's in Totnes. But I don't want to leave here feeling the failure that I am at the moment. I was supposed to make the boys and Derrycombe merge with each other. I haven't been able to do that yet; my flock occasionally compete, but it's against the town, not with it."

Without saying so she offered it to Lucy as a reason for the sadness locked up inside her, and to accept it was all that a friend could do.

"Well, you know what Ben would say: 'town's powerful cussed, my dearie, but hearten up; it don't do to expect nothin' but the worst'!" Lucy suggested hopefully.

Cressy did her best to hearten up, but thought Ben had been right about something else as well. Within the space of another twenty-four hours the river had become steadily more swollen with melting snow, and its present level was higher than she could ever remember seeing it. The wind was blowing up, and she'd learnt enough from Andrew about the effect of wind on waves to pray that a sou'westerly gale did not coincide with a high spring tide while the river was in flood. People stood in uneasy groups on the harbour wall, staring at the water rushing past their feet, but a paralysing confidence that God would take care of Derrycombe seemed to confirm that they need do nothing to help themselves.

With the rest of the town, Cressy took part in the last night of Helen's pantomime; the uproar was louder than usual, and she wondered whether the audience was trying to deafen itself to the noise of the gale blowing up outside. At the end of the performance Helen pushed her new collaborator on to the stage so that she could be thanked for the designs that had made the production memorable. Cressy watched Marguérite standing there, flushed and happy through her own efforts at last; at least that was a step forward that wouldn't have seemed possible six months ago.

Cressy knew that Giles was somewhere in the audience with the Ollertons, the three of them proudly brought as guests of the boys. They'd wanted to buy her a ticket too, but she'd been glad of an excuse not to join the party; being prompt, dresser, and scene-shifter as required, she was allowed in free. She hoped Giles could spare a fraction of the attention he devoted to Credland's to notice the change in his stepmother. Marguérite had even been able to accept calmly the news that Colin was going to remain permanently in America. Cressy remembered Giles' warning that she must restake her own claim to

229

Colin before it was too late. He probably now despised her for the usual fumbling mess she'd made of getting what she wanted, but she didn't know for certain – their only conversations nowadays were brief and brutally businesslike.

When the pantomime audience was finally persuaded to go home, Giles dropped an exhausted Helen off at Lantern Cottage, but Cressida was able to decline the invitation. She would enjoy a walk home through the wild night, and Ben had offered himself as her escort. For once he had very little to say and when the light from a street-lamp illuminated his face she was startled by its anxiety.

"Something's very wrong, isn't it, Ben?" she asked suddenly. "We've been whistling in the dark too long, hoping for Derrycombe's usual luck to see us through."

"Whistlin'? They 'aven't even got *that* much go in 'em at Town 'All," he said bitterly. "Giles Credland's right, Cressy, we need *young* people who can do more than talk and scratch their 'eads."

He couldn't worry his little maid with the full extent of his anxiety, but he was glad to say goodnight and walk away before she could winkle it out of him. She and Helen Marlow would be all right at Lantern Cottage but there were going to be people at Derrycombe tonight who wouldn't be.

Cressy went indoors, but not to go to bed. She was infected by Ben's fear, and by a premonition of her own that some catastrophic possibility hovered over them. She persuaded her tired mother to bed, then changed into slacks and sweater to settle down by the telephone. If there was work to be done, someone – Bart or Lady Evelyn probably – would tell her so; meanwhile she sat waiting, trying not to remember the fate of Poldinnick.

Giles wasn't equipped with the sailor's instinct that had troubled Ben but he, too, when he got home with Marguérite after the pantomime, consulted the barometer found in a Dartmouth antique shop. According to the dealer, it had been Admiral Blake's, and Giles had taken pleasure in reinstalling it where it belonged. He thought the Admiral would have been alarmed by what the instrument was recording now.

Marguérite was still reliving the night's triumph in her mind and wondering what her next assignment from Helen would be, but the rising shriek of the wind flinging itself round the house reminded her that she would never have been able to live there alone. She watched Giles' face as he studied the barometer, and remembered that they lived on a lonely little promontory.

"Are we going to be blown out to sea?" she asked with a smile that almost concealed the fact that she was growing nervous.

"We're all right, provided the surveyor didn't lie when he said the roof was sound! In fact, we're all right anyway; the wind's blowing us into the hill, but Derrycombe's going to have an uncommonly rough night of it."

If Giles said they were all right she knew she could believe him. She often made an effort to wish unselfishly for a happiness which she thought eluded him but, as often as she wished it, found herself praying that however he eventually organised his life, he would find room in it for her. Noise besieged the house like an invader determined to find its weakest point, but her bedroom was warm, the invader was safely outside, and she was pleasantly tired after the excitement of the evening. She was already asleep by the time the telephone rang. Giles, wide awake and fully dressed beside it, realised that he'd been waiting for it to ring.

"Trouble, I'm afraid, sir." It was Sam Ollerton, sounding even more calmly deliberate than usual. "The harbour wall's just gone in front of us, and I think things are worse further down towards the jetty. Hard to tell whether it's river coming down or sea coming up, but there's a lot of water outside already and the level's rising all the time."

Giles listened and made up his mind. "You could probably all stay where you are upstairs, but better to put Alice and the boys in the mini-bus and bring them up here. Sleeping-bags too, because the boys will have to stretch out on the floor. If I'm not here when you arrive, my stepmother will see to you."

He rang off, but picked up the telephone again immediately to talk to the man most likely to know how the local services were organised. Sir Nicholas's voice answered so quickly that it seemed he must have been waiting by the telephone as well.

"My superintendent has just reported flooding in the town," Giles said briefly. "I thought you might know if the necessary alarms had been given."

"They *have* been given, for all the good they'll do us. The Derry isn't the only river over its banks, but that's not all. It's a spring tide tonight, coupled with a gale forecast to blow up to Force 10. Conditions all along the coast are the worst in living memory."

Giles realised that the longest speech the Squire had ever made to him reflected the extent of the emergency.

"Well, if everybody else is asking for help, we'd better reckon on managing on our own." He rang off before the Squire could explain that he was about to leave, and that Andrew was already on his way down with a portable generator in the Land Rover. Brusque swine, Bart said to himself, but reliable; and competence tonight was going to be more useful than old world courtesy.

Giles knocked on Marguérite's door, and a moment later she was blinking in front of him, pale-faced and frightened.

"S – something wrong, Giles?"

"Not here, but we're bringing the boys up to the house as a precaution. There's flooding in the town, and there'll probably be more. Will you strew them and their sleeping-bags around the bedrooms when they arrive?"

"W – what about you?"

"I'm on my way down to the quay. Sam will bring his wife, so she'll be able to help you."

She wanted to implore him not to leave her alone in a house that might easily blow out to sea if he were not there to personally anchor it to the ground. She was very afraid, and not at all sure that she could think what to do with a dozen teenage boys who were known to be wild. But Giles was expecting her to be calm and untroublesome; she knew it was how Englishmen required their women-folk to be in times of stress; somehow she must behave like Lady Evelyn, Helen Marlow, and Cressy rolled into one.

"Of course, I'll – I'll get dressed and be ready for the boys."

Her air of dignity was touching because it concealed real fear, and he acknowledged the fact by bending down to kiss her cheek in a gesture that surprised them both. Five minutes later she watched the rear lights of the car disappear along the lane. It was time to get dressed, stay calm, and put aside for the moment the memory of the first show of affection Giles had ever offered her.

He drove with caution because the headlights showed him the trees being flung about so violently that some of them might already be down and spreadeagled across the road. But the gusts of wind blowing straight in from the sea seemed to propel the car along as though a giant strode behind, pushing it with a careless hand. There were still lights west of the river where he was, but over on the other bank where a line of lamps should have been strung like a necklace along the quayside from the bridge to the end of the jetty, there was only darkness, broken here and there by the faint flicker of lights that suggested cars nosing their way through flooded streets. The blackness where there should have been light seemed to add another dimension of horror to the wildness of the night, and he drove with a mounting premonition of the disaster that was engulfing them. In imagination he saw a wall of water hurling itself in vain against barriers like Bolt Head and Start Point, and raging on to find softer options – the Derry estuary for one – only to clash head-on with rivers already in flood.

He turned onto the bridge, tried to steady the car against the onslaught of wind funnelling straight up the river, and edged his way across into what seemed, in the glare of his head-lamps, to be a lake now being fed all along the quay as water poured over the harbour wall. There had been no sign of a mini-bus passing him. Why not? Sam and the boys should have been clear of this lower side of the town by now and safely on their way to the Admiral's House. He abandoned the car on the highest piece of ground he could see, pulled on fisherman's waders, armed himself with the most powerful torch he possessed, and splashed towards the hostel through steadily deepening water

Something loomed out of the darkness in front of him, a rowing boat full of people going the other way; his torch lit up the wet face of Jim Gurney.

"Can I go on walking?" Giles yelled above the wind.

"Not for much longer. Better help yourself to a boat, sir, there are quite a few floating about. Powerful lot of confusion along the quay a-piece . . . everybody needin' to be brought out of the cottages down there."

"Some light would help . . ."

"Young Squire's there now with Mick Selby, fixing up a generator . . ." His voice died into the darkness as he poled his boat-load
on, and Giles turned into the wind again, almost bowled over by the
force of it and by the water now surging round his thighs. God damn
it, where *were* Sam and the boys? Two more boats went past, with
torches held up to serve as riding lights; his own flash-light fell on
faces he recognised, but they were not the faces he was looking for.
He was alongside the hostel at last, hammering on the door, when a
figure dimly identified as Dan Pengelly drifted up to him, standing
on something that revealed itself as a makeshift raft.

"Not there, Mr Credland . . . Sam's further down the quay . . .
boys there too," Dan shouted. "You won't get there by walking,
though . . ."

"I know, find myself a boat! Thanks." In a moment or two it was
exactly what he did. A rush of water that sent him sprawling also
landed beside him a rowing boat that he managed to hold on to. He
heaved himself inboard, and propelled it along in the only way he
could, by pushing against each bit of wall he came to. The exertion
was great, but he wasn't aware of it, nor of the fact that his hands were
soon lacerated by the roughness of stone walls. Ahead of him Pollack's
generator must be working because he could see light, shining on water
that spread endlessly into the surrounding darkness. It was all the night
seemed to contain: water, the banshee shrieking of the wind, and men
desperately trying to shout instructions to each other. A powerful lot
of confusion, Jim Gurney had said, and he was right.

A piece of driftwood bumped against the side of the boat and Giles
made a grab for it; with something that could be used as a paddle,
he felt more in control of his leaky craft. Then as he came to the
first of the cottages he saw Sam, outlined against dim candlelight
inside a room, trying to dangle a small child through a first-floor
window into the arms of someone in a boat down below. With the
advantage of greater height and longer reach of arm, Giles safely
fielded the child, but his anxiety overflowed in a roar that Sam
could hear.

"I told you to take Alice and the boys to the house. Where
are they?"

"Alice is all right . . . top floor; boys are here, helping. Now, sir, next one coming down . . ."

Delivery had to be taken, and the work went on from there: old ladies who wouldn't leave flooded homes without their cats, elderly men clutching treasures of their own which included anything from a prized family Bible to their 'best' false teeth, only worn on special occasions. Giles gradually worked his way along the terrace, accounting for all the boys. Masterminded inevitably by Billy Street, they were working in pairs, taking to the safety of the upper floors every piece of furniture they could heave or push up the stairs. Andrew Pollack, bumped into briefly as he ferried a boat-load of people in the direction of St Fritha's church hall, went so far as to shout that the boys were making themselves useful.

"Having the time of their lives, no doubt," Giles grunted. "But the bloody little rebels are going to be in trouble for disobeying instructions, all the same."

"Quite right, discipline at all times, even times like these!" Andrew gave him a tired grin and disappeared into the night, leaving Giles to the reflection that, quite apart from the results of its battering, Derrycombe was never going to be the same again in other ways. The boys might be accepted at last for what they were – part of Derrycombe – and he and the Pollacks might manage to continue talking to one another. Lady Evelyn, met carrying blankets into the church hall, smiled at him when he arrived with half a dozen children, and the girl working a coffee urn – Cressida – was being helped by Colonel Fitzwilliam Carstairs – another hatchet sunk beneath the night's flood waters! He walked towards her, to say he knew not what, but she moved away and there was time to remember that he had work of his own to do.

At last a water-borne consultation on the quay, now indistinguishable from the river, confirmed that no more could be done until daylight came. No one was unaccounted for, and tired and wet as they were, the men clustered round the Squire felt satisfied. It was time to grab a little sleep, before another high tide brought the next moment of danger. Giles collected the boys as his last boat-load, and poled them to the rear of the hostel. Little Andy Street, unanimously selected as the one most likely to make a successful cat-burglar, was hoisted through a window with instructions to find Alice and shepherd her out the same way. She took the unusual experience with a calmness that moved the boys to cheer her arrival in the boat, and then Giles delivered them to the mini-bus, thoughtfully parked by Sam on the nearest unsubmerged slope.

"Provided my car's still where I left it, I'll follow you," Giles told Sam. "My stepmother expected you several hours ago, incidentally, so I'm not sure what state you'll find her in."

Sam looked slightly sheepish. "Sorry about that, sir, but once the boys knew there was trouble further down the quay, I couldn't seem to interest them in the idea of going to the Admiral's House."

"I dare say not. Well, for God's sake take them there now, wherever else they think they'd rather go."

He watched the bus climb the slope onto the bridge, then heaved off his boots, started the car, and followed it. Three minutes later he was swinging left-handed onto the water-logged road that ran along the western shore. In one of the intermittent lulls that broke the roar of the wind he could hear the insistent rushing sound of the river. Then another noise, not much greater than a heavy sigh, echoed towards him and disbelievingly he identified what it was – the rumble of disintegrating masonry. While he stopped the car instinctively his mind grappled with the enormity of what had just happened. The people who'd insisted that the bridge was weakening under the burden of heavier traffic than it was intended for had finally been proved right; the middle pier had given up the struggle to support its double span, and simply collapsed into the river like a tired camel folding its legs.

He thought of Sam steering the laden mini-bus across only minutes before, felt weak with thankfulness, and then the remembrance of something else made him cry out, "Dear God—" Another car *had* been crossing the bridge after him, because he'd seen the glare of lights in his rear-view mirror. He backed and turned, cursing because his sore hands were wet with the sweat of fear and slipping on the wheel. Then his own headlamps shone on what had been the gentle slope up to the middle of the bridge . . . there the roadway broke into a crumbled frill that now ended in nothing. But Pollack's Land Rover clung to it like a fly to a wall, with its rear axle hanging over the edge, and its near-side wedged against the broken parapet. Someone, Andrew presumably, was huddled over the wheel, and beside him sat ... Cressida.

Chapter Twenty-Two

INSTINCT clamoured that he should hurl himself at the stranded Land Rover and drag Cressida out; logic said that while he was manhandling Andrew's unconscious body, she would slide with the Land Rover into the blackness of the river. He found himself running back to the car; Sam was already there, and the mini-bus was parked a hundred yards along the road.

"Saw you stop, sir . . . something wrong?"

"The bridge's collapsed. A Land Rover is hanging over the gap in the middle, and Pollack and Cressida are inside it. He seems to have been knocked out."

"Christ!" It was a prayer, delivered in Sam's anguished voice. "What can we do?"

"Not trample about out there, or what's left of the bridge will break up and go into the river. As soon as I can get a rope round the towing hook, our only hope is to pull it clear."

"I weigh less heavy than you . . . let me get the rope on it."

"No thanks, Sam. Send Alice to the first house she can find with a telephone still working; she must warn the police, and ask for an ambulance to come to the west side of the river. Then bring the boys down here; we may need them. But I mean *here*, Sam; they're forbidden to get any nearer the bridge than this. If they can't promise obedience this time, they must stay where they are."

Sam nodded and set off at a run. A moment later, with one end of the rope fastened to the front bumper of his own car and the rest of it coiled round his shoulder, Giles stepped onto the stump of what had once been Derrycombe bridge.

Cressy watched him carefully travelling along the beam of light thrown by the headlamps of a car she couldn't see. She felt no

239

surprise. In a world where even the ground beneath their feet could no longer be relied upon, the only certain thing was that he would not allow them to stay there hanging in space. She couldn't twist round to see what had happened behind them, because Andrew's weight pushed her against the nearside door resting against the parapet. She could do nothing to help, only sit very still, listening to the river rushing headlong just beneath them. She would just sit and pray and wait for Giles.

She lost sight of him for a moment and panic almost won, then he spoke from the window on Andrew's side, half wound down as usual, because he always insisted on driving with it that way.

"I'm almost afraid to breathe for fear of dislodging you, but can either of you hear me?"

She turned her head carefully and looked at him; handsome is as handsome does and she would never see him in future as anything but beautiful.

"I can hear you, Giles, but Andrew seems to be hurt." She marvelled at the calm sound of her voice.

"Can you reach the hand-brake and put it on?"

"I did, the moment we stopped." In the dim light that reached far enough to throw a small glow on his face she thought she could see him smile.

" '*Good* little maid', as Ben would say! Now, listen carefully, Cressida. We're going to pull you off the bridge as gently as we can because the bridge is . . . is crumbling a bit behind you. The moment you hear Sam blast the Rover's horn, it means we're ready. Shift into neutral and release the hand-brake immediately. I've already put a rope round the hook in front, and we shall be holding you; you can't slip backwards and there's nothing to fear." He managed to say it with perfect steadiness and, in their present circumstances, she thought it was a heroic lie.

"See you on the bank, then," she said with a slight wobble in her voice, "only tell Sam to blow *hard*, please."

He nodded and disappeared, and she was left lonely again. 'Hold infinity in the palm of your hand and eternity in an hour', Blake had said, but eternity was the minute or two it took before she saw him step in front of the car parked on the bank, blocking out the light for a moment. Then above the rushing noise of the water she heard the Rover's horn, glorious as the sound of the last trump. She couldn't find neutral, sobbed "God, *help* me, please," felt the gear disengage, and fumbled for the hand-brake.

The Land Rover gave a jerk but wouldn't move; its rear wheels, below the broken edge of the bridge, refused to be dragged over it. There was a sudden jolt as they slipped lower because the jagged edge crumbled still more under the impact of the wheels. But the pressure dragging them forward didn't waver. The rope was attached to something she couldn't see, but Giles was heaving on the rope like a man possessed of some titanic strength, and behind him a line of smaller figures toiled with the same passionate determination. She tried to whisper to Andrew that everything would be all right because Giles and the boys were there, but still he didn't stir beside her. There was another shuddering jolt and suddenly the Land Rover was no longer tilting, they were squarely on what remained of the bridge, and the rest was easy.

The boys broke into a demented dance of triumph as they reached the bank, and Andrew's weight was lifted from her as Giles wrenched open the other door. She fell out into Sam's arms, and felt his face, wet with sweat or tears, against her own.

"Wheels kept spinning in the wet, Cressy, without Giles and the boys you'd still be there." He seemed overcome with remorse that he hadn't been able to make the Rover do more, and she kissed his cheek. "Without *all* of you we'd still be there," she insisted unsteadily. Then she forced herself to walk round the front of the Land Rover. Giles was still bending over Andrew in the driver's seat.

"I think he saw the bridge begin to crack behind us," she muttered. "There was a tremendous jerk, as if he'd tried to accelerate very hard."

"Which explains the bang on his head; he wasn't wearing his seatbelt. His pulse is steady, so perhaps there isn't too much to worry about, but we won't disturb him till the ambulance comes." At last Giles permitted himself to look at Cressida. "What about you . . . do *you* need checking over?"

What she needed most was the comfort of his arms, but the roughness in his voice reminded her: in time of crisis he would provide practical help, great strength, and all the courage in the world, but tenderness he would not offer.

"I'm all right," she said after a moment, "but I must go with Andrew to the hospital."

"You'll do nothing of the kind. Sam will drop you off at the cottage on his way to the Admiral's House. I shall see Pollack to the hospital."

She wanted to argue, but reaction was drenching her in weakness and it took all her self-control not to be humiliatingly sick in front of him. Then Alice clinched the matter by appearing out of the darkness to put her arms round Cressy.

"Let Sam take you home, my dearie. I'm going in the ambulance too, otherwise Mr Credland won't mention that his hands need seeing to."

There seemed to be nothing more to say. She put out a hand to Billy and Trevor and tried to smile at them. "You may have to start pulling again, as far as the bus!"

*　　*　　*

When Giles drove Alice back to Derrycombe a cloudy winter dawn was just beginning to break. The trees still tossed in the wind, but the worst of the gale had moved on. The next high tide might, with luck and Heaven's help, be no worse than normal, and at least it would reach them in daylight. They drove past the roped-off end of the bridge, and saw the dim bulk of something wedged across the nearer arch – a fallen tree had been carried down by the flooded river and acted as a battering-ram against the middle pier.

"Poor old bridge," said Alice quietly. "Not its fault at all."

When they got home Marguérite and Sam were in the kitchen drinking tea. The boys had been persuaded to sleep at last.

"Sorry you were left alone for so long," Giles said with unusual gentleness.

She smiled at him, still astonished whenever she bothered to think about it, that she'd managed to survive the storm-ridden hours alone. "Sam says the boys did very well last night, so I hope the people who didn't want them here are feeling rather stupid this morning." Her eyes fell to the dressings on his hands and she gave a little shudder. "Cressy and Andrew on that bridge . . . if you hadn't all been there . . ." but with new-found restraint she said no more, except to ask after Andrew.

"He'll be all right. The bang on his head that knocked him out has left him with concussion, that's all." He accepted the tea Marguérite poured for him and gulped it down. "With luck, we might get a couple of hours' sleep before the tribe upstairs starts stirring. They'll wake up ravenous – appetites sharpened more than usual by a rare feeling of virtue!"

"We shall be able to feed them," Marguérite said with pride. "I remembered to take bread and bacon out of the freezer."

"You've done very well," Giles told her, and meant it.

By mid-morning, with Sam driving the mini-bus again, they were crossing the river by the old narrow bridge that spanned the Derry at the upstream hamlet of High Cross. The flooded banks were a reminder of the previous night, but it wasn't until they were approaching Derrycombe on the east side of the river that they could see what awaited them there. The quay and its adjoining streets were submerged by a lagoon that stretched down over the jetty and merged with Start Bay. Lamp-posts stuck up out of the water like mournful exclamation-marks, rubbish and bits of timber from smashed boats drifted sluggishly on the surface, and the air smelled sour with river dankness.

Billy looked round his silent companions and thought they needed cheering up. "Quite Venetian, if you ask me." The experienced traveller's world-weary drawl, coming from someone who'd never been further east than a bus trip to Exeter, struck them as exquisitely funny, and the moment of horror that had gripped the boys was dissolved in laughter.

They left the bus and splashed their way cheerfully to the church hall, with instructions to make themselves useful until they were collected again. Beds had now been found for the people made temporarily homeless, but they still congregated there, held by an unspoken need to stay together. They were tired and anxious, but the story of the bridge collapse was already common knowledge and losing nothing in the telling. When Sam walked in with his

243

troop a tentative clap or two grew into a wave of applause that the boys were disconcerted to find was directed at them. They grinned sheepishly, wondering what to do next, until Trevor was inspired to haul out of his pocket the mouth organ from which he was never parted. The sound of it drifted round the room, and people who had been feeling very sorry for themselves began to smile. Derrycombe was still there, things might have been a great deal worse.

Giles, walking in after the others, was intercepted by Ben, on duty in the porch as what he called lee-ay-son officer. First, he had to make a fervent speech of thanks for the rescue of his little maid. "Young Squire, too, o'course . . . but there'd 'ave bin no one could take Cressy's place, ye see."

" 'A lass unparallelled'?" Giles suggested after a moment.

"Someone say that?"

"Chap called Shakespeare."

"Well, I couldn't 'ave put it better meself," Ben agreed generously. "Now then, Mrs Marlow and Colonel's in charge inside, 'cos her leddyship's gone to see young Andrew, but Squire said if you showed up, to go to Town Hall; you can get there now with waders on."

A special meeting of the Council had already begun when Giles arrived but Sir Nicholas, looking grey with tiredness, stood up at the sight of him.

"We'd hoped you'd come, reckon you ought to be here. First, though, Evelyn and I will never be able to thank you adequately for what you did last night."

Giles hid bandaged hands behind his back and wondered whether the Squire would still be feeling grateful when he was asked to sell a piece of land that would make the sports field they needed for the hostel. Then he felt ashamed of the thought; Nicholas Pollack would probably now insist on *giving* him the field he wanted. But what he wanted even more was the acceptance of his own view of Derrycombe by a man who'd stubbornly opposed it.

"This is how I see it," said Tom Snape more firmly than usual to a meeting that for once seemed eager to grapple with important issues. "The town has a right to expect us to do more than get up at Council meetings and argue about when to fly the flag over the Town Hall. I know Nature was against us last night, but *we*

244

failed something lamentable too. We've got careless, I reckon; the warnings were there to see, but we gambled on doing nothing and lost. It's only God's mercy that we didn't lose Derrycombe lives as well."

It was plainer speaking than Giles had expected. Then it was the Squire's turn to open fire.

"We did what any citizens would have done in the circumstances last night – no worse, and probably no better than others were doing all along the coast. Now, all we can do until the flood goes down is make sure no one suffers hardship. Then there'll be the job of clearing up the mess and assessing what damage has been done. After that, my friends, comes the most important task of all: planning afresh for the future. The subject has been discussed before, and opinion has divided the town." The Squire thrust his hands in his jacket pockets and came to the difficult bit. "No one has opposed Mr Credland's views more strongly than I, but I must say now that I was wrong. Last night proved that we must have young, vigorous people in the community. To keep them here we must offer what Mr Credland's scheme has started – training, employment and the means to enjoy themselves out of working hours. Belatedly, but better late than never, I hope, I should like to offer him my help."

The silence in the room was profound, and Giles was acutely aware of a dozen pairs of eyes fixed on him. Like the boys in the church hall, he was finding that opposition had been easier to handle than gratitude.

"I'm grateful to Sir Nicholas for his generous offer," he said finally; "any help is welcome. But I have to admit that last night taught *me* something as well. I hope the Credland workshops are only the first of such schemes, because I believe them to be necessary, but I now realise that whatever is done here must be accepted by the town as a whole, not foisted on it by the insistence of some. There's been controversy lately, but had Derrycombe been fundamentally divided against itself, it would have foundered last night. Its position is always going to make it vulnerable, however much we try to strengthen its defences, so its chief strength must be the one we relied on a few hours ago – the fact of being a united community." His tired face broke into a smile that none of them had seen before. "My gang are basking in public approval at the moment, I gather. We can't expect it to last; one of them, almost certainly Billy Street, will soon fall from grace and do something to irritate you. But if you can all accept the principle that they and the workshops should be here, then we can, as the Squire says, plan for the future."

There was a murmur of approval round the room, and then the subject of the future was put aside while they applied themselves to the problems of the water-logged present.

*   *   *

It was nearly a week before all trace of the lagoon disappeared into a river that was once more flowing in its natural course. The quay and its adjoining streets were visible and swept clean of the flotsam thrown up by the flood; the harbour walls were being repaired with a speed that even wrung a grudging word of praise out of Ben for the County Council engineers; and though people still camped in upper rooms while ground floors dried out, at least they were back in their own homes again. The broken bridge remained the most powerful reminder of the storm, and Cressy tried not to look at it whenever she went by. Andrew, still pale but home again, was inclined to be irritable at having been unconscious throughout so much excitement.

Cressy went back to work, relieved to be told by Sam that Giles was away again. She hadn't seen him since she'd been driven away from the bridge, and preferred not to see him until she'd sufficiently rehearsed her speech of resignation. It was no thanks to her, but the boys and Derrycombe had finally accepted one another; she could leave them now and launch herself on a brave new career.

Secure in the knowledge that Giles was away, she went one evening to check up on Marguérite. Sketches were strewn all over the drawing-room floor, and her hostess explained with simple pleasure that she'd been invited to submit costume designs for a production of *Lady Windermere's Fan* in Plymouth.

She sounded genuinely excited, but it wasn't the febrile enthusiasm she'd once brought to the task of killing time. At last she was creating something, and Cressy stayed with her longer than she meant to, discussing the clothes that an Edwardian hostess might have worn from breakfast to ball-time. She finally got up to go, and heard almost in the same moment the sound of the front door being closed – Giles was home after all, and must be smiled at and said goodbye to.

He threw down the coat and briefcase he'd been holding, saluted his stepmother, but addressed himself to a girl who clearly wished she wasn't there.

"Just off, Cressida? If you're walking home I'd better make sure you don't get lost – it's black-dark outside, as they say in these parts."

"I know these parts very well, black-dark or otherwise," she said briefly. "There's no need for you to come with me." Even to her own ears it sounded ungracious and she tried again. "You must be tired if you've been travelling all day."

"I'm tired of sitting in planes and cars; a walk will be welcome."

So that was that! She said goodnight to Marguérite and walked past him to the door, but outside she had to concede privately that he'd been right about the blackness of the night; there was neither moon nor starlight, and while her eyes were adjusting themselves to the darkness she strayed off the path and felt herself hauled back onto it again.

"Told you so – black-dark," Giles's voice murmured with relish in her ear. She peered ahead of her after that with passionate determination not to have to be retrieved a second time, and they walked in silence until they'd negotiated the drive and were out in the lane.

"All well at the hostel?" he enquired politely.

"Almost too well! I keep waiting for something to break the spell of saintliness."

"It soon will. Billy's halo will begin to itch, if no one else's does."

Cressy realised that the moment had come to begin her little speech, but something else also had to be said. "I tried to thank

them for pulling us off the bridge. I never managed to thank you
. . . I should have done." She was grateful for the darkness now,
hiding the expression of sardonic amusement his face no doubt
wore. "The boys are all right, settled at last, so I can think of
leaving the hostel; it's time I found myself another job."

"It's not quite what they think you need. I was privileged to
overhear Billy and Kevin discussing the matter, and have it on
their excellent authority that you need a man!"

Feeling that she'd suddenly been winded, she struggled to find
something to say. "I'm almost past praying for in their opinion,
being in my twenty-fifth year but, like Mr Micawber, I shall hope
that something turns up."

"The boys aren't the only ones to enlighten me," he said after
a moment. "Marguérite insisted that you wouldn't be hurt by the
news of Colin's engagement to Kim Wallace because, if you'd ever
loved him – which she seemed to doubt as well – you no longer did.
Her other certainty, though, was that you were doing your best to
conceal great unhappiness – which is pretty much what Billy and
Trev, in their own way, were also saying."

Cressy thought of the efforts she'd been making, the smile
constantly pinned to her mouth, and the exhausting attempts at
cheerfulness. She needn't have bothered if everyone was determined
to picture her on the verge of a decline. "People are so damned
motherly," she pointed out resentfully. "They always have been –
ever since I was a child in Derrycombe."

"It's no good being petulant about it. I'm afraid they take
an interest in you. Andrew Pollack does too, and he recovered
consciousness in the ambulance feeling compelled to talk. He said
you'd never loved him at all in the way he needed you to (which
I had realised); and you'd only loved a vision of Colin which the
poor sod would never have been able to live up to (which I hadn't
realised but Marguérite had). That, insisted Andrew, only left *me*
as the cause of your unhappiness."

"He'd been working most of the night and just received a
knock-out thump on the head," Cressy said coolly. "You can
scarcely blame him for not making much sense."

"I hoped he *was* making sense, but couldn't then do anything about finding out. Now, with duty done in all directions, I insist on finding out whether Andrew's effort to repay what he saw as a debt was a piece of huge self-deception or not. Was it, Cressida?"

They'd covered another twenty yards before she managed to find her voice. "I'm not sure of the question you're asking . . . I thought we'd found our way to some sort of friendship, but it didn't last, because you don't really need it . . . or attachments of any kind."

They were approaching the outskirts of the town, and the first street-lamp. Giles towed her towards it so that he could see her face. The light threw shadows on its pallor, making it theatrically beautiful and sad.

"I need you as a friend all right, but infinitely more so as a wife," he said gently. "I don't know whether I can change enough to make marriage bearable for you. I don't look like anyone's idea of an ideal husband; I certainly don't behave like one; and I'm used to being self-sufficient, and much too much in the habit of giving orders. But I knew when I saw you stuck on that damned bridge that I should be dead inside for the rest of my life unless I could – could get you off it and browbeat you into marrying me." His voice stumbled on the words, and his hands held hers in a grip that hurt while he waited for her to say something in reply.

Cressy hesitated for a moment, then plunged into what still troubled her. "You'll think I'm always harking back to Colin. Perhaps after this we need never do so again, but what happened to bring you back from Paris a bitterly hostile stranger? It wasn't just the fact of having to haul your family out of trouble yet again and pay a large sum of money in doing it – you came back hating *me*."

Giles shook his head. "Hating everything in life, but most of all the need to accept that I'd been misled in you. I'd almost convinced myself even by the time I got to Paris that true kindness would have been enough to send you flying over there, but Colin lost no time in making it clear, by repeated nods and winks, that you were back in his bed again as soon as you arrived. It would have been a pleasure to leave him to his pack of vultures; but I did what you'd wanted – rescued him; and my only relief was to hurt you instead."

"Do you still believe Colin's version?"

"No."

She examined his face gravely in the lamplight, almost afraid to believe that joy might be within reach at last, and made a stammering mess of her reply.

"I wouldn't m–mind marrying you, but s–soon, please, in case something else—" It was as far as she got before she was pulled into his arms and his mouth found hers. When he lifted his head to look at her she was shaken by the tenderness that gentled his harsh features. Self-sufficiency might take a while to die, but die it would, she felt certain. Then his mouth began to smile. "I didn't finish telling you what Billy said – he's a young man of infinite perception who will probably finish up General Manager of Credland's one day. He was strongly of the opinion that the man you needed was *me*!"

While she was speechlessly torn between the need to laugh and to agree, the unmistakable sound of Ben Davy's voice came floating on the night air.

"Whoa there, Giles me boy, what a stroke of luck! I reckoned on 'avin to trot all the way to Admiral's 'ouse. Cressy 'ere too? We got the cream o' Derrycombe, as you might say!" His manner seemed to suggest that there was nothing in the least surprising about finding the cream of local society deep in conversation under a lamp-post in the dark; it might have been something that happened every day. "You got somethin' to get off your chest too, Cressy love? If so, 'tis your turn first."

"Thanks, B–Ben . . . well, I wondered if I could b–buy some new – some new pyjamas for the boys." It sounded lame to the point of idiocy, but it was the best she could do.

"Why not?" Giles agreed solemnly. "Perhaps bedsocks too?"

The thought completed her ruin, and she collapsed helplessly against him. His arms enfolded her, but over her head he grinned at Ben.

"We were discussing marriage, not the boys' night attire. You can be the first of our friends to receive a wedding invitation!"

" 'bout time too," Ben said severely. "Pair of you 'ave dithered long enough. There's young Lucy doin' 'er bit for the future of Derrycombe, but she can't keep it goin' single-handed, if you takes my meanin'."

His meaning was hard to miss, and Giles promised that they would do their best. "That wasn't what you were coming to see me about, was it?" He asked the question by no means certain that Ben would say no.

"Well, in a manner of speakin', it *were* about future of Derrycombe," Ben agreed. "We was talkin' in Smuggler's Arms about the flood. Struck me we needed somethin' to remind us not to be so hem-careless in future, some kind o' memorial to a night when town might 'ave got washed out to sea. Well now, as I see it, future's in hands of people like yesself and young Squire, not that lot of old women we got on Town Council, so I told 'em in the Snug I'd ask you and Andrew to put your 'eads together."

He stared at Giles, trying to estimate how the idea was being received; pr'aps it wasn't the best night to have tackled him . . . then again, pr'aps it was! After a moment Giles nodded his head.

"The Town Council will certainly have to be consulted, Ben, but I think it's a very good idea. An engraved stone, maybe, incorporated into the new bridge when we get it built."

The lamplight shone on Ben's satisfied grin. "Knew you'd think o' somethin'. I'd better nip back and tell 'em in the Snug. Night, Cressy love. Glad you chose right at last; we've bin gettin' mortal anxious!"

When he was safely out of earshot she looked at Giles, torn between tears and laughter. "Nothing changes! They were watching over me when I was four, and they're still doing it!"

"Well, I can't say I blame them – you take a hem-powerful lot of watching over, as Ben would say."

His face in the lamplight was serious again, making her ask an anxious question. "Didn't you like the idea of the memorial, after all?"

"It's not that . . . I was thinking of something else Ben said: the future of the town is in the hands of people like Andrew Pollack and me. I didn't bargain for that when I bought the Admiral's House."

"You don't *have* to accept the responsibility."

"That's just the trouble – I think I do."

She thought that, between them, he and Andrew would make

251

sure. "Credland's *and* Derrycombe – shall you have time for a wife?" she asked teasingly.

His face looked suspiciously grave still. "I shall have to make time. You heard what Ben said: Lucy and Christopher can't be expected to manage on their own!"

Rather to his surprise, it was her turn to look serious. "It's the price of being needed . . . we *do* need you. Your days of being a solitary man are over. Do you mind?"

His smile answered before he put it into words. "I don't mind anything at all . . . with you."